THOUGHTS ARE FREE
Book 2 of the East Berlin Series

Also by Max Hertzberg

The East Berlin Series
Stealing The Future (2015)
Thoughts Are Free (2016)
Spectre At The Feast (2017)

Other Fiction
Cold Island (2018)

Non-fiction
with Seeds For Change
How To Set Up A Workers' Co-op (2012)
A Consensus Handbook (2013)

After the experience of the East German political upheaval in 1989/90 Max Hertzberg became a Stasi files researcher. Since then, he has also been a book seller and a social change trainer and facilitator.

Visit the author's website for background information on the GDR, features on this series and its characters, as well as guides to walking tours around the East Berlin in which these books are set.

www.maxhertzberg.co.uk

THOUGHTS ARE FREE
Book 2 of the East Berlin Series

Max Hertzberg

 WOLF PRESS

I 2 3 4 5 6 7 8 9 10

Published in 2016 by WOLF PRESS.
www.wolfpress.co.uk

Copyright ©Max Hertzberg 2016.

Max Hertzberg has asserted his right under the Copyright, Designs
and Patents Act 1988 to be identified as the author of this work.

Cover photograph copyright ©Georgie Pauwels, licensed under the
Creative Commons Attribution 2.0 International Licence.

Maps derived from OpenStreetMap. Copyright © OpenStreetMap
and contributors. www.openstreetmap.org/copyright.

Text licensed under the Creative Commons Attribution-Non-
Commercial-No-Derivatives 4.0 International License. View a copy
of this license at: www.creativecommons.org/licenses/by-nc-nd/4.0/

Wolf Press, 22 Hartley Crescent, LS6 2LL

A CIP record for this title is available from the British Library
ISBN: 978-0-9933247-2-7 (paperback), 978-0-9933247-3-4 (epub)

Set in 10½ on 12pt Linux Libertine O and 11/16/24pt Linux Biolinium O

Thoughts Are Free

(German, trad.)

Our thoughts are free,
Who may guess them aright?
They pass fleetingly,
Like shades of the night.
No-one can know them,
No hunter can shoot them
With powder and lead:
Our thoughts are free.

I think what I will,
And what gives me pleasure.
It's all very still,
And all in good measure.
My wishes and longings
Let no one be mocking.
It will always be
That thoughts are free.

And if they locked me
In a dark dungeon,
That would clearly be
A labour in vain;
For my own thoughts, they
Tear down the barriers
And the walls that be:
For thoughts are free.

That's why I forever
Cast off all worries,
And nevermore will
Let whims plague me.
For in our own hearts we
Have laughter and fun.
And thereby we see:
That thoughts are free.

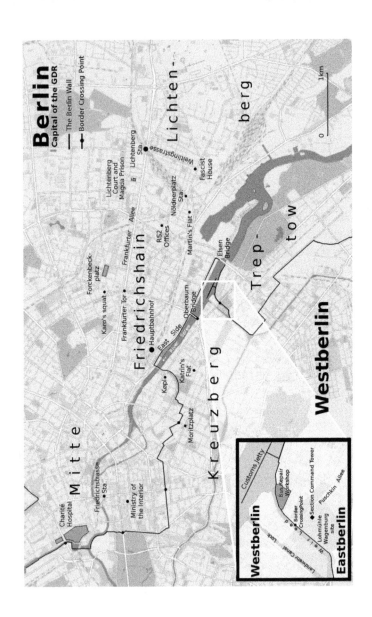

Map of Central Berlin
showing detail of the area around the
Border Crossing Point Puschkin Allee

DAY 1
Monday
14th March 1994

20:11
Martin

The noise was neatly quarantined. A hundred people were marching—they were chanting, shouting, jeering.

But in the surrounding streets: silence.

Windows and doors were shut. Shops darkened, shutters rolled down. The only movement was the slow, snaking column of the demonstrators; the only sound was the chanting: *Foreigners go home! German jobs for Germans! Tear down the Wall!*

The skinheads marched at the head of the demonstration, a waddle of goose-steppers leading the pack. Shaven heads, faces contorted with hate, bomber jackets, paraboots with white laces. Behind them bullish men in ill-fitting suits. At the back, a few dozen people, normal people—the kind you could meet on the street, at work or in the queue at the tram stop—shepherded along by a fistful of skins carrying black-red-gold placards: *Germany: one Fatherland.*

How could anyone take them seriously—their self-importance, their stilted arguments? And yet they were managing to tap into the fears of our time, they were gaining in strength and numbers. Many people in the GDR were unsettled by current immigration levels—higher than at any time since the end of the war: Russian Jews fleeing persecution, Vietnamese and Algerian contract workers stranded by the shipwreck of the Communist regime, refugees from the Balkan wars, idealists arriving from other countries, eager to support our cause. And we needed them all: without their support the labour shortage would bankrupt the country within days.

And a bankrupt GDR would suit the fascists just fine.

Behind the marchers came half a dozen cops, shields dangling from left hands, helmets clipped to belts.

In the wake of them all came the police lorries. I stood next to the operational commander and his lieutenant on the back of a W50 truck, the tarp pulled back to give us a clear view of the demonstration. A police radio dragged at my shoulder, the earpiece keeping me abreast of the reports being made and the orders being issued.

Concentration anti-fascist repeat anti-fascist demonstrators Jessnerstrasse, crackled the radio. *Concentration Antifa repeat anti-fascist Pettenkoferstrasse.*

"Numbers?" demanded the police lieutenant next to me.

The static stirred, snapping and whistling. We were following the march down Frankfurter Allee and the wide railway bridges over the road ahead of us interfered with radio reception.

"Say again! Say again!" The lieutenant shouted into the microphone, but there was no need. We could see over the heads of the marchers—a black-clad knot of Antifa had run out of a side street on the right. About a dozen of them were wearing motorcycle helmets.

The march in front of us disintegrated. The skins from the back were moving up through the ranks of the followers who cast about themselves, unsure what to do, where to go. A few looked back at the police lines behind, as if seeking advice.

"Squad C into position," sighed the captain behind us. Without hesitation the lieutenant repeated the order into the radio mike, looking over his shoulder to watch the riot cops jump down from their transports.

In front of us a second group of Antifa emerged from a street on the left, running across the central reservation, spearing into the demonstrators, isolating the skins from the other marchers scattered along the roadway. The cops headed towards the skins who were already encircled by punks and squatters.

There was a moment of sudden stillness—the skins stood in the middle of the road, facing outwards in a ragged square, placards ripped off poles to make wooden staves. Around them the anti-fascists, just out of reach. A loose ring of police kettled both groups.

With a shout the action started. The Antifa clumped together and pushed against the skins, who hit back with fists and poles. The police used their truncheons, lashing out without discrimination.

"Disperse them," murmured the captain. He had turned away and was watching the group of fellow travellers being directed by the couple of cops left near the trucks. A few wanted to stay and watch but most seemed relieved, almost happy to be sent home.

"Disperse, disperse!" shouted the lieutenant into the radio microphone, but there was no-one to hear him. The cops in the mêlée didn't have radios. There weren't enough of them and they had no plan. They were pumped up on adrenaline and were reacting only to what was happening around them.

It was a mess.

Martin

I was in the canteen when the sergeant came to get me. Sitting at a table, all by myself, leaning against the wall and ignoring the cup of coffee and the slice of poppy-seed cake before me. The other tables had been pushed together and cops sat around them, slapping each other on the back and drinking beer.

"Shoulda left them to fight it out! All as bad as each other," laughed one. "But did you see the fascists' faces when the Antifa stormed across the road?"

This country was going through so many changes, yet I still found it hard to work alongside those who had once been against us. Before 1989 the police had played their part, standing shoulder to shoulder with the Party and the Stasi, repressing social and political dissent. But now the Party was no longer in power and an uneasy dance of reconciliation had started, a wooing between the police and the politicised population. Somehow I'd been caught up in the machinery, assisting the Central Round Table but assigned to the Ministry of the Interior, often working together with cops.

"Comrade Captain Grobe?" A sergeant stood in front of my table, saluting. "We thought you might be interested in something. A detainee we're interviewing. The duty officer suggested you come to see for yourself."

He led me up the stairs and down a long corridor of brown polished lino, institutional green walls broken by heavy, padded doors. He stopped at one of these and pressed the bell set to one side.

While we waited I looked through a grimy window, down to the courtyard. A row of trucks were parked up, in front of them stood a dozen or so green and white liveried police patrol cars. There were no signs of life down there, just concrete, becalmed vehicles and the blank windows opposite. Last time I was here—just a few months ago—the yard had been boiling with movement and exhaust fumes as a squad assembled in preparation for a raid on a squat. It hadn't been a pleasant experience for me, even less so for those who were inside when the doors were kicked in.

Behind me I heard a door open, and I followed the sergeant into the interview room.

A uniformed police lieutenant was sitting behind a large desk—empty except for a phone and intercom device, and a buff file lying in front of him. The lieutenant held a pen, which he laid down on the thick file as he looked up to see who had entered. In front of his desk a table was set end-on, a couple of chairs to either side.

At a nod from the lieutenant we moved into the room. He didn't say anything, and I kept my silence too. It wasn't until I turned to shut the door that I saw the detainee, sitting on a low stool behind the door; his hands pressed on his thighs, his knees drawn up tight to make room for the door that was pushed against his legs. I quickly looked away, but not before taking in the stone-washed jeans, the white t-shirt showing arms sheathed in dark tattoos and the heavily greased short-back-and-sides haircut.

The sergeant went to the lieutenant, leaning over his desk to whisper something. A curt nod from the officer, then he left, opening the door carelessly so that it rebounded off the prisoner's knees. I sat down at the table, and the lieutenant slid a file over to me. Flicking through it, I could see the first page was a custody record, presumably for whoever was sitting behind the door. After that were a handful of unused statement forms, followed by a few dozen blank pieces of paper. I looked at a virgin, ash-grey sheet, my eyes tracing the splinters of wood in the fibrous paper, then I thumbed back to the custody record, checking the personal data: Andreas Hermann, born Leipzig 1976, detained at the demonstration this evening. An initial charge of rowdy behaviour under paragraph 215 section 1 of the criminal code was being investigated and prepared. I tried to meet the police lieutenant's eye but he was staring at the man on the stool.

"Where were you today at 1600 hours?" he snapped.

The detainee flinched slightly, I wouldn't have noticed if he didn't still have his knees pulled up so tight. The slight jerk of the man's head travelled down his torso and limbs, making his feet tremble. But he gave no answer, continuing to stare at a point somewhere above the lieutenant's shoulder.

"Fine. Tell me: when was the last time you went to Alexanderplatz?"

Again silence, the same stare over the lieutenant's shoulder.

It was a familiar set up. The sterile interview room, the implicit offer of the comfort a simple chair with a back could provide: a seat at the table versus the reality of the hard stool. The discomfort, the prohibition against leaning against the wall, the indignity of sitting behind the door. Or alternatively the interviewee might be placed in the middle of the room, back to the door, unable to see who was coming in, whether they were bearing a message, choke cuffs or a cosh.

"Do you go to the Alex often? Meet your friends there? Or do you prefer to hang out in Lichtenberg?"

Silence.

How often had they I sat in rooms like this? The endless questions, sometimes in relay, one interviewer replacing the next, only the detainee remaining the same, required to answer the same questions, again and again, hour after hour, day after day.

"But you don't live in Berlin-Lichtenberg."

The lack of sleep was worse than the arbitrary beatings. The lack of sleep played with your mind. You no longer knew what time of day it was, whether it was even day or night.

You lost track of what you'd said or not said, what you'd meant to say or not say.

"Spend a lot of time there, do you?"

The lack of sleep made you paranoid, unable to trust yourself. It didn't take long, only a couple of days before exhaustion broke you.

"So you stay at a friend's?"

But they couldn't be using those tactics any more? These new times must have put an end to torture?

"Because it's true, isn't it, that you spend quite a bit of time in that part of town?"

I looked at the custody record again, as if it could show me what interrogation methods were planned for this Andreas Hermann.

"How much time do you spend at the premises Weitlingstrasse 122?"

This time there was a reaction. The detainee moved his head, away from the spot above the interviewer's shoulder, slowly sweeping across desk and table, until he was facing me, his hard eyes challenging me.

"Think you're clever, don't you? But we have him," he said, in a slack Berlin drawl, his words whistling through the gap left by missing front teeth. "We know who he is, your *Zecke*, your little informant. And you know what? We know who you are too. You'll be next. No worries, you'll be next." His head tracked back to its original position, facing the wall, above the lieutenant.

I continued watching the detainee, but out of the corner of my eye I could see that the lieutenant hadn't reacted at all.

"How long have you been registered as living at your mother's address?" the policeman asked.

Silence.

DAY 2
Tuesday
15th March 1994

At 7 o'clock on Tuesday the 15th of March here are the news
headlines from Radio DDR I. Good morning.
Berlin: *The Information Office for Jewish Immigration from the*
Soviet Union has announced that there will be a further two
thousand arrivals in Berlin this week. Temporary accommodation
for the newcomers will be made available in the capital and in the
Brandenburg Region, including the towns of Potsdam,
Oranienburg and Bernau.

08:32
Martin

Predictably, the morning meeting at the RS2 office was
dominated by news that the police were running an IKM. We
were part of the investigation into fascist activities in Berlin
but the officers of Department K1 at the local *Kripo* hadn't
bothered to let us know that they had a mole in the fascist
scene. I'd managed to get hold of Laura on the phone last
night, while I was still at Marchlewskistrasse police station
and she'd immediately swung into action, making an official
request for access to the relevant files. If we were going to do
our job then we needed to know what was going on. And we
wanted to know why we'd been left out of the loop.

"We have to step up the investigation. Your news just confirms that," Erika said. "Nik from RS1 has been helping out but we're still struggling."

I considered my own workload for a moment. I had nothing particularly urgent on my desk—I'd been working on the information pack for the three referenda coming up next month, but I'd already passed it back upstairs to the Ministry for them to have a look at. It would take the bureaucrats a while to respond. The other biggish case I was dealing with was a historical investigation into a Nazi attack on a punk concert back in 1987, and I was making hardly any progress on that anyway. I agreed to help out with the investigation into current neo-Nazi activities.

I went to another office with Erika and Laura to discuss the case. They'd started last autumn, but had been much hampered by the fact that we had neither a clear remit nor a direct mandate for our work at the *Republikschutz*. We had been set up by the Central Round Table back in 1990, but after the experiences with the Stasi over the last forty years there was no appetite for a formal counter-intelligence service. So they'd given us some offices and a budget and told us to support the Round Tables on any matters of 'national security' that might crop up. Staff had been chosen from the ranks of pre-1989 dissidents—the idea was that since we'd been on the receiving end of the secret police's attention we'd be wary of developing any Stasi-style structures or tactics. Since then the *Republikschutz* had grown, making up three teams: RS1 and RS2 were based here in Berlin and RS3 was in the south of the Republic.

"We haven't got very far over the last few months," Laura admitted. "It's mostly been about mapping structures, tracing activities."

This surprised me, Laura was good at making things happen—she brought organisation and efficiency wherever she went—which had earned her the reputation of being severe. But she wasn't severe, just straightforward and focussed.

Laura pushed a couple of stacks of folders over the desk towards me, each a good thirty centimetres thick.

"What about their connections with the West?" I asked.

"Nothing useful since that first break last September when we got those photos," Erika said. "You know, the ones I showed you—they'll be in that pile somewhere."

Of all my colleagues I was probably the closest to Erika. We understood each other well, often asking one another for an opinion, and last autumn she'd shown me photos taken inside the house in Weitlingstrasse, right here in Berlin-Lichtenberg. The house had been first squatted then rented by fascists, and the photos showed wide men wearing wide suits, and of piles and piles of propaganda material. We'd immediately suspected a political-ideological diversion directed by the West—not only did some of the men's suits look Western, but in our broken economy it would have been practically impossible to get the materials to make and print that many placards, banners, leaflets, posters and bumper stickers. It was hard not to jump to the conclusion that it had all been smuggled in from the West.

"So if you haven't had any decent leads, what's all this?" I asked, gesturing at the mountain of paperwork.

Laura frowned, but it was Erika who answered.

"The police have been sending us the carbons of any crime reports with a suspected far-right element. Basically we're spending all our time looking at the reports and sending summaries to all the police forces here in the capital and the regions."

"Martin," broke in Laura, keen to get to the point. "We believe—that is, the police believe that the fascists are going to mount some kind of offensive in the run up to the referendum on the Wall. That's why we feel we need to be more proactive."

The fascists were intent on bringing about a union between the two German states. There was no clear or logical reasoning behind this desire, just antagonism towards the progressive society we were building in the GDR, and a raw, Teutonic patriotism. They felt that getting rid of the Wall would be a significant step towards a union with West Germany, and they'd be right. The Wall was a hugely emotive issue, it had caused so much pain for so long that it had been necessary to wait for a few years before opening that debate across the nation: in the media, in workplaces and neighbourhoods. Months of dialogue had followed, just to frame the question that would be asked in the referendum. And now the rising tide of nationalism might sweep away all those patient efforts in just a few weeks.

"So where do we start?"

"I'm going to go through all these reports again, see if anything stands out or whether it's all just random violence," said Laura in a businesslike manner. "Erika's going to talk to an academic at the Humboldt University about social factors behind the rise in far-right activity."

"The other thing we need to check on is whether any more demonstrations have been registered by far-right organisations," Erika chipped in. "You were there last night, and they've already announced another for Sunday. We need to see what they have planned in other places—try to work out whether there's a pattern to the public appearances. It's not just the demonstrations and violent crime reports we're interested in—we think we should be looking at leafleting, information stalls and other public appearances. It might give us an indication of which areas they'll be concentrating on in the lead up to the referenda."

Martin

I took one of the piles of files back to my office, but before I made a start I had a few loose ends to tie up.

Top of my list was to interview an ex-cop. In 1987 he'd been posted outside the church building when 30 Nazis gatecrashed a concert. He and his colleagues hadn't lifted a finger to help the punks being beaten up inside. I'd been given the task of going over the paperwork again, seeing if I could find evidence to support rumours that the *Volkspolizei* and the Stasi had had a hand in events that night. I hadn't found anything useful in the Stasi archives, and I'd been stonewalled by all the cops I'd interviewed so far.

It had taken me a while to track down this particular cop because he was no longer a police officer, but was now in the Border Police Service. He was on duty this morning, and I knew where to find him.

I left the office and got on my bike, cycling over the river to Treptow, then turning onto Puschkin Allee. When I reached the border crossing point there was a short queue. A border guard and his sergeant were watching customs officers open up suitcases and the bulky bags of a small group of pensioners heading West. Even though I kept my distance and couldn't really hear what was being said I could see that the officials were being polite and patient, the civilians in turn weren't cowed by the presence of officialdom. They even seemed to be poking fun at the men on duty—the pensioners burst out laughing, while the official checking luggage blushed and carefully closed a suitcase. It was in such minor exchanges that the major changes in our country could be seen. Just four years ago such a scene would have been unimaginable. In those days border crossings were a place of fear and paranoia, subject to continuous surveillance and the arbitrariness of soldiers and state officials. In those days the Wall had been an invisible fact of life, too dreadful to contemplate or acknowledge.

But after we took to the streets in 1989, after we deposed the Communist Party everything had changed.

Finally, the pensioners moved through the gap in the Wall and I showed the border guard my RS identity card before asking where I could find Corporal Giesler.

The guard saluted and directed me over to the Section Command Tower, a hundred metres off to one side. Before I could take back my pass the sergeant stepped forward.

"You're the guy who arrested the Minister last year?" he asked, taking my ID off the guard and opening it up to check the name there.

I nodded, waiting for him to continue. We stood looking at each other for a long moment.

"I just wanted to say, I admire you, I mean ...." the sergeant stuttered, paused, then carried on: "I mean, what you did. Last year." He held out his hand for me to shake.

The sergeant's enthusiasm surprised me. My relations with the security forces had been less than cordial since the events of last autumn. I nodded again, pasting a smile onto my face, and took my pass back, embarrassed, unsure how to react. But the sergeant still had hold of my hand. I looked at him again. He was young. Acne still scarred his reddened face. Looking uncertain in his oversized uniform he was as at least as flustered as I was. More so.

"Thanks." I pulled my hand from his grasp and started along the cement pathway towards the watchtower. My admirer kept pace with me, not saying anything, but still watching me.

"How are things here?" I asked finally, filling the silence.

We'd come to a stop where the cement slabs of the border crossing met the cobbles of the road. The outer, West-facing wall was behind us now, built along the bank of the weir channel while the line of the *Hinterlandmauer*—the Eastern edge of the death-strip—was still a few metres in front of us.

That East-facing wall was no longer there, the death-strip now was alive with colourful wagons and trucks.

The sergeant followed my gaze. "Well, they can be a nuisance."

We looked over the jigsaw puzzle of wooden and aluminium-sheet wagons, the kind that were usually to be found on building sites to provide workers with a place to have a cup of coffee or shelter from the rain. They'd been fitted out with wood-burners, kitchens and beds and dragged here by trucks and tractors. Stacks of cut wood were left over from winter, lines of washing, empty beer bottles and toys surrounded raised beds of soil, young leafy salad plants and brassicas peeping out. This was a *Wagenburg*, an alternative community, an alternative way of living.

"They jump over the Wall," the lad in uniform said. "Every time we take a ladder away they put up a new one. They don't want to show us their identity cards. I don't understand it—once they climb over the Wall they can't get any further unless they want to get wet." He chuckled and gestured at the deep water on the other side of the Wall. "So they come along the bank to cross the bridge—they pass within a couple of metres of us—and then they have to show their papers at the West Berlin checkpoint anyway. It doesn't make any sense."

I nodded in sympathy. The Wall no longer had any power to imprison us—people felt free to live next to it, to talk about it, to joke about it. Even climb over it. The Wall had always been an economic necessity, but a controversial one. Now it was mutating from a buttress for an illegitimate government to a thin line of protection from the greed of capitalists, a modern day customs barrier. Without the Wall the West Berliners and the West Germans would be over here, buying up our food and consumer goods. Our currency was weak, sold on the black market for as much as ten Eastmarks to one Westmark: our struggling economy couldn't withstand the purchasing power of Westerners buying up our scant stocks. We'd already experienced that, back in November and December of 1989 when the Wall first opened—food shortages throughout East Berlin and along the inner-German border were the result. So we kept the Wall, and we kept the customs checks on the crossing points.

"You know these people, don't you? They understand you. Can you talk to them?" he asked me.

It was an unusual request. A bold one, but one that suited the times. Instead of submitting an official request for 'administrative co-operation' that would be lost, found again, delayed then queried as it passed through the bureaucratic channels, he had simply asked me, person to person, citizen to citizen.

I shook my head: "I don't know these ones, no."

"But you know some other ..." he looked again towards the *Wagenburg*, "people like this, don't you? You worked with them on that case last year? I read about it in the papers, you were on television, on the news." He wasn't going to let me go that easily.

"I'm here to speak to Corporal Giesler," I said, changing the subject.

The sergeant misinterpreted my unease and stiffened. "*Jawohl*, comrade Captain. Comrade Corporal Giesler is on comms duty. I shall take you to him now."

He turned again, ready to march off to the watchtower, but I put a hand on his arm to stop him.

"What's your name?"

The sergeant half-turned, unsure whether to stand to attention or not. "Staff Sergeant Müller, comrade Captain."

I held out my hand and offered a smile. "How about we drop the formalities? I'm Martin."

Müller relaxed again, he shook my hand. "Rico," he said as his acne burned.

★

Rico took me up to the observation level of the watchtower. Giesler had stood to attention as soon as we appeared through the hatch at the top of the ladder.

"Nothing to report, comrade Staff Sergeant," he announced when his superior had fully emerged.

"At ease, comrade Corporal. The comrade Captain from RS wishes to speak to you." With a nod to me Rico descended down the ladder again.

Giesler continued to stand behind his desk adorned with telephones, radio sets and banks of dead lights. I looked him over, trying to work out the best way to approach him. He was older than me, still muscular, but his skin was grey and saggy. Pale grey eyes glared at me from beneath fine grey eyebrows and a widow's peak. I wondered what had made him change his *Volkspolizei* uniform for that of the Border Police; whether the move had anything to do with the incident I was investigating.

I decided to try the friendly approach.

"As you were, comrade Corporal. I shan't take much of your time. I'm just clearing up some paperwork from the old days, and I wanted to check whether you had anything useful to add."

Giesler sat down again, his eyes never leaving me.

I went to the window and looked down at the wagons and the punks below, and started to speak without turning around. "It's to do with an incident in Prenzlauer Berg on the 17th of October 1987." Although Giesler was behind me I could see his silhouette reflected in the window before me, but there was no shift, no start of recognition.

"Does that date mean anything to you?" I turned around to face him again. "It was the night a church building was attacked by rowdy elements. You were there that night, observing comings and goings. I just need a few details clearing up."

"I'm sure I don't remember, comrade Captain. I can only

suggest you look at the report I filed at the time." Giesler was now eyeing the phones—perhaps hoping that one would ring —but beyond that he showed no nervousness.

"It's just a minor detail." I sat down on a chair next to the desk, leaning forward, elbows resting on my thighs. "Did you have orders not to intervene when the fascists attacked the concert-goers?" I asked in a low voice, staring intently at Giesler.

He gazed blankly back at me, waiting a few moments before answering. "I've already said, comrade Captain, that I have no clear recollection of the incident."

I stood up and took hold of the pulley that held open the steel hatch at the top of the ladder, paying out the rope and letting the steel door bang down. There wasn't much space in the watchtower so I was still less than a couple of metres away from Giesler.

"Comrade Corporal—it's just you and me now. Nobody can hear-"

But Giesler had also got up. With just two strides he was out from behind his desk, and standing directly in front of me, the buttons of his uniform blouson grazing my chest.

"With respect, *Captain*," he snarled, "you'd do well to forget about 1987." He edged closer, trying to push me back. "For some of us the old times are still here."

Karo

"Hi Katrin, it's me."

The buzzer let me in and I went up the tenement stairs. Katrin's door was ajar when I got there.

"Karo!" she gave me a hug and dragged me into the kitchen. She flipped a switch on the coffee percolator and we sat down and started chatting.

"I've not seen you for ages! How's it all going?"

"Full on! Totally full on! You wouldn't believe what I've been up to!" But I stopped because I could tell something was bothering Katrin. "What's up?"

It was about the volunteering she was doing at the AL offices (I tried not to sneer about the fact that Katrin was volunteering at the West Berlin version of the Green party—maybe I did, a little, but she didn't notice so it was OK). Seems that Annette, Martin's ex, is really worried about the far-right *Republikaner* party.

"Annette was telling me that the AL members with seats on the Senate are worried that they'll lose them to the Reps. And if the same happens to the FDP then it looks like other parties could go into coalition with the right-wingers."

"Yeah, we've got the *Volkskammer* elections coming up in the autumn—it's looking like the fash are going to get quite a few votes." It made me really angry to think about this stuff and I got up and started pacing around the kitchen.

"Is Papa involved in any of this? Is he involved in dealing with the far-right?" Katrin was watching me move around her kitchen, even I could see she was worried. I stopped poking around her tea jars and went back to the table.

I had to think for a bit, but I didn't really know what Martin was up to. I shook my head.

"It's just that, I dunno. He's been a bit preoccupied lately. I was wondering whether he was involved in some case, you know, as part of his job. About the Nazis, I mean."

"Dunno. Haven't seen him for a while. But he's alright, isn't he?" I thought about it for a bit. "Martin's always alright."

Katrin just shrugged.

"Look, I tell you what—I'll keep an eye on him and let you know what's going on. I'll go and see him tomorrow, get him to come to a gig with me. A bit of a bop will sort him out!"

I thought it was a great idea but Katrin didn't look so sure.

12:22

Martin

I cycled back to the office, thinking about Giesler. I couldn't work out whether he was frightened or trying to frighten me. Either way, it was clear that I wasn't going to get any information out of him.

I decided not to bother with a full report on the interview, I'd just include him in the list of cops who wouldn't talk to me. That would save some time. In any case I had already decided to try to interview the other side—see if the punks who were at the concert had anything new to say. I'd read the police reports and the samizdat publications of the time, but it seemed possible that the punks would feel more able to speak openly now.

When I walked into the RS2 offices our secretary, Grit, was waiting for me with a telex print.

"Can you sign this?"

I read the message, it had already been initialled by Laura and Erika. It was from the Ministry—we were being told to back off Lichtenberg *Kripo*, stop asking for information about the mole they had in the fascist scene. I went over to Laura's office.

"Do you know what this is about?"

Laura sat back in her chair, a report dangling from one hand, her glasses perched on top of her head. "You've read it haven't you? Well, you know as much as I do."

"But why would they tell us to back off?"

"Martin, why do you have to make everything complicated? What's it matter, anyway? They probably just need a few days to sort things out—that's going to claim all their attention and they don't want us breathing down their necks. They'll have their reasons."

I signed the chit and gave it back to Grit.

Once back in my office I spent a few minutes trying to find my *To Do* list. It turned up under my chair, sandwiched between sheets of expenses claims that I should have filed back in January. I leafed through my notes, trying to decipher the scratched out and annotated lists. Karo's name was there—*ask if Karo knows anyone who was at concert in 1987.* But since the Nazi demo last night I was beginning to think I should prioritise current Nazi activities, and not those of six and a half years ago.

Looking further down the list I realised that Dmitri was overdue a call. He was an officer in the FSK—the agency that had taken over from the KGB since the coup against Gorbachev—and he was the main liaison between the FSK's Berlin office and the Central Round Table. I was the other side of that equation, representing the GDR's interests. There was rarely much content to our meetings—most of the administrative complexities of hosting the Group of Russian Forces in Germany were handled by other offices at various levels of the government. Dmitri and I represented a high-level and trusted connection, just in case we ever needed it.

I dialled the number for Dmitri's office. The phone lines to the Russian Forces' quarters in Karlshorst were always very crackly, echoes and ghosting voices lingering in the background, as if the listeners had never gone away.

"*Da?*"

"Dmitri Alexandrovich, it's Martin here."

"Martin Ottovich! Always a pleasure to hear from you, my

friend! Is it time for us to sup vodka again? So long, such a long time since we last had a chat."

Dmitri sounded a little preoccupied; his voice was warm and friendly but his mind was clearly on other matters. I didn't ask, the old caution was still with me: don't speak too freely on the phone, and watch what you say to the Russians. I trusted Dmitri, he was a good person and a friendship had grown between us, but I didn't trust his outfit, neither the FSK nor any of the other remnants of the occupying army.

"When shall we meet, Martin? No, wait, I will look at my calendar."

I could hear shuffling noises and muttering down the receiver, as if Dmitri was having to shift heavy piles of paper around on his desk to discover his diary. Finally, he picked up the receiver again.

"You know, I am glad you call, there is much to talk about ... But here, I have my calendar. Next week? Is next week good for you Herr Martin Ottovich?"

We agreed to meet a week on Wednesday at his office.

"Martin, we have much to talk about," Dmitri was repeating himself, which was unusual for him. "I shall tell you all next week, but until then be careful, my friend."

DAY 3
Wednesday
16th March 1994

Jüterbog: *There has been a further arson attack on accommodation used by Jews fleeing persecution in Russia. Last night a firework was thrown through a window of the asylum-seekers hostel in Jüterbog. A woman and two children were taken to hospital after inhaling smoke. According to the Round Table Committee on Extremist Affairs this is the sixth such attack this year.*

09:12
Martin

I finished typing up a report on my lack of progress in the 1987 case and filed away my copy. I took the original and the second carbon into the front office to give to Grit for filing and forwarding to the Ministry of the Interior.

Returning to my desk I started looking through the files on the fascists that Laura had insisted I look at. But my mind kept sliding off and returning to what the young sergeant had asked me to do. Rico, he'd said his name was: Rico Müller. It didn't feel like there was much I could do about his problem, and anyway, it wasn't my responsibility to do anything about it.

But still, I felt some kind of affinity with the border guard.

He was engaged enough to try to come up with alternative solutions, to ask me if I could help. Horizontal links—precisely the kind of thing we needed to encourage if we didn't want our revolution to run out of steam, if we didn't want a new elite to appear, organising our society for us, telling us what to do and how to think.

The obvious option would be simply to have a chat with the people in the wagons and trucks. Had Rico already done that? I hadn't thought to ask him. But the punks on the site and Rico were worlds apart—I didn't doubt that both the border guard and the wagoneers had the best interests of our Republic at heart but they would have different ideas of how our nascent utopia should be nursed. Rico saw the world through a filter of orderliness, predictability, clarity. The punks had a more chaotic, spontaneous vision of how society should function.

I had sympathy with both philosophies of life, but right now I had enough on my plate. Like these files detailing recent fascist activities in the capital. It was vicious stuff and it made for depressing reading. Apparently random violence was being meted out by the skins—foreigners and punks were the main targets, but muggings and assaults on pensioners had also increased in areas seeing fascist activity. After a while I stopped reading the detailed case files, concentrating instead on gaining an overview from the situation reports and the tabulated statistics. That didn't make for easy reading either, and I was glad of the distraction when Grit came in.

"The State Prosecutor's office rang, they want to meet up tomorrow," she said as she handed the memo over.

I scanned the chit. Henschel, the prosecutor in charge of the case against Evelyn. What did he want to speak to me about? As far as I was concerned I was finished with that case, I'd played my part and put her behind bars.

Karo

I'd had a bitch of a day, but it looked like Martin was having an even worse time. He was reading some report but kept turning back to the circulation list clipped to the front. He looked like he wanted to stab his eyes out with his pencil.

"So this is the headquarters of the mysterious *Republikschutz*," I said, kicking a screwed up memo out of the way. "Aren't you going to offer me a coffee, Mr. Bond?"

Martin put his report on top of a million other identical files on his desk. I tried to work out what it was, but all I could see was a pink stripe across the front and VVS stamped in one corner.

"Only joking!" I said hastily when Martin got up and started lumbering over to the kettle. "Don't worry about the coffee, I just came to say hi."

He sat down again, looking at me. So far he hadn't said anything.

"Aren't you pleased to see me?" Maybe Katrin was right, maybe the big man was under the weather.

He grinned at that and I grinned too, just to encourage him a bit. We did that until the smiles wore loose.

"What are you up to these days?" He managed to squeeze a question out.

"Well—you'd be dead proud of me! I'm training to be a Neighbourhood Facilitator. I really like the idea of it, but the course is just dragging on and on and on," I rolled my eyes to show him just how fucking boring it all was.

He grinned again at that, but I could tell he didn't have a clue what I was on about, so I told him about the programme.

"It's like, now we've got all this freedom—we can say what we want and virtually do what we want—well, that means there's more scope for conflict. People are falling out left right and centre, I dunno, about politics, about what colour they're gonna paint their houses, about solidarity work, noisy neighbours," (I made sure to do rabbit ears around *noisy* because I knew it would wind Martin up). "A million things. You know the score."

Martin did know the score, I could see him thinking about it. I always know when he's thinking about the old days because he looks like he's got some brain-disease and I can tell exactly what he's thinking: cops and the Party. Right then he was probably yearning for the days when you couldn't fart without getting written permission in triplicate.

"So, we're setting up a neighbourhood facilitation team. It's a step before the official arbitration process. We help people resolve their arguments, to talk to each other and understand each other's points of view. And we mediate if that's what's needed."

Martin still hadn't said anything, well, not really. I reckoned Katrin was right about her dad. I leaned over Martin's desk, trying to avoid the paper stacked everywhere.

"Listen Martin: you, me—we're going out tonight. We're going to have a laugh. You need brightening up—you look like a squad of soldiers on a wet May Day parade."

18:16

Karo

They were giving Martin the cold shoulder, and I felt guilty about that because I was the one who'd brought him here. We'd done a deal: I take him to the see the local Antifa group, and he comes to the gig afterwards.

"... so he's trying to find out a bit more," I was saying to the lads around the table. "Because they're getting bolder, getting out more, and the demo the other night-"

Bert had been watching Martin the whole time, really staring at him. And now he interrupted me.

"And why the sudden interest in the Nazis? Bit late in the day isn't it? We've been dealing with the shites for years.

Now the State's suddenly taking an interest so we're just meant to let them take over?"

"You're right-" Martin tried to answer but Bert cut him off again.

"I know I'm right, but what I don't know," he leaned towards Martin, getting him to lean in too, "is why you're still here!"

"Bert, back off. This is Martin. He's sorted, really." I put my hand on Bert's arm. He was being a macho arse as usual. "Just hear him out, yeah?"

Bert stared at Martin a bit longer, just to get the message across then nodded and leaned back.

"Look, I know the score," Martin said. He was looking around the group now, trying to work out who to talk to. It was obvious he didn't like Bert, and I didn't blame him. But Bert has his uses.

"This is a problem we've been ignoring for far too long. And you're right, you're practically the only ones who have been dealing with it." Martin had gone into making-a-speech mode, but fair play—the Antifa group were giving him a chance. "Now the police have become involved—I know, I know." Martin held his hands up, as if he could ward off the sarcastic laughter. "I'm sceptical too. Look—all my cards on the table—I'm with the *Republikschutz* and if I'm completely honest with you I don't know whether we can trust the cops to do the job right. They should have done it ten years ago and they didn't, but this time round they've got us breathing down their necks."

No-one had told Martin to fuck off yet, so he was doing well.

"The cops reckon the fascists are gearing up to something big, not just the usual casual violence on the streets or at football matches. They've got a plan. And that's why we're involved-"

"Hang on a minute!" Bert was back in the game and was

stabbing a hole in the table with his finger to make sure we all knew he was making a point. "Why should we trust you? You say you're from RS, but that's not a democratic organisation! Nobody's ever asked me if I think it's a good idea to have the RS! You know what? I've got better things to do than have chats with someone in a slouch hat and trench-coat." He sat back and crossed his arms.

"I'm not going to piss you around." Martin wasn't ready to give up yet. "I agree, RS isn't democratic. I could say all the usual stuff, that we answer to parliament and to the Round Tables but if you ask me what I think—I'll tell you it's just not enough. Right now, though, it's what we've got. And right now, I need a drink."

Martin left us and pushed his way through to the bar. I had to admire him—that was a pretty cool move. It gave the Antifa a chance to think about what he'd said.

"Can we trust him?" one of them asked eventually.

"Look, Martin's a windbag, but you know what, he's fucking cool. He's genuine, you know, we're all on the same side. You gotta give him a chance."

The lads all looked at each other and did whatever it is they do when they're making a decision, and I caught Martin's eye. He was at the bar, necking a bottle of pilsner. When he came back nobody said anything. They all just looked at him, like it was up to him to make the first move.

"Can I sit down?" he asked.

Nobody answered so Martin just plonked his bottle of beer on the table and sat down.

"Any questions?"

"Yeah." Bert was the first in the queue. "What do you want from us?"

"I need to know how the fash operate. The cops don't do that kind of thing—they see a criminal offence and detain the suspect, they think that's all they need to do. But now even they've twigged that something bigger is happening. I reckon you're the only ones who really understand how the fascists are operating."

"And what's in it for us?" Rex demanded. I like Rex, he's the most human of them all—like he's not just in it to have a fight with the fash. Thinking about it he'd probably be really useless in a fight, he's dead skinny. No muscle.

"Nothing. There's nothing in it for you," Martin answered. They didn't like that, but I had to smile a bit, I could see where Martin was going with this. "Because I reckon you're like me. I reckon you're not doing it for yourselves, but for all of us, for the whole of society. We need to deal with these fascists, and you're the ones who've been doing that for, what? Six, seven years? If we work together maybe we can make more headway."

That was it, I knew I could relax. Martin had won. He knew it too, and took the initiative.

"How about we start over? I'm Martin, I work with the RS, and right now, I'm really worried about the fascists here in our country, specifically in Lichtenberg. I'm hoping you can help me out. I'm hoping you can give me some background information about them—how they're organised, who's in charge, what they're up to?"

"Rex. Just like the beer." Rex offered Martin his hand to shake. He always had to make a joke of it, and yep, he was holding a bottle of Rex beer from Potsdam, the one with the lanky fusilier on the label. "Who you asking about? The skins? Yeah, well, it's not actually them you need to be worrying about. It's the fascist organisations behind them. The skins are just being used by the suits, they're just the boot boys, out for a laugh and a ruck." He took a swig of beer and put it down, dead prissy, dead centre on the beer mat.

"The skins weren't well organised when they started off, not here in Berlin. They just got together for drinking and fighting. *Lichtenberg Front*, then there was the *Movement of the 30th of January*, after that *National Alternative*—that's where it all started in this town. And somewhere along the way they got organised. We don't know when, we didn't work it out until after the cops stormed their squat back in April 1990. It might have been the *Reps* who got them organised—we know there's a group of 800 of them in Marzahn and another 300 members in Lichtenberg. Maybe that's how they made links with the West, through the *Reps*."

The *Reps*: the *Republikaner* party, they were the ones that Katrin was telling me about just yesterday. Martin told me once about how he reckoned they'd been doing counter-revolutionary stuff back in late 1989 and 1990. Now Rex was saying there's over a thousand members here in East Berlin!

"So, there's the skins," Martin checked in. "And in the background there are party members, some from the West, and they've more or less got control of the skinhead scene?"

"Yeah, except it's not that clear cut. Not all skins are fashos, some are just nationalist, some are even red-skins. And a few skins want more than just a scrap, they're into political stuff in a big way. And then you've got the hools, having a ruck after football matches."

"So if we want to stop this cancer we have to get to the party organisation?"

"Yeah," said Rex. "We've tried to find out more, but we've got our hands full, y'know dealing with the skins and the hooligans. It's the same story everywhere: Leipzig, Rostock, Dresden, Jena .... We can't do everything!"

Martin had a think about that while Rex took a swig of beer.

"If we manage to find a way in to the party organisation, if we find anything out, would you be prepared to help?"

"Depends on what you need, Martin. Depends on what you need."

"What? Even if it means the end of our revolution?"

Karo hesitated for a moment, I could see doubt creep into her eyes, just for a second or two, before it was discarded. She swayed a little, then finding her balance again, she waved her hand in my face.

"Yes," she bawled at me, with the force of conviction deeply held. "Even then!"

DAY 4
Thursday
17th March 1994

Berlin: In a ceremony taking place at midday today, parts of Lenin Allee will be renamed Kropotkin Allee. Local Round Tables in Friedrichshain and Prenzlauer Berg settled on the new name earlier this year, but no agreement could be reached in the district of Lichtenberg where the road will continue to be known by the old name. In a separate ceremony to be held next month, Leninplatz at the western end of the road will be renamed Bakuninplatz.

08:26
Martin

My colleagues noticed my hungover as soon as I walked in.

"What happened to you?"

"Late night. Punk concert."

They shared a grin. My connections to the punk scene were a source of amusement for my peers.

But there was something else. My colleagues were sitting in my office, they'd obviously been waiting for me, and all had an expectant air about them. I stood in the doorway wondering what was going on.

"Your turn to get the bread rolls," murmured Klaus with the half-grin he used when something amused him.

I looked around the room, only now taking in the plates and knives that were piled on my desk, along with a tiny kohlrabi, a bowl of lamb's lettuce and a couple of glass jars: five-fruits jam and what looked like some kind of spread.

"Sorry," I murmured as I moved around behind my desk, pushing the plates to one side to make room for my elbows.

"Can we carry on?" asked Laura, snappy at the delay. "We've already started with the agenda—we've finally had notice of who's going to be on the Ministerial Committee."

The Minister of the Interior had been replaced last autumn by a temporary committee, accountable to both the *Volkskammer* national parliament and the Central Round Table. The plan had been to try out the system before extending it to other Ministries. By announcing new committee members both parliament and the Central Round Table were indicating that they thought the experiment a success and worth continuing for the time being.

"The good news is that a couple of good people are going to be on the new committee: Mario Schreiber and Antje Willehardt."

Before 1989 Antje had been involved in the same dissident group as Erika, and she nodded, pleased at having a friend involved. Mario had been active up in Prenzlauer Berg, often to be seen in the *Umweltbibliothek*, but mostly working as an artist, pushing against the tight boundaries the Party had set around free expression.

"Who's the third person?" asked Klaus.

Laura shook her head, "Somebody from the CDU, never heard of him. Dietmar Rosen."

"Dietmar Rosen?" Klaus nodded. "Yeah, calls himself Timo. An old-timer, in the CDU back when it was still a block-party supporting the Communists. Now he's pro-unification."

A compromise appointment then, chosen to appease the authoritarian and pro-West factions in parliament.

★

"Frau Professor Doktor Weiss is an anthropologist. She co-ordinates a research group focussing on far-right activities."

Nik from RS1 had come over for the meeting, and was listening to what Erika had to say about the prof.

"Professor Weiss has compiled statistics on the acceptance and social standing of skinheads and their ideology. But I think what's interesting to us are the socio-psychological factors at play. Before 1989 some people were right wing because they didn't fit in, they couldn't find their niche in the socialist society, or they weren't prepared to. However, since the revolution started the numbers of young people with links to far-right movements has increased rapidly. Professor Weiss suggested that this has to do with the social upheaval we are experiencing: loss of direction and expectations; behaviour patterns that were previously rewarded—such as obedience and rote-learning—are no longer encouraged. Far-right organisations are offering the personal and social discipline that we used to have under the old system. It's essentially the way the Communist Party worked before: intolerance, structural violence and repression. Many people like to have that clarity."

"So you're saying the kind of person who felt at home in the Party and the FDJ in the old days are now more likely to join a far-right group?" Nik offered as a summary.

Erika didn't answer but flicked through her notes, "There's more: before 1989 the dual perception encouraged by the Party—the way of seeing everything as either right or wrong, black or white; the categorical, top-down determination—that's also the way the fascists want to see the world. They think they're right, and everyone else is wrong. And if you're wrong then you don't have any right to an opinion."

"The discipline thing interests me," I said. "The local Antifa told me that there's a clear hierarchy. Those at the bottom are exploited by a politically sophisticated inner circle. Did your prof say anything about that?"

"Yes—we saw that during the attacks on refugees at Hoyerswerda, as well as Freital, Thiendorf and all the other places. Same in West Germany, in Solingen and Mölln— different society and culture, but same set up. We should find out more about that inner circle—we can be fairly sure that quite a few of them have come over from the West."

Nik went over to the table where the police reports were laid out. He poked around a bit, then came back with a summary of observation reports from the last couple of months. He laid the paperwork on the table before us, pointing first to one page, then another.

"Here, see this: it looks like several groupings met up on this particular weekend at Weitlingstrasse 122, that coincided with visitors from the West. The same thing, on this date." Nik took the report and riffled through the pages again, finding what he was looking for, then turning the file around so we could see it. "Here, on this weekend. It happens several times, always with more people coming and going than is normal, and always with several well known fascists from West Berlin and West Germany, once even from Austria."

"So they're having meetings. The different groups are getting together and talking to known figures from the West," Laura said, thinking aloud.

"Or they're doing some kind of training." Nik added.

"What kind of training are they going to be doing?" I asked. "They don't need to be told how to beat people up. So it would have to be something else ...." In my head I sorted through the alternatives, and only one seemed remotely likely. "Something like political organising, say for the referenda in a couple of weeks, and after that the *Volkskammer* elections."

That was one possibility, but there'd be others. We really needed hard information. We needed the kind of inside information the *Kripo* must be getting from their informant— the information they weren't passing on to us.

Karo

Today's the day I get to take Frau Kembowski shopping.

Frau Kembowski is ace, she's really old-school, but we all love her. She was in the resistance in Nazi times and ended up in a concentration camp. But because she wasn't in the Communist Party they wouldn't give her a Victims of Fascism Pension.

She lives next door to our squat and has never complained about the noise and the parties, but maybe that's because she's deaf as a nut.

It started out with us just taking her bottles and waste paper to the recycling shop and spending the deposit money on beer. But when we noticed that she can't see very well either, and didn't get out much, we got a rota sorted to take her shopping and to the park and stuff.

"Mind the step Frau Kembowski—it's a bit uneven here!" I shouted at her.

"Oh deary me, haven't they repaired it yet? Things seem to be going from bad to worse in this country of ours ...." she wittered on.

"Yeah, but we don't want the fucking Party back, do we?"

Frau Kembowski tut-tutted loudly but I knew she didn't really mind me swearing. It's a bit of a game we play.

We'd got the shopping sorted and now we were on the way to the post office. When we got to Frankfurter Tor there were a couple of Nazi-skins handing out leaflets and abusing anyone who didn't take one. I knew exactly what would be on that leaflet: *Foreigners go home!* and *Tear down the Wall!* If I'd been on my own I would have gone and told them they could fucking go home themselves, or maybe gone to get some friends to help me make sure they did. The fuckers shouldn't be hanging around here, this was our *Kiez*.

While we were watching, some normal looking people stopped to chat with the skins. Frau Kembowski shook her head when she saw that and toddled off the other way, dragging me by the arm. "Come on deary, we'll go this way shall we?"

So we carried on up the road and I decided I'd deal with the situation later.

When we got to the post office the queue snaked out the door but we just went past all the people, with Frau Kembowski warbling *Veteran coming through!* It's fun queue-jumping with Frau Kembowski.

Once inside I steered Frau Kembowski to a counter where a bloke my age was being served. The other cashiers were dealing with old biddies and I could see they were digging in to spend the day counting their change and checking their savings books while everyone waited for them to get out the way. I barged in at the head of the queue so that we'd be next. The bloke being served had this really weird package. It looked like a hockey stick wound up in brown paper, and he was having real problems trying to pass it over the counter. It was really funny, he nearly swiped the grey withdrawal forms and the scales off the top while the old ladies looked on and tut-tutted.

When it was our turn Frau Kembowski asked for ten stamps for letters, and she had the exact money ready in her hand.

"Have you got the Kropotkin Allee commemoration stamps?" she quavered.

"Kropotkin's sold out already," replied the cashier, and proceeded to ignore us, waving forward the next person in the queue.

"We'll have the old ones then," I said to her in my rock-hard voice.

The cashier sighed (why does everyone in the GDR sigh all the fucking time? It's like it's catching) and poked around in a folder until she found a leaf of stamps with Beardy Marx on them. "Two Marks fifty," she snapped.

Frau Kembowski gave her the money and a really nice smile on top, and that seemed to do the job or else the cashier must have felt guilty because she started rabbiting on to Frau Kembowski.

"You can tell who's still a Party member, you know. They may not have the pin on their lapel any more, but they always ask for old Karl." They shared a smile and I dragged Frau Kembowski back out into the sunshine.

"You know what, young Karo?" Frau Kembowski was breathing heavily, and no wonder, the way she was wrapped up in that thick coat and big hat. "I do believe things are getting better in our country."

By now we were at the curb and had to wait to cross the road.

"Why's that Frau Kembowski?"

"Well, I think that's the first time anyone has ever said anything civil to me in a post office, and I've been around for a while too. Petty officials taking the drudgery of everyday life out on the customers, that's how it's always been. Just plain fucking wrong!" Frau Kembowski cackled.

15:22

Martin

The State Prosecutor, Ottokar Henschel, was waiting for me just inside the doors of the lower courthouse in Lichtenberg. It was another of those massive buildings built in the time of the last Kaiser—high ceilings and echoing corridors. I went up the steps and in through the doors, holding my hand out. Henschel took it in his insipid grasp for a moment before letting it fall. He marched off, expecting me to follow him. He didn't look very happy.

"The President of the Court, Professor Doktor Kirchherr, wishes to speak with you—he's not satisfied with the standard of evidence," he said over his shoulder as he strode down the stone flagged corridor. "He has a suggestion, but he wouldn't tell me what it was."

I was confused: if I was to meet the judge in charge of the case then why had I been asked to come to the local court rather than the Supreme Court on Littenstrasse? Before I could ask Henschel he was rapping on a heavy oak door. He stood aside, letting me enter first.

The polished stone floor of the corridor gave way to darkened oak parquet in the room. High windows provided enough light to show off the tall ceilings and dark wood. Robing tables stood off to one side of the room, hooks in the panelling above them. But occupying the centre of the room was a large desk, and very much in charge of that desk sat the President of the Divisional Court.

The judge looked up as we came in, but didn't stand to greet me, just nodded sourly, as if everything that was bothering him in his life were my fault. In a sense he might be right: at least some of his problems were down to me. I was the one who had worked out the role ex-Stasi officers were playing in last year's Silesian Crisis, and I'd arrested the two main figures in the plot. Now Kirchherr was in charge of hearing the case against Benno Hartmann and Evelyn Hagenow.

I wasn't sure how to address the judge. President? Your Honour? I settled for a mumbled *comrade*. He took my hand and pressed it, not too hard, but hard enough to show he intended to imprint his status upon me.

"You are Captain Grobe?" he enquired while looking pointedly at Henschel. The prosecutor took the hint, muttered something polite and left the room.

"Captain Grobe, I have a problem and, given the quality of the case that has been made so far in my courtroom, I have little confidence that you will be able to help me. But on the other hand, we must pursue every possible avenue." He rearranged his papers while he spoke, then raised his eyes to meet mine.

He had clear blue eyes which contrasted with the salt and pepper eyebrows bristling above. Those eyes dug into me, as if demanding a confession. I looked away, and, spotting what I was after, took a chair and placed it in front of the desk. I sat down, prissily crossing and re-crossing my legs. When I was finally comfortable, and felt that the judge had waited long enough, I answered him.

"How do you think I can I help, comrade?" I deliberately emphasised the comrade this time, watching for his reaction.

A frown played at the corner of the judge's mouth. "Captain, times have changed. I was a judge in the days of Democratic Centralism, when the Party viewed the judiciary as one of their many executive organs. That is no longer the case: we are no longer the executive of any governing body in this Republic. Nevertheless, I am asked to preside over a hearing in which the case brought before me—clearly of social importance—has certain ...." The judge cleared his throat. "Shall we say certain *deficits*? Allow me, Captain, to be indiscreet. The evidence against Hartmann and Hagenow is—and I'm putting this politely—mostly circumstantial, and flimsy at that. Am I merely to follow popular opinion and instruct the jury to find them guilty?

"Yet these modern times demand something different, do they not? In turn, I fail to see any opportunity for making this a case of restitution. I cannot see how the principles of restorative justice can be applied. What exactly can the accused restore, and to whom?"

Kirchherr paused for a moment, fixing me with his stare again. Before continuing he picked up a stainless steel propelling pencil and examined the point for a moment.

"Captain, if you will allow me a further foray into the intangible—the West Germans have always taken great delight in stating that we do not have, nor ever have had, a *Rechtsstaat* here in the GDR. They say we do not follow the rule of law, that we are not a constitutional state. They ignore the fact that our laws have always been entirely in accordance with our real, existing constitution. And now we take great pains to comply with the laws that have been both democratically informed and formed. But none of this helps me in the peculiar case I have been appointed to oversee."

In a nervous gesture that belied his calm exterior the judge was pressing the button at the top of his pencil to release the lead, then pushing it back in with the palm of his hand. I wondered whether his flowery speech was also a symptom of his agitation, or whether he always talked like this.

"As I have already remarked, the prosecution is failing to present a convincing case. These are no ordinary accusations the court is hearing—they are entirely political. It is a distinctive case, and how, I ask myself, am I to deal with it? I hesitate to use the word *fair*, yet I wonder how we might treat this case *otherwise*, how may we find a *different* way to proceed?"

I could appreciate his problem. We hadn't managed to find any substantial documentary evidence in this case. When it came to prosecuting Mittag, Tisch, Honecker, Mielke and all the other leaders of the Party we had had hard evidence of criminal complicity—in manslaughter, torture and embezzlement. There was no question of trying them as political cases—all had been heavily involved in not only immoral but also criminal activity.

But now, even though both Benno Hartmann and Evelyn Hagenow had almost definitely been involved in at least one murder, we had nothing but circumstantial evidence. All the hard evidence we had gathered pointed only to a minor player who had conveniently turned up dead.

But it wasn't my problem, I felt like I'd done my part. Now it was down to this pompous member of the old system to work out how to deal with the trial.

"I am considering other options," the judge droned on.

Having put the pencil down he was rubbing his nose between thumb and forefinger. "Let's say, for the sake of argument, that the case were to be dismissed, subject to the application of certain conditions, and if such conditions were of an, er, *satisfactory* nature ...." He looked at me from under his eyebrows, expecting a response to some question he felt beneath his dignity to actually ask.

I tried to work out exactly what the judge might be suggesting, but he'd already picked up the threads of his disquisition.

"In the case of Hartmann there is little difficulty. He has already requested, in writing, to be released to the West and promises never to return to the GDR. I am satisfied that his promises are sincere.

"Hagenow on the other hand is a different proposition. She has made clear to me that she regards this as her country, and that she believes she not only acted, but intends to continue acting in what she sees as its interests." He paused for a moment, a silent sigh, eyes turned upwards at the ceiling. "I was wondering whether your department might have any suggestions?"

His question absorbed me for the moment. How could my department have any suggestions? The judge saw my confusion, and helped out.

"Let us put it this way: Miss Hagenow seems to believe that she was serving her country, and wishes to continue to do so. She has suggested to me that you and she may be able to work out what she termed 'a deal'. She explained that you may be reluctant, and asked me to mention what she phrased *certain problems in Weitlingstrasse.*" He looked at my startled face for a moment, then nodded in satisfaction.

"What did she mean?" I asked him.

"I don't know. But I can see that it means something to you. So, Captain, what's it to be?"

I had no suggestions, and my immediate reaction was to

refuse her this chance. What was she after? Forgiveness? Redemption? But what was happening around the fascist headquarters in Weitlingstrasse was a big issue, big enough that I felt I should talk to my colleagues, in fact we should refer this matter up to the Ministerial Committee.

But first I had a question for the presiding judge.

"What happens if we don't want to do a deal with her, or if we can't?"

For the first time the judge was visibly less than sure of himself. He glanced down, cupping his chin in his hand for a moment before answering:

"I don't know. Within the judiciary we are proud of the fact that we no longer have political prisoners in the GDR. But what are Hagenow and Hartmann if not precisely that? They are being tried for a political crime, treason, if you will, although that is not what it says in the charges. Their guilt is plain, their agitation and intrigue against the revolution cannot be condoned. If I find them guilty they will become prominent political prisoners, yet if I find them not guilty .... I'm sure you see the difficulty. This is why I agreed to investigate a somewhat unorthodox course of action."

I could see his point, but I was damned if Evelyn was going to get off the hook that easily.

Judge Kirchherr was keen for me to talk to Evelyn. In fact State Prosecutor Henschel had already arranged for her to be brought over from the prison next door. Which explained why we were in Lichtenberg rather than at the Supreme Court. I'd been backed into a corner, and I would be meeting Evelyn Hagenow, like it or not.

Evelyn and I had known each other for years. We had never been good friends, but had moved in and out of each other's lives with a regularity which suggested we were close. But last year I'd had her arrested for treason, and she'd been on remand ever since.

I had been left alone in the robing chambers, but didn't have long to wait before I heard a discreet knock on the door.

"Enter."

Evelyn came in, followed by a warden. Her wrists were held in front of her, bound with choke cuffs, and she waited patiently while the guard unclipped the handles and unwound the chain. She didn't say a word the whole time, she just stood there, looking at me.

"Evelyn, please sit down."

She sat down slowly, smoothing the blue tracksuit bottoms over her thighs, then she looked up, her eyes closing for a moment as she slipped into her role. Behind her the guard left the room, gently shutting the door as she went.

"Martin," she started, her voice warming with every word. "I knew you'd come. I knew you'd be the one to see that I can help-"

"What do you want?" I asked. My voice was hard but unsteady. I wasn't ready for this, but you could bet that Evelyn had been preparing this meeting for weeks, if not months.

She didn't answer immediately, she just looked me in the eye for a heartbeat or two.

"I want to help."

I tried not to show any reaction, but I knew that no matter how hard I tried Evelyn knew me well enough to see right through me.

"You know I want to help, otherwise you wouldn't have agreed to see me. And you know that I really can help."

"I wasn't given a choice. The judge just told me to wait here-"

"And of course Martin Grobe always does what he's told, doesn't he? You can tell that to your hat, I know you better. You were intrigued, weren't you? Go on, admit it."

I didn't admit it. I leaned back in my chair and crossed my legs, pretending to admire the fine wooden panelling. I

45

suppose I wasn't very convincing.

"What's it like? Outside, I mean. I know it's sunny, I can see that much through the glass bricks in my cell. But what's it like?" She knew my weak points, she knew exactly what to say.

"You know what it's like outside, they just brought you along the road." I struggled a bit, trying to get off her hook.

"No." Evelyn shook her head. "They brought me here through a tunnel, I haven't been outside, not properly. Not since last September."

I knew she would have been outside, but only in those exercise cells—small rooms with wire mesh instead of a ceiling. An armed guard looking down on you from the catwalk above. If you stopped to look at the sky he'd tell you to keep moving.

It was no way to keep a person, no matter what they may have done.

"It's spring," I said, feebly.

"Oh, silly Martin," laughed Evelyn, "I know that. But what's it *like*? In the parks, the woods, on the streets?"

The laugh was false, an act, but the questions were serious. I decided to humour her.

"It's warm. Very warm. The crocuses finished last week, the daffodils are starting to go brown. The plane trees are budding, you know that sticky, glossy bud they have? I cycled down Puschkin Allee the other day, and the trees are still dark and wintry, but when you look, you can see they're just waiting to burst out. There's willow catkins along the river Spree-"

"So early, it's all so early!" Evelyn laughed again, and this time it sounded real. "Oh Martin, I just want to get out of these buildings, I want to run through the Treptower Park, I want to see all the grass growing, the Prussian garlic pushing through the soil next to the river, is the dog's mercury out, are the cherry trees in blossom? Just imagine, I'd hear the cuckoo and the woodpecker, if we were there early enough in the morning the blackbirds would be singing. If you took me away from here right now we'd go down to the Rummelsburg Lake and we'd look down the river—we could see for miles and miles, we could watch the cormorants and the herons, see the gulls soaring through the blue sky!"

For Evelyn the walls of the court house had disappeared, she could see the woods of the park, the open spaces of the wide river. Her eyes danced with the joy of her vision.

I couldn't meet her eye. I was the one who'd put her in jail, I was the reason she couldn't see the blue skies and the growing spring.

DAY 5
Friday
18th March 1994

Berlin: *Striking workers from the Chemical Triangle will today call for hard currency investment in their industry. The workers from various plants in the Leipzig-Halle-Bitterfeld area, who have been on strike for over a fortnight, will hold a demonstration in the capital this morning.*

10:27
Martin

There was no morning meeting today—my colleagues were at the Ministry, having a pow-wow with some big cheese. I'd managed to get out of it, arguing that we couldn't leave the office completely unattended. That's why I was here when Nik came calling. I was typing up a report on yesterday's confab with the President of the Court and Evelyn. The judge had asked me to make a choice, but I didn't feel it was a choice for me or my colleagues at RS, it was one for the Ministerial Committee. I was pecking away at the typewriter, wishing I didn't have to write all these reports all the bloody time—pages and pages of them, most of which would probably go straight into the archives without even being read. A peculiarly German disease, I was telling myself, just as Nik tapped on the door frame.

I got out from behind my desk, and plugged in the kettle, placing two cups on the table and started hunting for sugar.

"No need for sugar," said Nik, patting his waistline.

I shrugged, and poured the hot water over the grinds, the warm aroma of coffee filled the office. I passed Nik his cup, and waited for him to tell me why he'd come calling.

"I was on my way over here when I ran into a demonstration on the Unter den Linden. Chemical workers, you know, the strikers." He lifted a few files off the visitor's chair and looked around for somewhere to put them, before giving up and plonking them on top of another pile. "There were lots of them—at least a couple of thousand. But really, what's the point? Who are they demonstrating to?"

The area around Leipzig, Halle and Bitterfeld, usually called the Chemical Triangle, had been devastated by open cast mining and the chemical industry. With the fall of the Party in 1989 this process had been reversed. Several mines had been shut and chemical production had been cut back while the plants were renovated. This came as a relief to the local population—air quality had already improved, the water coming out of their taps was once again safe to drink—but it came at a cost: jobs.

For some workers the only option was to move elsewhere to take up other work. And who wants to do that?

To be fair, they weren't the only ones in such a situation, lots of people were having to relocate as the economy restructured and industry was repurposed to cater for domestic needs rather than the Soviet dominated international market of COMECON. Sometimes this worked well—factories could be refitted and workers retrained. But at other times it was associated with real social upheaval on a regional level, such as in Bitterfeld, Espenhain and Leuna.

While I was thinking about the workers of the Chemical Triangle Nik had gone into the reception area to fetch his briefcase.

"Here's something to cheer us up." He pulled out a paper bag, put it on my desk and ripped the side open, revealing a couple of slices of cake. "I'll brew more coffee, shall I?"

I went into the front office to get plates from the cupboard and when I got back Nik was standing by the bookshelves. He was looking at a little plastic yellow box.

"Is this what I think it might be?" he asked.

"Guess."

"Socialist Work Award?" He opened it up and chuckled, pulling out a cheap alloy medal. "When did you ever earn a Work Medal?"

"I didn't. One of the punks gave it to me last year. Said it had been his mother's. She's dead, but he reckoned that she'd have wanted me to have it." I shrugged. "It would have been rude not to take it."

Nik sat down again, still smiling, and slid a slice of cake onto his plate.

"You know, they impressed me today on their march."

I cocked an eyebrow at him, but Nik was too busy finishing off his second cup of coffee to respond immediately.

"Some skins turned up," he finally carried on. "About twenty or thirty of them. They tried to join the march, but the chemical workers weren't having any of it, they didn't want the skinheads marching with them. Scuffles broke out. The police intervened. They were trying to pull the skins out of the march, after all, the skins had no chance: thirty against two thousand! And instead of being grateful, the skins started bawling about their constitutional rights, freedom of expression, all that stuff. Hypocrites! Then one of them started singing, and as soon as that happened all the skins stopped fighting, they stood in a line and sang. Every last one of them sang."

"They sang?"

Nik shook his head at the memory. "You'd never rate it, really. They just stood there in a line, as if they'd rehearsed it.

They sang that old song: *Thoughts Are Free.*"

I sat there at my desk, sipping my coffee and feeling angry.

"Yeah, exactly. That was my reaction too," said Nik, reading my mind.

We both finished our coffees in silence, and between us hung the image of a gang of skinheads standing in the middle of a demonstration, singing a song of revolution and freedom.

"Anyway, what was it you came in for?" I asked eventually. "You seem to be spending more time here than at your own offices."

"I told Laura that I'd come and have a look through some police reports—she said they'd be on her desk."

I watched him go over to Laura's office, then got on with my own work.

11:12
Karo

COMMUNIST SCUM!

I couldn't see anybody on the street but the red paint was still wet, dripping down the wall of the offices where Martin works. I shrugged and rang the doorbell.

One of Martin's colleagues let me in, some old dude I'd never seen before, about the same age as Martin. I was going to ask him about the paint job but the guy just looked so grey and tired that I didn't bother.

When I knocked on Martin's door he had his irritable face on, as if he was expecting someone else and wasn't too happy about it. But then he saw me and chilled out.

I sat down in front of his desk but felt embarrassed. I'd come here to apologise, but I wasn't much good at that kind of thing.

"Do you want a coffee? Or there's a bit of cake here-"

"Martin, shut up a minute will you?" I was looking at my

feet, but told my head to look at Martin. He'd stopped blethering and was waiting for me to say something.

"I wanted to say sorry. Y'know, for shouting at you the other night." I looked at Martin. Now he was examining his feet. Or his desk because his feet were hidden somewhere underneath.

"No, no. I actually agree with you," he said. "And anyway, it was the wrong time to talk to you about something like that."

"I was pissed."

"Yeah. So was I. A bit."

My fingers were doing that knot thing, you know, when they sort of start squeezing each other and you wonder whether they're ever going to come apart again. I stopped doing it.

"But I'm glad you came to the concert. Even if we did argue. Did you enjoy it?"

Martin looked a bit lost for a minute. "Yes, I did," he fibbed, his eyes sliding off over the desk.

"You liar!" I grinned. "Are we OK then?"

"We're OK."

"But what you were talking about—look, I'm against the Wall," I couldn't really stop myself blurting it out, and now I'd started I couldn't stop again. "This time round we've got to stop the power structures from becoming established. We don't need things like ID cards, like the Wall. We can't give the state that kind of control over us!"

Martin didn't say anything, and his eyes went glassy.

"Of course," he said after a bit. "The ends shouldn't ever justify the means you said. But if we keep the Wall I can control who comes in, who goes out, what goods are coming in and going out. It's a practical thing, an economic thing. That's the whole point of it. Without that Wall we won't have the chance to do what we need to do to keep our country going."

I heard what he was saying. He was saying that if we got rid of the Wall then the GDR would follow soon after.

"But so long as we have a Wall we can't be free!" I was almost shouting now.

Something moved behind me, a swish of clothes, it was Martin's colleague. He must have come to check what all the shouting was about.

"But if we can't have a GDR without a Wall, and we can't have freedom with the Wall then there's no answer is there, young lady?" the colleague said.

"Who the fuck asked you, anyway?" I snarled at him, and he backed away, giving Martin a look as he went.

"Welcome to real life," I heard him breathe as he went.

"Who the fuck's that?" I asked Martin.

"That's Nik. Leave him alone."

"Nosy twat!"

I took a deep breath, Martin and this Nik had really got on my wick. I needed to calm down.

"Yeah, I know all of that," I told Martin, "What you and your Nik said. But we've got to do what we think is right, haven't we? Give me some credit, will you? It's not like I was born yesterday."

"How about that coffee?" asked Martin, getting up when I nodded. "It's good that you came round, I wanted to ask you a favour."

"Give me the coffee first and I'll think about it. Can I have that bit of cake too?"

Martin

When my colleagues returned I decided to go home. An earworm was playing like a broken record in my head—the tune wouldn't let me go. In such situations I usually just listen to the song, several times over if needs be. Most of the earworms that invade my conscience are from my own music collection so it's just a case of finding the right LP.

But *Thoughts Are Free* wasn't in my collection.

I was in the kitchen, looking out of the window, down to the S-Bahn tracks below. A red signal glared at me from further along the embankment. *Thoughts are free / Who may guess them aright?* How did it go after that?

I left the flat again, going down the stairs to the cellar, opening the flimsy padlock on the wooden trellis that guarded my corner. I looked around the small cubicle: shelves stacked with boxes, preserving jars, empty beer bottles, an old cuckoo clock. It was the boxes I was interested in, and I moved them around, trying to read the faded pencil scrawled on the sides and tops. Coughing in the dust, I pulled a box down. It was heavy, almost slipping through my fingers. Opening it up, I looked inside. At the very top a big, hardback book: *Vom Sinn unseres Lebens.* Beneath that, school books, exercise books, a pencil box, a wooden ruler. This was the right one. Pulling the books out, glancing at covers and spines before placing them on the floor. There it was. A yellowish-brown cover: *Songs for the JG.* I opened it up, pausing for a moment at the rounded, childish writing on the flyleaf. *Katrin Grobe, 14 years.* Turning to the last page I scanned down the contents list. There it was—flick back through the book until I got to the right page.

Our thoughts are free,
Who may guess them aright?
They pass fleetingly,
Like shades in the night.
No-one can know them,
No hunter can shoot them
With powder and lead:
Our thoughts are free.

Reading the words, my finger tracing the notes up and down the staff, my mind went back to a damp day in the woods. Saxon Switzerland: a holiday, just me and Katrin. Her mother had already gone, it must have been the summer after. We were walking through the woods towards the *Bastei,* one of those fantastical stacks that the wind has carved from soft sandstone. It was raining, a light drizzle that collected and coalesced on the close beech canopy before dripping into the thick mist below. We couldn't see very far, our world was made up of emerald light, pewter beech trunks and the bronze of last year's leaves covering the earth. We walked hand in hand along the path, gradually becoming aware of the singing that seeped through the rain —deep, slow yet joyous. By the time we could make out the words of his song, he was in sight. Standing beside the path, bare-headed, hands behind his back, face raised to the verdant roof above him.

I think what I will,
And what gives me pleasure.
It's all very still,
And all in good measure. My wishes and longings
Let no one be mocking.
It will always be
That thoughts are free.

He was singing for the pleasure of it, for no audience but the surrounding trees. We stood listening as the tune washed around the woods, and it seemed to both chill and warm us.

> And if they locked me
> In a dark dungeon,
> That would clearly be
> A labour in vain;
> For my own thoughts, they
> Tear down the barriers
> And the walls that be:
> For thoughts are free.

A beautiful song, a dangerous song. A song in the rare land between official acceptance and overt resistance. A song that was uncomfortable for the Marxist-Leninist Workers' Party—the Party that knew best, that couldn't allow its subjects to have their own thoughts. A Party that had to accept the song for its pedigree: revolution, freedom, resistance against imperialism and fascism. A Party that dare not ban such a song outright.

> That's why I forever
> Cast off all worries.
> And nevermore will
> Let whims plague me.
> For in our own hearts we
> Have laughter and fun
> And thereby we see:
> That thoughts are free.

A song that wound its way through the trees, wound its way into our hearts. A moment apart from a grey world, a moment in the fairy kingdom of the beech forest and the solitary singer in the mist.

Martin

I rapped on the steel door of the watchtower and a *Grenzer* opened up, only letting me in after I'd shown him my official papers. I climbed up the metal ladder, past the mess level to the darkened observation deck at the top. As I poked my head up through the hatch I saw Rico holding a muttered conversation with a customs officer. They both turned as I came up, and Rico crossed over to me.

"Martin, thanks for coming. We've got something you might find interesting." Rico held out his hand, looking pleased to see me again. "This is my colleague from Customs Administration Service, *Obersekretär* Kalle Reinhardt."

The customs officer, a tall thin fellow, older than Rico but still with youth on his side, had been peering through the north-west windows. He motioned for us to join him, holding out the binoculars for me. I didn't need them—in the gathering dusk I could quite clearly see the small group of punks climbing a ladder, then rolling over the top of the wall, less than 150 metres from the tower.

"Apparently they're on the way to a squat, it's called the Køpi," I told them, "They have concerts there practically every night. It's on Köpenicker Strasse, just the other side of Engeldamm. And there's another trailer site there too."

Although the Køpi and the nearby *Wagenburg*—Schwarzer Kanal—were in the East, the most direct route between here and there was to cross the Wall twice, heading through the last corner of West Berlin. There was no border crossing near the Køpi, so jumping over the Wall at that point was the only option.

"Reports of provocations have been received from that sector too." Rico nodded. "They're climbing over the Wall on Engeldamm."

We observed the punks until the whole of the small group had disappeared over the rounded asbestos tube that topped the whitewashed concrete of the Wall.

"Have you spoken to them about it?"

"The Section Commander is keen to avoid any conflict. He says we have more important things to worry about than a few chaos-mongers."

Kalle exchanged a glance with Rico, something passed between them, a message, a negotiation, some kind of agreement.

"Perhaps you'd be interested in this?" he said, and shinned down the ladder.

Rico and I followed him, and we left the command tower, walking over the sandy grass towards the other side of Puschkin Allee. Once over the road we picked our way across hard-packed earth, hemmed in by abandoned guard-dog kennels, followed by battered cobbles criss-crossed by redundant tram tracks. We entered a door in the side of the bus repair workshop, a semi-derelict red-brick building from the turn of the century. Up several dimly-lit flights of stairs, all the doorways bricked up, until we reached the attic level. From there we went out onto a walkway that crossed the tar-paper roof, about three metres from the edge. The roof sloped down to my right, and I could see the factory lights shining through the saw-tooth skylights. Ahead of us— merely a shadow marring the sparkling reflection of the moon in the river—I could make out the customs pier. But to the left another railing marked the edge of the building which loomed over the weir lead that ran parallel to the Landwehr Canal.

That was the border to West Berlin.

Kalle and Rico were leaning on the railing that edged the catwalk, watching the weir channel.

"We've had a tip-off: watch the bushes on the far bank. If the information is correct then we should see some activity in the next half-hour or so," Kalle whispered to me.

A lazy wind came off the river, blowing across the roof. I

pulled my collar up, and zipped my jacket as far as it would go, leaning back against the railing, burrowing my hands into my pockets. But Kalle was right, we didn't have to wait long. Rico tapped me gently on the shoulder and pointed across the channel to Kreuzberg. The moon wasn't yet half full, and clouds nudged past, casting the landscape into shade. Only the cement works and cranes on the riverside could be seen—the buildings and bushes that covered most of the ground in front of us were as murky as the inky ribbon of water below us. Eventually I made out shadows, denser than the background gloom of the bank. They were manhandling something into the water—a rubber dinghy, perhaps a rigid inflatable. Whenever the wind dropped the lapping of oars cut through the dissonance of traffic drifting over from West Berlin.

Kalle headed along the catwalk and we followed him, around to the right and down some steps. From here we could see the customs pier—part of the border defences—and the gap in the piling that extended to the Oberbaum Bridge. Kalle pointed down that way, but I was too busy watching the mouth of the weir lead, waiting for the dinghy to appear, and I didn't notice the speedboat until its buzzing engine caught my attention. Presumably it had come from one of the old harbour buildings on the Kreuzberg side of the river, halfway between here and the bridge, but it dashed up the river towards us, engine whirring loudly, its bow wave breaking on the banks and piles. A swerve to starboard and it disappeared into the mouth of the Landwehr Canal.

I turned away from the river, wanting an explanation of what just happened, but Rico just nodded towards one of our customs boats. It had set off from the pier, and was making way down the river, presumably looking for the place where the speed boat had launched. But Rico wasn't interested in our customs launch, he was now watching the little dinghy, its nose just pushing out of the mouth of the weir. It hung around, allowing its bow to catch the stream, careful not to be drawn out into the river, the oars being used to keep position.

It was a good few minutes before the customs launch came back our way, searchlight stabbing the banks until it focussed on the dinghy. The two figures in the small boat could be clearly seen now, casually paddling backwards, moving further back into the weir lead, back into West Berlin.

The customs boat stayed in the river, its light following the slow progress of the boat until it disappeared under the lee of our building.

"What the hell was all of that?" I asked Kalle and Rico. Kalle looked away, while Rico gave me a grim smile. They went back along the catwalk, leaving me to follow.

"They're testing us, to see how fast we react, what we notice," Kalle told me, looking over his shoulder as he went. "They know their rubber dinghy is very hard to spot on the radar and that we're relying on visual contact from the observation towers on the pier and in the *Osthafen* on the other side of the river—you can't really cover the mouth of the weir from the Oberbaum Bridge. The problem is that the Wall was built to keep people *in*, not smugglers *out*. Our observation positions are facing the wrong way," said Rico, not bothering to whisper any more, assuming there would be no more action this night. "And the speedboat, it went into the Landwehr Canal—and that's a lock mouth. But they wouldn't have gone through the lock, they would have just pulled the boat up the bank in front of the lock gates." He pointed towards the edge of the roof. "The whole width of the weir lead down there is in Kreuzberg. As soon as that dinghy moved beyond the line of the river bank it was in West Berlin."

★

Back at the Section Command Tower Kalle brewed up some coffee in the mess.

"Anything to report?" Rico asked the *Grenzer* at the signals desk.

"Yes, comrade Sergeant." The soldier at the desk turned the logbook round for Rico to look at.

Rico read the log, his finger tracing each entry.

"Here, look—while they were messing about on the river a third boat crossed from the Kreuzberg side of the canal, dropping off a package further down Lohmühlenstrasse," he said to me before turning his attention back to the *Grenzer*. "Has a signal already been sent to Staff and the GKSi?"

"Yes, comrade Sergeant."

Rico grunted appreciatively. "I better get on with my report too, but first let's have that coffee. Kalle—how long do you need to brew a cuppa?" he shouted down the hatch to the mess below. "I hate nights like this."

We climbed down the ladder to the mess level where Kalle had a pan of water on the electric ring.

"Is Giesler not on duty tonight?"

Rico and Kalle shared a glance, much the same as they had when I'd turned up earlier.

"No, he put in for a transfer after your visit on Tuesday. And now he's gone." Rico shook his head and Kalle busied himself with taking cups out of the locker. "I don't know how he managed to organise the transfer so quickly but good riddance if you ask me. That one had history."

DAY 6
Saturday
19th March 1994

Berlin: The new General Secretary of the Communist Party, the PDS, will today call on the government to ensure decisive action is taken against the fascist threat facing the country. In a speech this morning Karl Kaminsky will tell his party that only a strong, central leadership can steer the GDR out of the current crisis.

08:07

Martin

It was past eight when I left home, heading down the still cool streets toward the office. If I hurried I should just about make it in time for the morning meeting.

I hadn't slept well—it had been late by the time I'd got back last night, and then I'd had trouble getting to sleep.

Excuses I told myself. *It's not about how well you slept, you've got a job to do—it's lack of discipline. Faith,* another part of me replied, *not enough faith.*

Perhaps I had too many questions about whether and how I was contributing to our Republic. In the old days it was so easy—easy to imagine a perfect way of organising our society, easy to ignore the real-life problems, the complex logistics of keeping eighteen million people rubbing along.

But the problems didn't end there, the reality was that not

all of those eighteen million souls wanted us to succeed, many had radically different ideas of what our country should look like.

Put that way, we had no chance, I thought to myself.

Too much thinking, old son, too much thinking.

By now I'd got to the office, and was examining the new graffiti on the wall outside.

We'd agreed to come in this Saturday morning to catch up on the meeting we'd missed. So far we'd finished the general part and had moved on to the fascist case.

"I saw Nik yesterday," I told the others. "He told me he saw the fascists try to gatecrash the chemical workers' demo. But the chemical workers weren't having any of it, they literally distanced themselves from the skins."

"Speaking of Nik," responded Laura. "He wanted to drop in this morning but he couldn't get here on time. He's had a look at some of the police reports and he's suggesting we let someone he knows have a look at the material. She used to be an agitation and propaganda expert working for the Party, and Nik reckons she can do something he calls 'reverse engineering'. I think it means having a look at what the fascists have been doing publicly, then taking back-bearings and working out what their intentions are."

Nik's idea wasn't bad, such an analysis could be useful, but it didn't sit easily. The Communists were exploiting the current upsurge in fascist activity—they had their propaganda machine running at full tilt—using a law and order strategy, blaming the Round Tables for being soft on the fascists, despite the fact that the current problem of fascism in our country had its roots in the years of the Communist dictatorship.

"Is this analyst still a Party member?" I asked. "If she's still close to the Party then we can't just hand over the material—they'll cherry pick the juicy bits to back up their arguments for a firm leadership by the Party of the Proletariat!"

"I don't know, I'll ask Nik about any current connections to the Party." Laura made a note for herself and the meeting moved on.

I told them about the strange water ballet of the two boats last night, and how it didn't seem to make any sense.

"And what's that got to do with us?" asked Laura.

"This thing with the boats seems to be happening regularly, and customs suspect it's related to smuggling. I think it may tie into our theory that the fascists are smuggling their propaganda material in from the West. It seems sensible to follow it up, see if there are any connections."

Erika nodded in agreement, but Laura was frowning. "We haven't got any capacity for that kind of thing."

"Oh, Laura, we're only going through paperwork and observing fascist marches, I think this lead looks quite promising," said Erika, winking at me across the room.

"OK, let's do it. Martin, do you want to follow up on it—you seem to have the contacts already?"

"I'll talk to the Border Police and Customs."

We ticked off the next few points in short order: the fascists had registered another march in Berlin, and several more around the country too; Laura was to liaise with the Ministry—it was nearly a week since we'd found out about the IKM informant and we still hadn't been allowed access to the operational files.

"There is one other thing—about that meeting I had with the State Prosecutor on Thursday. Turns out it wasn't actually the prosecutor that wanted to see me—it was the President of the Court in charge of the case against Evelyn Hagenow and Benno Hartmann. Evelyn wants to do some kind of deal and the judge is keen on the idea." I filled them in on my meeting with the judge and Evelyn.

"But what does she want to do? What's she offering?"

asked Laura.

"To penetrate the fascist scene, to be an agent. To gather intelligence that can be used in a criminal investigation against them."

"Stasi tactics," Erika said, almost under her breath.

Laura ignored the interruption. "But the police already have an IKM there, and anyway, they'd recognise her!"

"No, they've been very clever. Think about it: there's not been a single picture of her in the papers or on the telly. They've been hiding her away, almost as if they've been preparing for this."

But it was Erika who asked the big question, the one that had been bothering me since I'd spoken to Evelyn.

"Can we trust her?"

No-one gave an answer. It wasn't up to us to decide whether or not to trust her. Our job was to pass the information upstairs, to the Ministry. Let them make the decision. We wouldn't be part of executing any plan anyway —that task would fall to the *Kripo*. To all intents and purposes we'd already done our bit. There wouldn't be any more contact with Evelyn, and I was glad of that.

Once everyone had left my office I rang the Customs Administration, asking when I could see the Chief Inspector of Customs. I spoke to a very helpful secretary who offered me an appointment with an underling in three weeks time.

"And what if I just pop round to the Chief Inspector's office on Monday morning?" I asked.

"That would be quite impossible!" I swear there was panic in that secretary's voice. "There won't be anyone available unless you have an appointment, good day." He hung up.

I'd probably do better to have a chat with my new friend in the Border Police. I rang his regimental HQ in Treptow, and once I identified myself they proved far more accommodating.

"Comrade Staff Sergeant Müller is on early shift this week —he will be at the Section Command Tower Puschkin Allee until 1400 hours."

I looked at my watch, I'd better get a move on if I was to catch Rico.

10:54
Karo

"Fucking wankers!" I turned the radio off again.

I only turned it on to get the music events listing on *DT64*. But some fucker had tuned the radio to DDR I and I got the news instead. Communist Party blaming the Round Tables for the fascist disease! Yeah, well, we tried their authoritarianism for forty years—they're the ones who gave us this problem. Bastards seem to reckon that we've already forgotten that we were the ones who chucked them out!

I decided to stop ranting at the empty room and tried to work out why the news had wound me up so much. I guess I was scared that they could still come back, things would be like the old days again, when people like me would be harassed the whole time, locked up now and again, not allowed to work or only given the shittiest jobs. When people would give up and try to leave the country rather than put up with the hassle.

And the fucking hypocrisy! The PDS pretending they're concerned about the rise of nationalists and authoritarians— jealous more like, because somebody else was using their tactics!

But they were right about one thing, we needed to act against the fash. I'd been ignoring it for too long. It was time to get involved, cos things were only going to get worse.

Martin

As I'd told Evelyn, the plane trees were budding early. Cycling up Puschkin Allee I could see the folded leaves glistening in the midday sunlight. The sight of them made me stop to look more closely, appreciating the freedom I had to do just that. Dismounting and pushing my bike between the large concrete flower pots that marked the end of the road and the start of the border zone, I kept an eye open for Rico, but the only people to be seen were the trailer residents.

Leaning my bike against the side of the tower, I banged on the steel door, my knocks echoing around the sandy park that was being laid out on the old death-strip. The door creaked open and a guard looked out. He pointed me towards the roof top of the bus garage on the other side of the street, where Rico, Kalle and I had watched the boats last night.

I climbed up the stairs, and went out through the tiny door onto the catwalk, making my way towards the figure looking down at the river. As I got closer I could see it was Rico.

"Hi Martin." He shook my hand before offering me a cigarette. "The duty officer said you might be coming by."

"I've got some questions about the smugglers. I tried talking to the big cheeses at the Customs Administration, but they just fobbed me off. I thought it might be better talking to someone on the ground."

"You want to have a word with Kalle? He's the customs officer in charge of this sector."

I shook my head, Rico could probably help just as well. "We think large shipments are coming in from the West, and we're fairly sure they're not coming in through the proper channels. There's a fascist group with huge amounts of printed materials, including banners and placards that obviously haven't been produced over here. So we're wondering how they might have got them across the border."

Rico laughed, almost choking on his cigarette.

"Are you serious?" he asked. "Ever heard the expression about the needle and the haystack? You saw what happened the other night, they're running rings around us—what you're looking for could be coming in at any point along the border. The Wall leaks like a sieve now, and it's only going to get worse. There's not enough Border Police to keep an eye on the whole of the Wall, and the border zone isn't at all secure since we opened up the death strip. Now they're talking about reducing our numbers. And that referendum coming up—if the people vote to get rid of the Wall .... We're going to have to get used to the fact that smuggling is here to stay."

"What kind of things are coming over the Wall in this sector?"

"Well, you know about that lot." Rico nodded over his shoulder, towards the wagons and trucks behind him. "They're probably taking beer over to the West, maybe cigarettes from Poland. They'll flog them over there and bring cannabis back. But that's nothing, there are rumours of more serious stuff coming in. Heroin, crack, and some chemical thing they're calling 'E'. We're trying to move towards intelligence led policing, but look at us, we're not really policemen, are we? We're just soldiers. For years, they told us to shoot anything that moved, now they tell us we need to be intelligent." He chuckled at his own joke.

"But back to your problem. Look, how big are these consignments, a pallet? Two? It could be coming in on a regular lorry—customs can't check every load like they used to. Or somewhere along the green border, round the back of West Berlin or along the inner-German border—bribe a guard to open up a maintenance gate and look the other way for ten minutes."

He paused for a moment to shake his head, tapping ash off the cigarette. Then he pointed at a barge being pushed by a tug, making its way downriver.

"Or what about them. They come in and out, loaded with coal and gravel." We looked down on the barge, its covers were open, showing several dumps of gravel. "All we can do with that lot is poke sticks in it. In the old days we'd have dogs sniffing, checking for the smell of humans, but it's not people smugglers you're after, is it?

"And come to think of it, what about the Baltic coast? You could have a fishing boat come out of Travemünde or anywhere in the West—a launch could just bring the goods ashore. And now Dömitz has been opened up you can bring small boats in from the Elbe, right into the heart of Mecklenburg."

Rico was piling on the options: there were so many ways in and out of our country, a country that just a short time ago had been hermetically sealed against the West. And the way Rico was talking it all sounded pretty obvious, yet in the office I'd imagined that we could somehow narrow down the options, work out the probable entry points for the fascist material. Now it just looked hopeless.

"Don't look so down in the mouth!" Rico clapped me on the shoulder, "there's always a way. Look, I wasn't here in the old days, before 1990, but there's plenty of guys in the ranks who were. We talk, you know, they tell tall tales of what it was like back then, the loneliness of being on guard duty on the border, just hoping that nobody would try to escape on your watch. Because if you saw someone you'd have to shoot them. If you didn't see them, or if you looked the other way, well, your life wouldn't be worth living."

The tug and barge were past us now, but had slowed down and given off a long, low whistle followed by a second, shorter blast.

"But that's not the point. In the old days the Stasi were

always sniffing around. They were always watching us, and at the same time, watching everyone who came into the restricted area near the border. They were on the look-out for people planning an escape over the Wall. Now that's what they really mean by intelligence-led policing, isn't it? Things don't change so much, do they?" Rico shrugged. "So, Martin, what I'm trying to say is, if there's a plan to get something across the Wall, there'll be people who know about it. And there's your weak point. The more people who know about a plan, the more chance there is of a leak. Maybe you need to concentrate on that angle?"

In his roundabout way, the young man was telling me that my only chance was to make an effort to find out what the fascists were actually up to, and not just try to second guess their plans in order to catch them at it.

My thoughts returned, once again, to the mole that Lichtenberg Kripo had in the Nazi scene. Presumably they were in the process of extracting him now that the Nazis knew about him, but why weren't we being given access to the intelligence that had already been delivered?

12:32
Karo

"You ready for this?"

I nodded, yeah, ready as I was ever going to be. I'd gone to see the Antifa group as soon as I'd got up this morning. They were doing training and they'd given me a try-out right then.

I was knackered. I'd shown them all my moves, all the judo and karate self-defence stuff I'd learnt over the years. They weren't impressed, but Bert said I could tag along. A few of the lads grumbled, but no-one said anything to me.

Martin

I'd been back for a few hours and was trying to relax. Freygang was on the record player, but the political lyrics kept bringing my mind back to the chat I'd had with Rico.

Before I could follow my thoughts any further the doorbell rang.

"Hi Katrin!" I gave my daughter a hug in the doorway. I was so pleased to see her I didn't notice how stiff she was.

She pushed past me, into the hallway, not saying a word. Closing the flat door I followed her down to the living room and stood leaning against the door frame, watching her as she fell onto a chair at the table. She didn't make any further movement, and I knew her better than to press her. So I let her be and went into the kitchen to put a pan of water on the stove to make coffee.

"Papa?" she said finally, from the living room.

In the pan small beads of air gathered around the surface of the water, slowly turning to a faint steam. I turned off the gas and went into the living room. Katrin was still sitting at the table, she looked exactly as she had done a few minutes before, but she must have moved because there, lying in front of her was an envelope, torn along the top. A letter. The white paper looked innocent against the colourful oilcloth.

But from where I stood by the door I could feel the cold fingers of a ghost reaching out to me. I took a step towards the table, towards the envelope. My eyes fixed on it, hardly taking in the West German stamp, just concentrating on the writing. It was intimately familiar to me: the swirls, the pressures, the scratches where the pen hadn't quite lifted off the paper to form the next letter of Katrin's name and address. I hadn't seen that writing for years.

The ghostly fingers slowly, tenderly, wrapped themselves around my heart, tightening and freezing me in the winter of their grip.

"It arrived yesterday," Katrin said. "I didn't know what to do. I didn't know whether to tell you, whether to hide it. Throw it away. Burn it."

I sank into the chair opposite Katrin, my eyes fixed on the letter. Questions swirled, but didn't make it as far as my mouth. *Have you read it? Why didn't you tell me as soon as you got it? Why tell me? Why didn't you hide this from me?*

"It's from Mama." The words broke loose, eddying from Katrin's mouth. Her eyes met mine as she said the obvious.

I looked away, away from the letter between us, away from my daughter's face. Up to the corners of the ceiling, grey webs woven with dust, swaying in the current of emotion.

"She asks if I want to have contact. With her. She says that now I'm 21 I'm old enough to understand the world."

My eyes descended again, focussing on Katrin's face, on the tears gathering in the corners of her eyes. A movement further down caught my attention, her hand was edging along the oilcloth, unguided but drawn towards the letter. I moved around the table, pulling my daughter into a hug, her face against my chest, her arms lying limp on the table.

We sat there all evening, silences punctuated by aborted conversations. Katrin had so many questions. So many feelings she couldn't find a place for.

"Why did she go?" she asked me.

I didn't have the answer, even though I'd seen it coming and had been there when it happened. I hadn't been able to stop it.

"She couldn't stand it. She felt that if she stayed there," it was here, here in the GDR, but it was a different country in those days, so I said *there*. "If she'd stayed there, it would have broken her. She wouldn't have survived."

"She didn't even apologise," said Katrin. "In the letter. She didn't make any attempt to explain or defend what she did."

Her mother's decision to leave seemed ineffable to my daughter.

That sounded like her, like Katrin's mother. She was strong, she knew herself, she knew her own limits. She'd decide to do something and then she would go ahead and do it, whatever the consequences.

"When did she go?" Katrin had been small, she'd just started school. But when exactly had her mother gone? In what month, on what day had she actually left the country? I didn't know.

Oh, I know when they came to search the flat, I know when and where we were each and every time they stopped us on the street, every time they took my wife into custody, releasing her minutes, hours or days later. I know when they tried to warn her—so often. I know when they came to warn me, waiting for me at work, on the way to the supermarket, outside the house: *Do you think we'll let you all leave? Do you think we'll let you keep the little girl? You can end this, make your wife withdraw her application to leave the GDR. Then you can get on with your lives.*

But I couldn't end it.

I know when they took her away that last time, the last time we saw her. She was dragged away from us, dry eyed, staring at us, fixing us in her memory as we stood in the doorway of our flat, too scared to follow them down the stairs. Katrin was hysterical, screaming, her clenched fists beating on my leg. The neighbour's doors all firmly shut, knowing better than to show any curiosity.

But I don't know when they let her out of prison. I don't know when they put her on a train to the West.

I don't know when she passed from our country to the other side.

Katrin kept her eyes fixed on the mug of coffee in her hands. She hadn't expected an answer, but she needed to ask the questions. The same questions that I had.

Karo

We were waiting in the bushes, just by the entrance to Nöldnerplatz S-Bahn station. Behind us was the gate to the railway yard, but at this time of night it was shut and locked.

"Isn't this a really stupid place to wait?" I whispered.

"This is the way they always come. Now keep quiet!" one of the hard lads said.

It was really boring, waiting in the darkness for some pissed up fashos to come sneaking into Friedrichshain. The idea was that they always come from the house they've got in Weitlingstrasse, and head this way to find a punk or foreigner to lay into. But only if the victim's alone—because five fascists against two or three punks wouldn't be an equal fight, would it?

"Do you do this every night?"

"No, just weekends. Now shut the fuck up. If they come now they'll hear us gossiping like girls."

I nearly did my karate moves on him, sexist pig. But I told myself I'd deal with him later. Right now I was here to get the fascists before they got us, and I was going to impress the fuck out of these chauvinist dinosaurs!

That's when the sexist pig stuck his elbow into my ribs. I was about to shout at him but then I heard some laughing coming from the subway that goes under the S-Bahn station. Six skins stopped just under the street light, passing a lighter round and sparking up their ciggies.

Ronny was at the front, and he held up his hand: wait.

The fash carried on, heading towards Kaskelstrasse, still laughing about something. As soon as they were under the next railway bridge Ronny's hand dropped, and we left the shadows, running quietly after the skins.

Ronny got there first, his arm went around the throat of the skinhead at the back, his fist smashed into the side of the fash's head. The other Antifa lads were just behind him, and the two groups collided, but there was no way I could see what was going on. There didn't seem to be any room for me to get in there, just a frenzy of shouts and fists. Ronny went down, and I got hold of his arms as paraboots thudded into his sides. But I managed to drag him out, and he was straight up on his feet and back in the middle of things. Just then, one of the skins made a break for it, went past me, so close I could have reached out my arm to touch him. But I didn't. I just stuck my foot out, and he toppled over, his nose ramming the concrete in a cloud of blood. The other skins must have legged it and left their mate to his fate, because my lot had surrounded the fash I'd felled. They were laying into him, big time. Boot after fucking boot was crunching into him.

DAY 7
Sunday
20th March 1994

Berlin: The parliamentary parties CDU and SPD are asking citizens to vote against the proposed devolution of power in next month's referendum. In a joint statement the parties called the Round Table system a stop-gap solution, and condemned it as both untenable and undemocratic.

12:42

Martin

I'd slipped into a new ritual: Sunday Mornings. Somehow, during the winter, and without even deciding to, I'd managed to ease off on the work front. I avoided working on Sundays, and I didn't take work home with me at weekends. Maybe it was because I finally realised that no matter how much I do, the revolution will never depend on me alone. For years, I'd been putting myself into this great project—heart, body and soul—and it was killing me. I was near my physical limits, and, after the stress of last autumn, my mental limits too.

Or maybe it had been Katrin, my daughter, nagging me: *there's more to life than this!*

And here I was, doing my Sunday Morning thing. Sitting in my favourite chair, sipping coffee, listening to records, or today, one of the tapes that my daughter had given me. She was introducing me to various funk and acid jazz bands from the English speaking world. She'd tried to excite my interest in this particular album by drawing comparisons with our home-grown Panta Rhei. I was relaxing to a bootleg of Incognito's *100° And Rising*, wondering whether or not it was actually similar to Panta's *Kinder dieser Welt* or *Gib dir selber eine Chance*. I could see why Katrin had made the comparisons, but the British band was bright and Panta Rhei was downbeat, owing more allegiance to classic blues. Perhaps it was because their best work had been before the start of the Revolution, when things were grey, and hope was scarce, manufactured only in small amounts by underground groups meeting clandestinely.

When Incognito bounced their way to *After the Fall* I got out of my chair, and, taking the cassette player with me, headed for the kitchen. I plugged the music in again, and Incognito carried on playing for me. Looking through the cupboards I wondered what to make for the house potluck lunch. We were becoming more and more creative when it came to cooking—the shortages of meat and milk products were making us re-examine our culinary culture—and I decided a mushroom and hazelnut pie would be a nice addition to the communal meal.

14:07

Martin

I pulled my pie out of the oven, satisfied with the golden-brown crust radiating warmth, the rising steam hinting at the gravy within. Wrapping it in a bath towel to keep it warm and to protect my hands, I negotiated the stairwell, heading for the *Kulturbund* rooms next door where the residents of my tenement held Sunday lunches. I was running a bit late, and most people had already started eating. I placed my pie on the side table, next to big bowls of red cabbage and bright vegetables, yeasty dumplings, letscho, a dish of kasha with root vegetables, a big pan of heaven-and-earth, a couple of kinds of sauces, several bowls of spring salads and a massive pot of *Rote Grütze* pudding.

I filled a plate and looked around for a place to sit. At the other end of the table Margrit, who lived a floor above me, gestured to the empty space next to her. I went over, rubbing her shoulder in greeting and sat down. On my other side was Frau Lehne, who was a bit deaf, and in any case preferred to enjoy her food rather than exchange small talk while at table, so I tucked in. The kasha was really good, and my pie lived up to expectations, garnering compliments from the other residents.

Once I'd finished my plate, I sat back, waiting a bit before going up for seconds. Margrit and I started talking, as usual, about our week, and when I mentioned that I'd been at the fascist demonstration she looked off into the distance, absenting herself from the chatter and clinking of cutlery on plates that surrounded us. After a moment she began telling me a story.

"A few years ago, at our factory, we had a Vietnamese woman in our work brigade. I say in our brigade, but she wasn't really. She couldn't speak German, and she never came along to any of the social events. But every day at work, there she was, stretching up to reach the workbench— she was too small for the standard issue stool that we all used. And one day she wasn't there any more. I didn't really notice for, oh, I don't know how long, a few days probably. Then I went to the brigade leader and asked where our colleague was, whether she was ill, whether anyone had gone to see her and check whether she needed anything. The brigade leader just shrugged and said I should talk to the union. So I went to the BGL office and tried to talk to them but they just shrugged and told me the *Fidschis* were none of my concern. This was in summer 1989, when we were all starting to get a bit uppity, so I didn't let the matter rest. I went to another brigade, one that was only Vietnamese contract workers. Problem was, there was only one of them who could speak any German at all. She said the same thing: *No, no. You leave, nothing for you*, was all she would say to me.

"So after work I went round to the hostel, the place where our factory put the contract workers. It was like student halls, only worse, they were really crammed in, triple bunk beds, a couple of a dozen people to each room. I had to blag my way past the security guard, and once I'd made it in, it took me a while before I could find anyone to talk to. So after asking a whole load of people I found this woman who could speak a bit of German. She told me that my colleague had been sent home, back to Vietnam. She was pregnant. That was it: she was pregnant. She was no longer suitable for work in our socialist homeland. All that propaganda about internationalism, about supporting the socialist brother-countries, but there I was in this hostel, men and women not allowed to mix, roll-call at six every morning, no integration with colleagues, no German lessons. Treated like prisoners, cheap labour, that's all they were. That is what the Party's proletarian solidarity looked like!"

I remembered the contract workers from Vietnam, Algeria, Hungary. Some had returned home in 1990, but many had stayed, seeing more opportunity and hope in our revolution than at home.

"I'll never forget her, but you know what I'm really ashamed of? I don't even know that woman's name. I didn't talk to her when she worked with us. In my brigade we all used to have a laugh, we'd all go to the canteen, go bowling together. But she was never there, she'd join her friends in the Vietnamese brigades. I never even asked her name." Margrit was staring at her plate as she talked, using her fork to poke at a few leftover crumbs of pie crust.

"And now when I see what's happening, just a few streets

away, I wonder whether it should really be such a surprise to us—if our socialist state was so racist, so lacking in respect for people, whether its own people or those who've come to help us with their labour—is it any surprise we've got this problem now, these racist, fascist bigots, running riot: pissing on people, pissing on our dreams?"

"But what can we do? What do you think we should do?" I asked her.

"Lock the bastards up, throw away the bloody key. It's what they deserve!" I was taken aback by her viciousness, but she hadn't finished. She gave me a half smile. "And yet we both know that's not really the answer, don't we? Why didn't they lock them up back then? I don't know. What do we do with these fascists? They're not the kind of people we can just *talk* to, are they?"

She paused again, obviously thinking, still poking the crumbs, pushing them along with her fork. Shove, shove, from one side to the other, then back again.

"We need a new way to deal with them. It's not like we can hold a referendum on whether to simply abolish racism and fascism. It's not enough to discuss it at the Round Table, talk about why we don't want them." She paused, still thinking about the problem, staring at her plate.

People had started to get pudding, so I got up and spooned *Rote Grütze* into a couple of bowls, taking them back to the table. I took the fork out of Margrit's hand and pushed her plate away, replacing it with a bowl. She was so deep in thought she hardly noticed the exchange.

"But you know what frightens me most about them?" She carried on as if I hadn't been away. "It's not the violence, although that's pretty awful. It's the absolute commitment, the unquestioning belief that they are right. We've seen it before, we've all seen that before, haven't we? But what scares me is that I too once believed. Years ago, when I first started work, I applied to be a Communist Party member candidate. I had the faith, but they didn't want me in the end. *An absence of political maturity* they said, and I'm glad about that now." She looked around for her spoon and picked it up, resting the blade of her hand on the table. "But you know what that means? It means that I could have been like them, unquestioning, unthinking, conforming."

A pause, while we both pondered Margrit's words, then she continued.

"And you know what? I wonder about it now, too. We have a belief system now. Sure, it's widespread, it's humanist, we're not going to beat people up if they don't agree with us. But how are we going to stop people if they're really set on tearing apart our dreams? People like these skinheads, or like those Stasi stooges you arrested last year. What do we do with them?"

I thought about the old *Politbüro*, the grey men who used to rule the country. They felt a humanist duty too, they thought that duty obliged them to issue orders to shoot people who tried to flee the country. They thought that humanist duty bound them to capture and torture those who thought differently.

The way we deal with those who think differently—the troublemakers, the ones who refuse to participate in our dreams—how we deal with them would be the making or breaking of us.

14:20
Karo

"Karo!" Schimmel was banging on my door, waking me up.

"The fuck? I was asleep, Schimmel!"

Schimmel didn't even stop, he loped across my room and pulled me off the mattress.

"You've got to see this, come on!"

I shook Schimmel off and left him standing there, arms dangling, face bright red, dead excited.

"OK then, what do you want?" I got up and pulled on a pair of jeans, then followed him down the hall.

Schimmel's room was full of junk. Metal and plastic boxes with wires and circuit boards and shit like that just lying around. It didn't make any sense to me, and it didn't look very homely either. He was squatting on the floor, in front of one of these boxes, a television balanced on top.

"Look at this!" he shouted, pointing at some green writing on the black screen in front of him.

I could see a load of Xs, and if I squinted hard enough I could make out the letters WOTAN BBS.

Schimmel typed something and the screen changed to some kind of list. Using the arrow keys Schimmel made the screen change a few more times.

"This is a Bulletin Board System used by the Nazis. Rex asked me to have a look at-"

"Whoa, slow down a bit! What you going on about Schimmel?"

"Look, it's really simple. This is a computer network, it's like ...." Schimmel took his eyes off the screen for a moment, looking round the room, trying to find a way to explain what he was doing. "Like a library, no, a filing cabinet. A message board. You dial in and you can leave stuff here, and see what others have left. Like files, or messages or whatever." Schimmel was still pressing lots of keys and the screen kept changing. A little box on the floor had four or five green lights that kept blinking at me.

"Dial in? You mean on a phone? We don't have a phone!"

Schimmel was concentrating, but he took a moment to grin at me. "I spliced into the line from that empty shop next door."

He was still stabbing away at the keyboard and I was about to have a go at him for waking me up for no reason when he yelled again.

"Here it is! I lost the connection before. Here, read this!"

I looked over his shoulder at the screen.

"This is the fash?"

"Yeah, I told you, I got the details from Rex. This is where they talk about what they're up to."

"What, so anyone can read it? Not even the fash are that stupid!"

"No, you can't find this unless you've got the phone number. And even then you need a password." Schimmel could tell I didn't know what he was on about so he tried again. "You get your computer to phone their computer, and they can share this." He pointed at the screen, all the information there. "But you can only do that if you know the phone number and have the right name and password."

"OK ...."

"And they write stuff like this." A few more clicks on the keyboard and a new load of type came up on the screen.

"So what's that, a list of their members?"

On the screen was a list of people's names and addresses. I didn't recognise any of them.

"No, I think it's a kind of hit list."

One of the names stuck out because almost all of the addresses were in East Berlin, but this one was a hospital in West Berlin. Schimmel pressed the down arrow and the lines slid up the screen to be replaced by yet more addresses.

"Shit!" Schimmel stopped pressing keys and pointed at the screen. "That's Martin!"

Martin

After the potluck I decided to give Incognito another go. I'd just pressed the play button when Karo banged at the door.

"Are you missing me?" I stopped when I saw her face. I don't think I've ever seen Karo look so serious. Schimmel stood in the hall behind her.

"Martin, you've got to look at this." Karo came right in, and was unreeling a computer print-out on my kitchen table. She jammed her finger onto one of the names. "This is you!"

I turned off the tape player and looked at where Karo was pointing. There was my name, Martin Grobe, and the address of the RS2 offices.

"What is this?"

"It's a list I found on a Bulletin Board used by the Nazis," Schimmel said from behind Karo.

I looked at Karo, hoping she could translate.

"It's like a meeting place for fascists, on a computer that they can all get access to."

Schimmel looked like he was going to argue with Karo's description, but she waved her hand at him. "It's a hit list—and you're on it!"

I picked up the end of the print-out and started looking through it. There was about twenty pages of names, all printed out in dot matrix, barely legible.

"Why do you think it's a hit list? Even if it is, there are so many names here that it'll take them years before I get to the top." I sat down and crossed my legs. I can't say I wasn't disturbed by seeing my name on this list, but after the events of last autumn I was public property—I'd been in the papers and on the telly. This kind of thing was only to be expected.

I started at the top of the list again, reading more carefully this time. "Look, practically the whole government is on this list, along with *Volkskammer* representatives, Central and local Round Table members—this is the list of a fantasist."

I managed to get Karo and Schimmel to calm down a bit, told them to make a coffee while I carried on looking through the list. "I'm going to pass the list on to *Kripo*," I told them, ignoring the face Karo pulled at the mention of the police. "And I'll take it into work. I'll go through our files, see if anyone on the list has come to grief recently. That way we'll know how seriously to take it."

Karo slumped onto a chair, her fear draining away. "But you're going to take it seriously?" she demanded. She waited for me to nod before going on. "OK, in that case, and since we're here anyway: I'm helping to set up a gig, up in Prenzlauer Berg. In the *Schlaraffenhaus*—it's going to be really cool. You wanna come? Say you will, because then we can keep an eye on you."

19:20

Martin

In the end I gave in to Karo's pleading and agreed to check out the gig. That's why a few hours later I off the tram at the end of Dimitroffstrasse, but outside the police station a group of people had converged, standing around a bloke strumming a guitar and crooning in a low voice. Somehow he managed to compete not only with the noise made by the band accompanying him, but also with the elevated railway and the trams going past. A small child strutted around in front of the singer, wearing denim dungarees, her hair was cut short at the front, rat tails dragging down the back of her neck. She held a pair of drumsticks and air drummed while the band played out. Meanwhile, the next act waited in the wings: jeans hanging loose around his waist, shirt open over a T-shirt advertising some Western band.

A drunkard stumbled through the crowd, arms paddling—clawing himself along, hands grappling the air.

Oblivious to the impromptu concert, crowds of people swelled around the knot of music lovers, growing and diminishing to the rhythm of the traffic lights controlling the pedestrian crossing.

The person next to me half turned and elbowed me in a drunken, friendly way.

"Drink!" he shouted, waving a bottle of vodka at me and smiling. His forehead was shadowed under the peak of a traditional *Heinrichsmütze* cap, but his face lit up periodically in the headlights of cars turning onto Schönhauser Allee.

He produced two glasses, and poured out some vodka, right up to the brim. Parking the bottle in his pocket, he gave me my shot, looked me in the eye, toasted me then necked the liquid.

"*Prosit!*" I swallowed down my vodka too.

"*Prosit!*" he said again, about to turn away, ready to find another recipient for his liquid generosity.

"Where are you from?" I asked him before he went.

"I am of German Democratic Republic," he slurred, but still rolling the Rs, "of G-D-R" He pronounced it the Russian way: *Djay-Day-Err*.

"You're new here? Welcome!"

"This is my home, *Djay-Day-Err*. I am here. Now I am happy and I am safe. And *Prosit!*" He moved on, readying the glasses for a refill.

19:39

Karo

I was sorting out the loudspeakers in the cellar-bar when Martin got there. A couple of band members were meant to be helping but they were just getting in the way and being generally annoying. So I left them to it and gave Martin a hug.

"Still alive then?" I could smell drink on his breath. "You stink! You started drinking already? Anyway, you're gonna love this, they're an amazing act—you're going to cream yourself!"

"O-kaaay." Martin raised an eyebrow at me.

"No, seriously, man. You. Are. Gonna. Love. The show!" I told the two hippies what to do with the wires and took Martin back up into the yard. "It's jazz. The band that shoulda played tonight, they bailed out. Post folk-punk-metal it was. But these guys offered to plug the gap, and I listened to a demo tape. Fucking. Ace. I mean, even I like them!"

Martin shrugged as if to say he reserved the right to leave at any point.

I punched him on the shoulder.

One of the drummers was a dude with really wide shoulders, red shirt stretched tight over his chest. Forearms like tree trunks. The whole time he was playing he had his eyes fixed on the other drummer. She didn't ever look at the drums, her hands and drumsticks just, like a blur—you literally couldn't see them—just beating away: bum-bum-bummmm. The guy with the trombone though, he was totally focussed on the microphone stand in front of him. He was pushing his hand and the mike right into the bell of his instrument. The double bass player was even more manic, it was really crazy—he was foaming at the mouth, and mumbling something that you couldn't hear over the noise, his eyes roving over all of us in the audience as if he was looking for the bastard who'd nicked the score sheet.

The saxophonist was the last of the group, and he was really chilled. He had this massive ragged beard that matched his wild hair, and he was doing this weird thing with his sax, wailing and screaming at random moments.

The sound they were making had less tune than your typical neo-grindcore punk—it was just a bass throb intertwined with higher notes. Completely undanceable, impossibly fast, no melody to follow. Totally ace. The dance-floor was chokka, everyone had their hands up in the air.

A disembodied voice sang the Internationale: *Völker hört*

die Signale! Auf zum letzten Gefecht! It was like some ghost wailing, and I was trying to work out how they did that. There was no tape player, I know because I set up the sound system. Where was that voice coming from? And then I worked it out. The guy with the trombone, he wasn't blowing into the mouthpiece, he was shouting into it! He suddenly switched the lyrics: *The spoils of revolution / Kronstadt, Budapest and Prague / where the spectre of Communism still haunts / still dragging its chains*. It was so ace, the ghostly hand of the past being totally twatted to fuck by this stupidly fast beat.

It made sense, so much sense. I wanted to write it all down, record it, tell everyone I knew how these people had got it, they'd really *got* it!

I tried to tell Martin about it, but he was dancing, really manic. He'd got it, I could tell.

He was pissed, well pissed.

It was good.

02:04
Martin

"Come on Marty! Let's go and see Annette! She'll be pleased to see us!"

It was past midnight. At least, the blurred outlines of the hands on my watch, they were both pointing somewhere near the top. Yeah. Middle of the night.

Annette? Why not? Something niggled, some thought trying to escape my befuddled brain. Something about Annette. I had fences to mend, I had to tell her how much she meant to me, that I'd missed her and was sorry we weren't together any more. She'd be pleased to see me, and I could tell her how I felt. And Karo was with me, we could go dancing, the three of us. In Kreuzberg.

We climbed the steps to the elevated railway, got on the ivory and yellow train that soon rattled into the station and we cheered as it dived down the ramp into the tunnel. We weren't the only party-goers aboard, an accordion started playing at the other end of the carriage, and I swayed around, more or less in time to the music, hanging on to a strap.

"You know that list you gave me? I sent it to K1," I told Karo, shouting above the noise of the accordion.

"K-*fucking*-1?" shouted Karo back. "Do they still exist? Fucking lowest of the fucking low! Fucking Stasi swine."

"No, no, no." I tried to put her right. "They're DVP, they're cops. They're different from the Stasi."

"Fuck off!" was Karo's answer.

We got off less than ten minutes later, at Märkisches Museum, swerving down the road, towards the border crossing point about a kilometre away. Karo still had her bottle of beer to keep her company, but I seemed to have lost mine. Was it still on the U-Bahn?

"I lost my bottle!" I exclaimed to the sleeping streets.

Karo just giggled and wobbled out into the middle of the road.

The border guards at Heinrich-Heine-Strasse stood just outside their hut, arms across their chests.

"Evening, comrades, do you intend crossing into West Berlin?"

Drunk as I was, I could still sense the disapproval, a priggish concern that if we entered the West in such a bibulous state we may sully the good name and standing of the German Democratic Republic.

"I, comrades ..." I started, before fumbling through my shoulder bag, looking for my identity papers, the ones that identified me as a captain of the *Republikschutz*. "My magic papers, magic will get us through," I breathed over to Karo, who giggled again.

But I couldn't find my magic RS identification. I looked over to Karo, who was carefully balancing her beer bottle on the kerb. Did she have my papers? No. But they're not in my bag and not in my pockets. With a sigh, I decided that a bluff would do the job, I just needed to be insouciant enough in the execution.

"My papers, comrade!" With a flourish I produced my blue civilian identity card.

The guard I was addressing looked over to his colleague, raising an eyebrow. The other gave a small shake of the head, and we were let through.

The West Berlin policeman on the other side deliberately looked away as we crossed the white line that delineated West from East, bad from good, rich from poor.

We stood at the huge roundabout of Moritzplatz, wondering which way to go. A cool breeze was blowing against my face, waking me up a bit. An empty cola can clattered along the gutter, and a sheet of newspaper pressed itself against my ankles.

"Where does your Annette live?" asked Karo, looking around, bewildered, paying attention to the edge of the pavement, aware that here in the West, even at this time of night, it didn't do to stand in the middle of the road.

"Too many fucking cars!" she shouted at a passing Volkswagen.

I was beginning to have doubts. I looked at my watch again. It was after two o'clock. I could see it clearly now, I was beginning to sober up. It was quite a walk from here to where Annette lived. My synapses started to connect again, my brain slowly working out that maybe it wasn't such a good idea to call on Annette right now. Or maybe ever again. I'd scared her off last year, when I'd last seen her. My job had scared her off. Maybe she didn't want to see me. No, if she wanted to see me, she'd have been with us tonight. No, no, no. Not a good idea at all.

I turned to Karo, feeling the need to impart this great

news to her.

"Karo, Karo, shhh! Listen: you ready? This is veryveryvery *important.*"

Karo drew herself up, standing to attention in front of me, wind ruffling her bright red hair. She pressed her thumb to her forehead, palm held straight out in a mock Pioneer salute: *always prepared.*

"I. Don't. Think." I said, enunciating each syllable so, so perfectly, "That. We. Should. Gotosee. Annette."

Karo shrugged and set off down Oranienstrasse, singing U2's *One.* I followed, not for a moment wondering where we were going.

DAY 8
Monday
21st March 1994

Berlin: The South Friedrichshain Neighbourhood Round Table has repeated requests for dialogue with residents of the Wagenburg *on the banks of the Spree.*

A spokesperson for the Neighbourhood Round Table stated that there was ongoing conflict with local residents and industry, including the Reichsbahn and the Border Regiment. The Wagenburg *has allegedly refused to meet local stakeholders.*

08:17
Martin

"Jeez, Papa! How old are you?"

I couldn't work out whether Katrin was pissed off or amused. Possibly a bit of both, I decided in the gaps between the hammer blows that were pounding the inside of my head. It was the same banging that caused my skull to swell and made black rings blur my vision. *Old enough*, I thought to myself, *to know how to avoid a hangover.*

"What are you doing here anyway? At least you didn't puke all over my flat."

One of us had been sick last night. I remembered that. We were ringing Katrin's bell, pushing it, holding it in. I was. That was it, I rang the bell while Karo puked all over the pavement.

"Here's some money, go and get some rolls. I'll get the coffee going and try to wake up Karo."

I looked at the coin in the palm of my hand as if I'd never seen Westmarks before: a West German eagle on one side, and some face on the other, maybe a president or a chancellor? I turned it over and over, noticing the words stamped on the edge of the coin: *Unity and Justice and Freedom*. Putting the money in my pocket I went down the stairs and out of the tenement block. A Turkish lady in a head scarf was throwing a bucket of water over Karo's vomit. She caught my eye and shook her head sadly, as if to say *young people today!* I looked down and hurried off.

Karo's vomit wasn't the only refuse on the street, I wandered past a footstool, horsehair stuffing trickling out of a rip in the vinyl covering. A little further on—sprinkled around the trunk of a tree that looked like it probably wouldn't bother with leaves this year—lay empty cigarette packets, a couple of crushed coke cans and a smashed beer bottle. Fag ends and splots of dried chewing gum littered the pavement. The West: so rich, so many things available in the shops, no shortages. But their streets were paved with carcasses of consumption.

A group of punks came towards me. It wasn't until they were almost level that I realised they weren't the young people I had taken them for but were all about my own age. Ragged, saggy leggings, ripped leather vests and jackets, studs and hoops in ears and noses, they came towards me, uncertainly following the drunken pavement, holding tightly onto their bottles of beer.

"YougoddaMarkforme?" one of them slurred in my general direction.

I shrugged my shoulders, bunching my hands in my pockets.

"Krotte, leave 'im be," shouted another punk from the back

93

of the group. "He ain't got no dosh, he's an *Ossi*! Got less than we 'ave, that lot!"

The group laughed harshly, and disappeared into a bar. Curious, I looked in through the open door, peering past the thick cigarette smoke that condensed into the street. Icons, religious reliquaries and statues hung behind the bar, draped with medals and crucifixes on chains. Many of the clientèle looked like they had moved in when the place opened and had never managed to leave again. Going by the patina of ossified dust and nicotine, that must have been a decade or two ago.

I smiled to myself and made my careful way to the bakery. Eyeing the distended golden crust of the rolls in the basket behind the counter I again considered the money I held in my hand.

"How do you get them so crispy and full of air?" I asked the lady behind the counter.

"Are you going to buy anything or did you come over here just to ask stupid questions?" she snapped back in Berliner dialect.

I shrugged and did some mental arithmetic. I had two Marks, so could just about afford six rolls with a bit of change left over. At home, I could get over twenty *Schrippen* for two Eastmarks—or on the black market I could exchange these two Westmarks for twenty Eastmarks and buy two hundred rolls. And at home they were solid affairs, full of bread; not like the crusty air bags that I was looking at now.

I was taking too long for the shop assistant and she'd started serving another customer. I waited patiently for her to turn back to me.

"So, what's it to be? You decided what you can afford?"

I was looking at the glistening layers of the Splitterbrötchen, the dark surface pocked with powdered cinnamon.

"How much are they?" I asked.

"Mark-forty."

One Mark forty. I looked at the two Mark piece in my hand, and dug into my pockets, fishing out my Eastmark change. I easily had about ten Marks worth there.

"We only take proper money—none of your dodgy scrap aluminium!"

The bread rolls were still warm, I could feel the heat through the colourful paper bag. It felt good in my hand, and I had to stop myself from curling my fingers around one of the rolls, squeezing until the crust splintered and the soft dough inside collapsed. They looked so good, these rolls. My mind fixed on that thought, keeping hold of it, past the waves of pressure that were still gripping my head with every footstep. It was all about appearances, how they looked.

Like the punks. They looked so young, but when they got closer, they were my age.

Here in the West things don't always appear as they seem. *Brilliant Martin*, I thought to myself. *With thinking like that you'll soon solve all the problems of the world.* But another thought was trying to make its way through my hangover. The boat the other night, or rather the boats. I hadn't been able to work out what they were up to, what the point of their theatrical manoeuvres could have been. But, the thought persisted, perhaps that was exactly what it was: a piece of theatre, designed to distract us. Even the boat that had slipped across the Landwehr Canal to deliver a small package was a double bluff.

No, a triple bluff—we were meant to believe that the small package was the reason behind the activity on the river Spree. Next time the *Grenzer* would be watching the Landwehr Canal, and maybe the river between Oberbaum Bridge and Elsen Bridge. Customs and Border Guards would be focussing along the canal and the weir lead. Any forces on the Oberbaum Bridge would be looking upstream. Which would leave the downstream sector of the river—towards Schilling Bridge—practically unobserved. And that was a section of the river that had another *Wagenburg* directly on the water's edge: no border guards on the ground there.

When I got back I found the kitchen table laid for two.

"Karo's still asleep," said my daughter. "She's snoring away, so I left her to it."

I nodded, there wasn't much to say, and I was still thinking about my new theory. We sat down and Katrin cut all the bread rolls in half: neat, no crumbs flaking away from the crust, the soft, doughy bread inside not balling up but sliced straight down the middle.

"Papa," Katrin said in that cautious voice she used when she wanted to talk seriously.

I looked up from my bread roll.

"Papa, thanks for the other day. I know it wasn't easy for you."

I shrugged, what are fathers there for? "Have you decided what you're going to do?"

A long pause while Katrin worked out how to reply, carefully considering how to put her words into place.

"I don't know," she finally said. "I wish I did. It's not like I'm thinking about it all the time. But I sit there in my room, I'm meant to be studying, and out of the corner of my eye I'll see her letter. Sitting there, on the edge of my desk. I don't even know what to do with the letter. I don't want to throw it away, not yet. And I don't want to file it away—that way I'll let myself forget about it and I won't ever decide what to do. So for the moment it's sitting there, on the corner of my desk, reminding me that I need to make a decision."

"It's OK, you know," I said, then broke off and started again. "I mean, it's your choice. To write to her. Or not. I won't be upset." I wondered how truthful my words were. How much would it bother me if my daughter wrote to the woman who had abandoned her when she was a small child? Abandoned us, both of us.

It was so long ago, another life, another State, another history. I couldn't be angry at her after all these years, no, not angry. But it still hurt. I understood only too well why she'd gone: the frustration, the feeling of being trapped, the claustrophobia. I'd had those reactions too but we'd each had different ways of dealing with them.

Except that Katrin's mother hadn't really found a way to deal with it—she'd fought her way out of East Germany, like a wild animal trapped in a cage fights to escape, no matter the cost. She'd left behind her family, so desperate was she to get out. Had I forgiven her? The years had softened the hard, sharp edges of pain, but it was still there. A scar on my heart, reminding me of past torment; aching when the weather turned, or when the moon waxed to full.

"Papa, I know it's my choice." She smiled and touched my hand with her long fingers. "I know. But first I have to decide whether I actually want to have contact with her. If I do, then I'll talk to you about it first." Her eyes sought mine, looking for understanding. "I promise. I don't want to cause you any hurt, but right now I don't even know what to think. I've no idea what to do, what the right thing to do might be."

My daughter had been speaking slowly, with lots of gaps. She was thinking aloud. Now there was another pause, a gap in which we both digested the words we'd said and heard. This conversation had been years in the coming, there was no rushing it. It would take a while to reach any conclusion. Love is complicated, how can it be described? How can it be quantified, weighed across the years and the miles and the borders that stood between the pair of us here in Berlin and the mother that hadn't been a mother for so long?

"Would it have been better if she hadn't contacted you?"

Another pause while Katrin considered her answer.

"Perhaps," she answered finally. "It's like I can feel her,

waiting. Somewhere in West Germany. Waiting for an answer." She was staring at our clasped hands, trying to find the right words. "I can feel her hope. Hoping I'll write back, forgive her. But I'm not sure it's me who should be doing any forgiving. She's nothing but an impression from the past, a ghost. It doesn't feel like it's up to me to forgive her. Maybe that's for you—maybe that's your job. I was so young, I hardly remember her. She was always there, but as an absence—I never found a way to talk to you about it because I could see how much she'd hurt you." She placed her hand briefly on my forearm, a light touch, then she was talking again. "What she did, that hurt you. When I look back at that time, I can't remember anything concrete, except that she broke you.

"And every time I think about picking up a pen, writing an answer, every time I do that, I can't. Because it's too complicated. I don't know what to think, what to say. *Hello mum*," she said, in a slightly ironic tone, quoting her unwritten letter. "*Thanks for sending me a letter after all these years. I'm fine, Papa's fine, hope you're fine. Lots of love, your daughter.* Doesn't really work, does it? There are too many strands binding the past and the future, and it's like I need to cut through them before I can know what I want."

Perhaps I understood, perhaps I knew what Katrin meant. Writing a letter to her mother wasn't just a simple correspondence, an action in the present. It meant dealing with the past but also looking into the future: just a letter or constant contact? Would it stop at letters, or would they meet? What kind of relationship would they have? What kind of relationship *could* they have? When her mother had left, Katrin had been little, a Young Pioneer in a blue necker-chief. Now she was an adult, making her own way in life.

And her mother would be different too—what she went through back then, all the things that might have happened since then, they would have changed her, moulded her.

When she put in her application for an exit visa she was ready for the harassment from the state. To some extent I could support her at that stage, even though I didn't agree, I wanted to stay, wanted her to stay too. But when they took her away, from that moment on she was by herself. I have no idea what she'd been through. She would have been in prison. Softened up in Hohenschönhausen, after that Hoheneck. Hell holes that break your spirit. Then they would have released her to the West. She'd never written to tell me what had happened. Or if she had, then the letter had never arrived. All I knew was that one day I'd received a summons. I was required to go to the police station. An anonymous room, an anonymous man sitting behind an empty desk. He informed me of my wife's release, that she was no longer a citizen of the GDR, that she had forfeited the privilege of living in the socialist state. He had meant release from jail, but for her it was a release from a prison that was the size of this country.

"I wish I knew what to do." Katrin was crying now. The tears came suddenly, they shocked me. She hadn't cried last Sunday when we'd talked about this. I hadn't seen her cry since 1989 when she followed in her mother's footsteps, leaving the GDR. In that year she'd grown up, our relationship had equalised: no longer a father and a daughter, the adult providing protection, advice and support to the child, but two adults, there for each other. More than that in fact, Katrin had become, in some ways, the stronger of the pair of us. To see her cry was hard for me. I went round the table, stood next to Katrin's chair and put my arms round her shoulders. She wrapped her arms around me, and we held each other tight.

A slight cough. "Am I interrupting?"

I turned my head to see Karo standing at the door of the kitchen, looking even more dishevelled than usual.

★

We left Katrin to her breakfast and headed Eastwards. Katrin had insisted that we go, she said she had a lecture, and didn't I have a job to go to anyway? So we left the flat, making our way down the dingy staircase of Katrin's tenement block, spent bulbs in the lamps, nicotine yellow gloss paint on the walls, worn lino on the steps. Along the side-street and into Skalitzer Strasse, following the U-Bahn viaduct where the orange trains rumble over the corroded structure. We were walking in silence, I was thinking about my daughter. She had been embarrassed by her crying, I decided. She was like her mother in that way.

Like her father, too.

But I was glad we were talking to each other. We weren't very good at sharing feelings even though we'd learned that we had to use whatever time we had together. There was no knowing when circumstance would divide us again.

"Martin! Earth calling Martin! Come in all cosmonauts!"

I'd stopped walking, Karo was shouting at me from in front of the checkpoint at the Wall. Before catching up with her I took a look around me. I decided that Kreuzberg wasn't all that great, it looked as run-down and unloved as most of East Berlin.

But Karo was still waiting for me, right next to the Wall that blocked off the western end of the Oberbaum Bridge. A squat guard tower peeked at us, the corrugated iron roof rusting into holes, windows covered by bars. To the right the rail viaduct crossed over the bridge, but the tracks were cut by several fences and a concrete wall.

We ducked through the gate and walked over the bridge, looking downriver towards the East Side *Wagenburg*. I couldn't see it clearly from here, it was just a bit too far away, but I knew it as a stinking place, rubbish piled high between trucks and wagons, people lying around in a drunken or drugged haze. A real contrast to the gardens and washing lines of the Lohmühle.

But my mind was still turning over the events of last Friday night. If the smugglers' main delivery was to be downstream of this bridge then the only feasible landing place would be the East Side: all fences already removed, no wall at the water's edge, no watchtowers between this bridge and the next, the perfect place for smugglers to land.

"Karo, what do you reckon, the East Side *Wagenburg*—good place for smugglers to bring their stuff in?"

Karo stopped and leant against the railing, gazing downriver. "Yeah. Suppose so. Why?"

09:37

Karo

I was standing with Martin on the Oberbaum Bridge, just enjoying the morning sunlight when he started on at me about smugglers. Before I knew what had happened he'd dragged me along to the East Side as if I was his personal tour guide.

I don't go there much—it's got a bit of a rep as a lunch-out zone. People who just want to sit around on their arses drinking schnapps all day and not giving a flying fuck about the revolution. Some say that it's because there's a lot of foreigners there, but you know what, everywhere I look I see foreigners, and they're all doing their bit. Except here. On the East Side nobody does fuck all.

We went through the gate and Martin made a bee-line for the edge of the river. It was still really early so none of the locals were up yet, we had the place to ourselves.

"What you looking for?"

"I don't know. Some signs of smuggling. Could be anything."

This smuggling thing was really getting old. I remembered our conversation at the Feeling B concert and decided to leave it—I'd promised Katrin I'd keep any eye on Martin, not argue with him the whole time.

He was mooching about, looking under the wagons, kicking at the piles of tat that were lying around.

"Martin, you can't just poke around like that! People live here."

"Yeah? And what about this," he said, a triumphant grin plastered over his coupon. He'd lifted the corner of a tarp and was staring into a nest of blankets. "You usually expect to find a stash of antique Meissen porcelain somewhere like this?"

"The bastards didn't give me my fix." I looked up from the crate of pottery.

This hippy was watching us. Thin, spotty. Track marks up her bare arms. I thought she was just ranting about something in her own head so I ignored her, but Martin wanted to know what she was blethering on about.

"Every Friday, about a quarter to ten. We get a fix. Good shit. They come and give us good shit." She sat down on the edge of the crate with the Meissen in it. "But I was late last week. I'd gone out, hadn't I, into town. So I didn't get any shit, did I? Bastards."

"Who? Who gives you shit?" Martin didn't have a clue what she was going on about.

"The guys. The men. The suits, y'know?" the hippy looked at Martin as if he was the one who'd lost it.

"So these guys." I decided to help Martin out—we'd be here all day otherwise. "They come and give you dope, good stuff. Always on Friday." The hippy was dead pleased that somebody understood her, she was nodding away like a member of the *Politbüro*. "And they give it to you for free?" She was still nodding.

"Quarter to ten, Likasay. Good shit. Bastards."

A quick look at the ground and I spotted the wheel tracks and the scratches on the concrete edge of the quay. I walked over to an old army tarp covering something big, taller than me, but not too wide. I peered through a rip in the canvas.

"Martin, check this out—fork lift truck!" I pointed at the tracks in the dust. "Every Friday they dole out smack to this lot so they don't notice anything and nobody's gonna believe them even if they do grass them up. Sweet. Then they bring a boat in, use the fork lift truck to shift this lot." I pointed at the pretty pots in the crate. "And you reckon they're delivering stuff as well?"

I thought Martin was going to object about the boat bit—I thought he'd just tell me they couldn't just bring a boat in under the border guards' noses, but he was stroking his chin and nodding slowly. In fact, I reckon he was well impressed with my reasoning.

"Oi!"

Oh fuck. This wasn't good. The hippy had vanished, and two skinheads were standing next to the fork lift truck, each holding a wooden chair leg.

"Martin! Run!"

We legged it. Dodging between the trucks and builder's wagons, trying to give the skins the slip. If I'd been by myself I'd have been straight out of there, but I had Martin in tow. I couldn't leave him behind. I jumped up onto an old flatbed and looked to see where Martin was. He was lagging well behind.

"Martin! Move it! Come on!"

He ran along the side of the trailer, below me, with one of the skins just behind him.

"Fuck you!" I jumped at the skin, landing on his back. He stumbled, dropping to the floor and letting go of his bit of wood.

"Martin—run!" I was on my feet before the skin. I grabbed his stick and without even thinking about it just twatted him on the nose. The skin screamed and dropped down again, landing on his knees, hands to his face. Blood fucking everywhere. I got out of there fast.

I was just behind Martin and the gate in the Wall was dead ahead of us, get to that gate and we'd be on the busy road, we'd be safe. Martin was breathing heavily, clutching his side.

"Come on Martin, come on!"

Just then the other skin darted out from behind a truck. He grabbed Martin by his bag, using it to swing Martin round, down on to the sand. I ran up behind the skin and whacked him, hard as I could. Chair leg to the back of the skin's head. I got hold of Martin's hand and dragged him up, towards the gate. He looked like he was going to argue, but I just pulled him along.

I got us out of there.

That was well close—if I hadn't dealt with those two skins then Martin wouldn't have made it. I don't know whether he got that, he was kind of dazed, and I don't think he would have liked the fact that I'd just twatted those two fuckers. I don't know how I felt about it, you know, after Saturday. That lad, the one on the floor, getting the shit kicked out of him by my mates. Just couldn't get it out of my head. The Antifa group had been on a real high after that, we'd gone to a social centre and everyone had to hear about how fucking heroic we'd been.

I'd left soon after.

And now I'd done it again. It felt kind of different because it was self-defence. But so was Saturday, except we got to them before they could do any damage to any of us.

"You OK?" I asked Martin. He was bending over, trying to catch his breath. We were at the Hauptbahnhof station now, we'd run all the way from the hole in the Wall that leads to the East Side. I had an eye open for the skins, in case they were still coming after us.

"OK. You win. I'm going to take you seriously about this smuggling stuff," I told Martin.

Martin wobbled over to one of the benches. "You want to give me a hand with the smuggling stuff?"

I hadn't said that, I'd just said I was going to take him seriously. Then again, I'd also promised myself I was going to take the whole fascist threat thing seriously too. So, yeah, I could help Martin out.

"You see, the next thing on my list is to have a chat with the people at the Lohmühle *Wagenburg*."

"Martin, what is your problem? What's the Lohmühle got to do with smuggling?" Maybe I was still wigged by what had just happened at the East Side, but I could hear myself getting louder and louder. "How many fucking times do I have to say it? It's like you're not taking me seriously!"

Martin looked a bit shocked, like he hadn't been expecting my reaction, but he should have done cos I'd already told him what I think.

"Look, I know what you're saying, but sometimes there are bigger things going on, we have to look at the bigger picture," he started, but then he backed off a bit. "Like we have to consider how to make it harder for the fascists to smuggle stuff into our country."

"And why are you telling me this?"

"Well, about talking to the Lohmühle people about jumping the Wall ... I was thinking that it might be better if it came from someone a bit more, you know, a bit more like them."

"Like me, you mean?" Now I was really wicked off, I'd expected better from Martin! "Dream on! You can do your own dirty work."

Martin slouched back and looked down. It was like somebody had stuck a pin in him and all the air had come out.

He started rubbing the side of his leg and pulling a face. That's where he must have fallen when the second skinhead grabbed him.

"My bag, damn!"

I laughed at him, we'd just escaped with our lives and Martin was more worried about his bag.

"My shoulder bag, Katrin gave it to me."

Could have been worse, if you ask me. But then I thought about last night, coming through the checkpoint.

"Martin, what was in your bag?"

"Just a hanky, paper, some pens, junk." He scratched his head and thought a bit more, then groaned. "My identity papers."

He didn't seem too bothered, he hadn't cottoned on to it yet, was probably just thinking about the hassle of getting new ID.

"That skinhead has got your *Ausweis*," I told him. "That skin has got your name and address!"

I watched his expression change from irritation to fear.

12:08

Martin

When I finally got to the RS2 office a burly, middle aged fellow passed me on the stairs. He wasn't wearing a uniform, but he was a cop if ever I saw one. Going into the offices I was greeted by unusual levels of activity. Laura was giving Grit a list of things to do, she sounded even more brusque than usual.

"Draft a memo to that effect for the Ministerial Committee, carbon copy to Police Headquarters. Then ring the district police—VPI Lichtenberg. Tell them we want copies of the medical reports, an up to date briefing on what's going on—yes, demand that someone comes down here to give us a full report in person. Then phone the General State Prosecutor's office, I want to know who is going to be in charge tomorrow, and I want to be briefed about what they hope to achieve. Inform them that one of us will be present."

I stood by Laura's elbow, watching our unfortunate secretary make shorthand notes, waiting for Laura to run out of steam. She finally turned to me, frowning.

"Martin, come with me." We made our way over to Erika's office. "Lichtenberg police have finally told us what's going on."

I waved a greeting at Erika, who just blinked in response. She had a police interview record in front of her.

"You've seen the newspapers?"

I shook my head, and took the copy of *Die Andere* that Erika passed over to me. Before I could scan the headlines Laura was talking again.

"Page four, bottom right." Then, exhaling loudly, "It doesn't matter, listen: the IKM we asked about, the informant in the Weitlingstrasse scene. He's dead. When Erika saw the article about a police informer dying in a West Berlin hospital we put two and two together. Lichtenberg K1 has finally condescended to bring us up to speed."

Laura paused for breath, her foot was tapping the lino, making me nervous. I hadn't seen her this way since 1989. Erika had gone back to the interview record she'd been reading when we came in. She seemed absorbed by her task, and she was bothered by what she was reading.

"Yesterday the informant turned up half-dead on the street outside the squat," Laura carried on. She'd taken the newspaper off me and had rolled it up tightly. "He was taken to the hospital in Friedrichshain, in a coma, trauma injuries to the head, severe internal bleeding, collapsed lung—the lot. They moved him to a hospital in West Berlin late last night so that he could get better treatment, but he was found dead this morning. Somebody had turned off his life-support machine-"

"Laura," Erika suddenly broke in. She was looking up from her report, her face drained of colour. One finger was pressed against the paper, marking a paragraph. But Laura wasn't to be stopped.

"The West Berlin police haven't any leads, and they seem determined to treat it as a cock-up by the hospital-"

"Laura! Martin!" Erika tried again, louder.

She was holding out the transcript, trying to get our attention. I took it from her, checking the title at the top. It was the record of the interview with the fascist that had been arrested at the demo last Monday: Andreas Hermann—the interview I had been present at.

"What about it, Erika, what?" asked Laura, annoyed at being cut off.

"This guy, he threatened the informant last Monday." Erika was looking at me now.

"Yeah, so what? What would you expect him to do?" I asked.

"No, Martin, look: not only did Hermann know about the informant a whole week ago, but he actually threatened the informant. And now he's dead. But Hermann also recognised you, and he threatened you. He said he knew who you were —that you'd be next!"

I looked at Erika, then at Laura who had taken the transcript off me and was scanning through it, trying to find the relevant part. At first, I was a bit taken aback, but I put that down to the chase at the East Side, and I got a hold on reality again. I'd been vaguely aware of the threat at the time, but hadn't taken it seriously. By itself it seemed to be just an empty threat, there wasn't really anything to be scared of.

"*You'll be next. No worries, you'll be next,*" read Laura from the transcript. "That's you he's threatening. Why you?"

"I doubt it's anything, just bluster from a violent young man. Bravado, he probably wasn't even involved in the IKM situation. Coincidence." I was trying to calm them down, but the fact that my colleagues were taking it seriously meant that I was re-evaluating the situation too. After all, that threat to the mole had turned out to be far from empty. Maybe it wasn't mere coincidence.

And now I was on some list, and now the skinheads we ran into this morning had my home address.

"Look Martin, we need to take this seriously. Since the Silesian Crisis you've pretty much become the public face of RS—if they think we're investigating them then it stands to reason that you'd be a target—you'd be the first target."

Erika nodded agreement at Laura's words, but I wanted a bit more time to think about it.

"So what's next?" I tried to deflect the conversation back to what the cops were doing. "Presumably K1 or whoever from *Kripo* told you what their next steps will be? They can't just leave things as they are." My ploy seemed to work, at least with Laura.

"They're going to raid the Weitlingstrasse house tomorrow, see if there's any evidence of involvement in the murder of the informant. One of us should be present."

"I'll do it," I offered.

"Well that's going to make you even more of a target—they're sure to recognise you!"

"Yes, but on the other hand, why should we risk anyone else? Right now I'm probably the only person they know in RS." I decided, for the moment, not to tell them about losing my *Ausweis*. "Best limit the faces they know—otherwise they may target you two or Nik as well."

"I'm not happy about this," Erika told me. "I'm not sure any of us should be putting ourselves at risk in this way."

"But we have to, because we don't trust the cops, do we?"

DAY 9
Tuesday
22nd March 1994

Berlin: *The Central Round Table has responded to the statement made by the CDU and SPD last Sunday. Round Table member Hanna Krause appealed for calm, saying that discussions around next month's referenda should be measured and based on facts rather than propaganda.*

05:54
Martin

I cycled past the fascist squat. All was quiet, no signs of life this early in the morning. It wasn't actually a squat—they'd squatted the building next door but now legitimately rented a whole tenement building from the Housing Association.

I didn't stop but carried on to the next junction and turned left. I locked my bike to a lamppost, blowing on my hands before jamming them under my armpits, trying to warm up my chilled fingers after the dawn cycle ride.

As so often happens when you're waiting, time telescopes and it feels like hours are drifting by. My impatience wasn't helped by the fact that I was nervous; the last raid I'd observed hadn't been pleasant, and quite a few people who had since become friends had been the victims of police violence that day. But, as I told myself in the grey darkness, this time I was less likely to feel any empathy for those who may be on the receiving end of truncheons and fists.

My thoughts were interrupted by a patrol car drawing up across the junction at the end of my side street. An officer got out, holding a white and black traffic baton, posting himself in the middle of the road. This was my cue; I walked back to Weitlingstrasse, waving the traffic officer away with a flick of my RS identification card, then went down to the squat. A scrum of uniforms was gathered by the front door, slowly funnelling in through the narrow gap. By the time I reached them all but a handful were inside, and I pushed my way in too. I could hear boots hammering up the stairs, but no swearing, no shouts of resistance or cries: the only sound was that of the bulls crashing around. I went into the ground floor flat, which was where the office was meant to be. A couple of cops stood around, staring at the empty space. A couple of desks, a few overturned chairs and a telephone wire hanging from the wall; nothing else to be seen. No fascists, no electronic equipment, not even a typewriter or a scrap of paper. I went into the next room: also empty except for a couple of wooden pallets leaning against the wall.

I stood for a moment, nonplussed, irritated by the echoing emptiness, then went back out into the hall, running up the stairs, looking in through open doors at each landing. Cops were standing around in the empty rooms, chatting and smoking. The only other occupants of these flats were dust and empty beer bottles.

Our birds had flown.

I went back down to the ground floor, where a sergeant was taking reports from other cops. Next to them was a low doorway, I stooped to go through, finding myself on a steep stairway. Feeling around, I found a light switch and twisted it until a bulb clicked on, lighting up the stained wooden steps. Careful not to slip, I made my way down to the cellars, looking into each of the three large, low rooms. These cellars were also empty except for bits of junk: a few crates of empty beer bottles, a tattered and ripped black hoody and a few wooden banner poles in the corner. I walked over to them, crunching across shards of glass and sandy grit, and kicked the stack of wood. Light-coloured timber, spruce or pine, about three by three centimetres, most just over a metre long, but a few were broken in half, jagged ends sometimes matching the negative impression of a neighbour. Many of them, particularly the broken pieces, had a reddish-brown discolouration, splashes that had soaked into the wood, in a few cases leaving a crusted layer on the surface.

I stood for a moment, looking at the stains. Shuddering, I made my way back up the cellar steps.

"All empty?" I asked the cop standing in the hallway, who was still taking notes while listening to colleagues' reports.

He nodded without looking up from what he was doing, and I went back out onto the street. A police lieutenant was leaning against a green and white Wartburg smoking a cigarette and toying with the microphone of the two-way radio hanging over his shoulder.

"Are you in command of this operation?" I asked, impatiently holding my hand up to ward off a junior cop that looked like he might drag me away from his chief. My gesture must have carried enough authority, because the bull stopped, looking towards the lieutenant for guidance.

"I asked you a question, Lieutenant!"

The lieutenant didn't seem too impressed with my performance, but did at least stand up straight.

"Are you Captain Grobe?" he asked. "I was told to expect you. Yes, I'm in charge here. Lieutenant Steinlein. Anything I can help you with, comrade Captain?"

"Lieutenant, I want to know why this house is empty!"

The officer shrugged, turning towards the sergeant who was heading across the pavement, his notes clutched in his hand. "Better ask the people you were expecting to find."

Karo

"Schimmel, we've got to do something!"

Schimmel wasn't awake yet. He just sat there, staring into his mug of coffee. I shook his shoulder.

"Schimmel, wake up! This is important! We've got to do something!"

Schimmel managed to look up from his coffee. He might have said something, I don't know, I was too busy pacing around the kitchen. I'd had too much coffee already, and I was pissed off. Pissed off with the two skins yesterday. Pissed off with the computer stuff that Schimmel had shown me the other day. Pissed off with Martin for not taking it all seriously enough. Pissed off with the Antifa group even though I didn't know exactly why.

And now I was feeling pissed off with myself for not doing more.

Martin

My colleagues were surprised to see me back so soon.

"They'd cleared out, the place was empty," I told them.

It was pointless speculating about why they would have given up the building they'd been using—the only reasonable explanation was that they'd been tipped off about the raid.

The number of people who'd known about the plans for the raid had been pretty much limited to our team at RS2, and the main police station in the district, VPI Lichtenberg. Obviously we'd be pointing the finger at the cops, and they would be returning the compliment.

"There has to be a leak at VPI Lichtenberg," said Nik. "First of all the fashos find out about the mole, then somebody— presumably the fascists—murder him while he's in a West Berlin hospital, even though nobody other than the Lichtenberg cops knew he was there. Now there's been a tip-off about the raid. The whole thing stinks."

Yes, it stank, but was it so surprising? I almost said that, but held back. Such remarks weren't going to help us decide what to do.

"We've already informed the Ministerial Committee that we're unhappy with the way the VPI Lichtenberg has dealt with the matter of the informant, so we can just update our position with a memo," stated Laura, as ever trying to deal with action points rather than speculation. "I think we need to stay on their case though. We can't just let them do what they did during the Silesian Crisis, it's not good enough to have a narrow investigation and ignore the wider picture. We should get authorisation to be more involved—that way the cops won't be able to complain about us breathing down their necks."

We all agreed with Laura's suggestions, but my mind was on more immediate matters.

"I think one of us needs to go down to the cop shop and lean on them, I mean this morning, not sometime next week. Right now they'll be trying to work out how to cover their arses, and we need to get to the bottom of this before they have a chance to get their story straight."

"I'm not sure you're the right person to do that," Laura objected. "Maybe someone who is less well known to the security forces would be more acceptable?"

We were just about to get into another argument when Klaus stomped into the office, a deep frown creasing his face. In his hand he had a copy of the *Berliner Zeitung*.

"Have you seen this?" he demanded as he sat down heavily in a chair opposite me, throwing the newspaper onto the desk.

I looked at the article Klaus was pointing out. The chemical workers were saying that several of them had been detained by the police and questioned regarding future plans for their campaign.

I passed the newspaper on to Laura, who scanned the article briefly and gave it to Erika. She shook her head in disbelief.

"Where's it all going to end? This is political policing, just like in the old days," she said quietly. "For three or four years they go round with their tail between their legs, afraid of offending anyone, and now they're growing in confidence again and they go after the chemical workers."

"It's not a police matter," Klaus said, obviously irritated by what he'd read. "And if anything actually needs to be done then we should be the ones doing it, not the cops."

"But it isn't a matter for us either, is it?" was Nik's reply. "The chemical workers aren't posing any economic or political danger to the Republic, they're just exercising their rights."

"Precisely!" Klaus responded. "They're exercising their rights. Their political rights. Just because that's uncomfortable doesn't mean the bulls should get heavy on them."

"But even if the cops are involved it doesn't mean we have to get involved, does it?" Nik shook his head.

"Nik's right," said Erika, so softly that her contribution was nearly lost in the scraping of chairs and rustling of the newspaper. "We're not here to hold the police to account, or interfere in their cases—no matter how worrying they may be. That's a job for the Ministerial Committee."

"But that's exactly what we are doing: holding the cops to account, monitoring their investigation. Why else was Martin at the raid this morning? Why else are we hassling the cops to tell us what they're doing about the dead informant?"

Erika didn't reply to Klaus's questions, she just looked at Nik and me, expecting us to respond. Neither of us did, but Laura had something to say.

"Klaus, listen: Martin's back from the raid already because

the squat was empty. We reckon they had a tip-off."

Klaus gave me a hard look, as if he blamed me. He pulled a half-smoked cigar out of his pocket and chewed on the end for a moment or two before responding.

"And the only place they could have got the tip-off would have been VPI Lichtenberg?" It was a question but he said it more as a statement.

None of us felt the need to answer, we just sat there, giving him time to think it through.

"Then we definitely need to go and read them the riot act," he said eventually.

"We can't just mix it all up because we're cross with the Lichtenberg cops!" Laura took the newspaper back off Erika and crumpled it up. "There are different issues going on here: there are questions around the mole and the potential leaks and we need to handle those separately from any concerns we've got about whether or not the cops are getting political again. Maybe we should put some pressure on the cops about the leaks—like Klaus said, we're already involved." She tossed the mess of newsprint on to my desk. "But the other issue, well, if the cops are taking political decisions about who they will allow to demonstrate and how people may use their right to freedom of speech then that can only be a result of decisions taken at a high level. Dealing with that isn't our job. But we can't just ignore it either. We can't allow political policing to begin again—the chemical workers aren't breaking any law, at least nothing important. We should ask the Committee to give us oversight powers in the interests of accountability, the same responsibility we had when we sent Martin along to observe the Weitlingstrasse raid."

We thought over Laura's suggestion, and eventually everyone agreed.

But Klaus had the last word: "And if the Committee says no then we should do it anyway!"

Martin

Somehow I got my colleagues to agree to let me be the one to talk to the cops. It wasn't far to the district police headquarters on Schottstrasse—just over the road from the Lichtenberg courthouse where I'd met Evelyn last week. Unlike most police stations in Berlin it wasn't built in an imposing style, it looked more like an ordinary pre-war tenement block.

The Kripo were based at the back of the building, overlooking a concrete yard. But first I had to get past the front office. While I was waiting for the officer at the front desk to get round to noticing my presence, Lieutenant Steinlein sauntered in, accompanied by several other uniformed officers. He hesitated for a moment when he saw me, then came over, wearing a smile that didn't reach his eyes.

"Comrade Captain Grobe," he said, giving me a relaxed salute.

I glanced over to the duty officer behind the front desk who was still studiously ignoring me, and took Steinlein by the elbow, steering him through the double glass doors that led into the police station proper.

"You're going to take me to the *Kripo* officer responsible for handling the IKM in the squat. When you've done that, I want you to fetch the written orders you received for the raid this morning, plus any other paperwork you have on this matter. Understood, comrade Lieutenant?"

Something in my tone must have warned Steinlein. He just nodded, no attempt to be as cool as was this morning at the raid. He took me straight to a door that looked like all the others on an endless corridor. The plaque on the wall said *Captain Neumann, Kriminalpolizei Department K1.*

Neumann looked up from his desk, irritated, as I opened the door and went into his office without knocking.

"Dismiss, comrade Lieutenant," I said over my shoulder, but Steinlein announced me instead.

"Comrade Captain Neumann! Comrade Captain Grobe from the *Republikschutz* to see you. The comrade Captain wishes to see all written orders regarding the operation this morning."

Neumann looked me in the eye while he countermanded my order and dismissed his subordinate. I looked straight back at the captain for a few moments, then sat down in the chair in front of his desk.

"Comrade Captain, I think we can dispense with the formalities and get down to what matters. You know why I'm here, and I'm sure you are aware that there will be consequences if you refuse to co-operate."

But Neumann wasn't taken in by my bluff, he just sat there, quite calm and collected in his brown corduroy suit, light brown shirt buttoned up to the collar, but minus a tie. A *bonbon*, the Communist Party badge, adorned his button hole.

"And your authority, comrade Captain Grobe?" he asked, holding out his hand for the written authorisation he knew I wouldn't have. I might get it one day—although that was far from certain—but the slow milling of government machinery meant it was impossible for me to have gained authorisation to investigate something that had happened just a few hours ago.

Round one to Neumann.

I leant back in my chair, crossed my legs, breaking Neumann's staring competition for long enough to pick an imaginary speck of lint from my knee, noticing as I did so that I was still wearing my cycle clips. I ignored them. Looking up at Neumann, I started round two.

"Comrade Captain, you know as well as I do that written authority will not have been issued yet, but make no mistake, it will be. And when it is, any early co-operation—or lack thereof—will be noted."

I was putting Neumann in a difficult spot. Although both of us held the same rank, he would be aware that I had the Ministerial Committee's collective ear, whereas he was just one captain among many others on the police force. That gave me the potential for a lot more clout, although he could count on his colleagues to block, hinder, obfuscate and fudge any internal investigations. And whether or not he was responsible for the leaks, or was aware of who may be responsible, he could hardly tell me about it without incurring the wrath of his comrades. He was a member of a militarist organisation with a strong *corps d'ésprit* and a harsh system of informal punishment for those who stepped out of line.

All in all I think it was fair to say that in Neumann's position I would think twice before co-operating.

Neumann lifted the left edge of his lips in a crooked half-smile. The right side of his face was immobile, pinched to a scar that ran down the side of his nose and past the corner of his mouth. Now that we'd stopped the staring contest I was finding it difficult to keep my eyes away from his damaged face. I focussed on his eyes again, waiting for a response.

He leant back in his chair, pulled open a drawer in his desk, removing a packet of cigarettes and a box of matches. Taking out a cigarette, placing it carefully in the left corner of his mouth, he looked up at the ceiling as he struck a match and lit up. He exhaled through the nose, then balanced his cigarette on the edge of a small glass ashtray.

"What is it you want to know?" Pause, "Captain Grobe."

"I wish to speak to the officer who handled the informant in the Weitlingstrasse squat."

"I'm sure that can be arranged. In the meantime, how else can I be of assistance?"

"Do you have any other informants in place in the fascist, hooligan or skinhead scenes here in Lichtenberg?"

"Captain, I can't possibly let you have that kind of information. It's a matter of protocol. And of safety for the putative IKMs, of course."

I considered my position. At some point I would have to start pushing back, but was this the right moment? I decided to give him an easy question, see if he had any intention at all of 'being of assistance' as he had put it.

"What operational procedures did you use to handle the IKM? How often did the handling officer and the IKM meet, how were crash meetings arranged? I want to know about briefings and debriefings, support mechanisms—the lot."

Neumann hesitated for a moment, a tiny delay which he tried to cover by reaching for his cigarette.

"We did everything by the book."

"And what book was that? The one written by the Stasi? The same one written by our Soviet friends, the Chekists? If everything was done by the book then why wasn't the informant given protection at the hospital?"

Another indecisive movement betrayed Neumann's uncertainty. "The handling officer wasn't informed of the IKM's transferral to the hospital in West Berlin."

At last, a break in his stonewalling. I wondered whether Neumann was preparing the ground to deflect the blame that was coming his way.

"Why not?" I demanded, leaning forward in my chair and taking a cigarette from his packet.

"The decision to transfer the IKM was made by the hospital. It has become common in serious cases such as this one—the patient benefits from procedures and equipment that are currently unavailable in the GDR. The hospital informed Police Headquarters in Keibelstrasse, but the night duty officer didn't think to forward the message on to us until the next morning."

He chucked the box of matches over to me—underarm, no force or malice in the throw. I caught them, and lit up my cigarette.

"And the protection detail at the clinic here?" I asked after taking the first puff.

"Two uniformed officers were detailed to protect the IKM while in Friedrichshain. They were from Station 51— Friedenstrasse. They informed their duty officer on return to the police station, but he didn't think to pass the information on to us."

As I thought: arse-covering. Point the finger anywhere that wasn't K1 in Lichtenberg. I didn't want to let Neumann get away with it that easily.

"So, Captain Neumann, let's see if I've got this straight. You have at least one IKM engaged in an extremely volatile operation. You're careless enough to let him get severely beaten, then without your knowledge he is taken out of the country and murdered in West Berlin. Is that a fair interpretation of events?"

"The West Berlin police are at present investigating the case. It would be a mistake to make assumptions about the nature of the death. We are co-operating with the West Berlin police in this matter-"

"Perhaps, comrade, you'd do better to start co-operating with *me*." I stood up and leaned over the desk. "And for a start you can send me a copy of all files relating to this IKM." I walked over to the door, turning back as I opened it. "Have Lieutenant Steinlein bring over the paperwork—I shall expect him by the end of the day."

12:11

Karo

Schimmel and I managed to get everyone in the house together for a meeting. I told them about what had happened yesterday, how Martin and I had narrowly avoided a beating, or worse.

"We've been ignoring this problem for too long. The fash

are back in Friedrichshain—not just coming by at night to catch a few stragglers. They were at Frankfurter Tor the other day handing out their hate-propaganda! And now this, what happened to me yesterday. God! We've got to take this seriously!"

"Yeah, Karo, I don't disagree, but we've all got our own projects on the go—like you've got your Brown Coal Coalition and the stuff with global warming and your facilitation course. I'm doing my refugee support. We're all doing our bit. None of us have got time to go hunting Nazis."

12:53

Martin

Things were looking busy when I got back to RS2. Grit was at her desk in the front office, hammering away at an electric typewriter, the carriage pinging and growling back at the end of each line. Through the open office doors I could see and hear that everyone was on the phone. Erika's door was nearest, and I stood on the threshold to her office, listening in to her phone call.

"Yep, urgent. You got it. Thanks, appreciated." She hung up.

"What's going on?"

"After you left we decided that we should follow up whatever contacts we have in the police, see if we could come up with anything about the leaks."

"What? Just phone up people and ask them to tell us which cops like a bit of a gossip?" When Neumann got to hear about this he'd be even more pissed off than he already was.

"Come on, Martin, give us some credit! We're being a bit more subtle than that: asking how many IKMs are on the go across the Republic, how they're handled. General sort of stuff."

I ran my fingers through my hair then shook my head.

These testosterone contests with cops never did me any good.

"Sorry. But look, I'm back, maybe I should let you all know about my meeting with K1. My office in ten?"

Erika nodded, and I told Klaus and Laura the same thing. Nik had already made himself at home in my chair and was using the telephone. I held up ten fingers, then motioned towards the kettle. He nodded before going back to his one-sided conversation.

I spooned some coffee into the big glass pot and got five cups out of the cupboard. I pushed a pile of paperwork to one side and ignored the domino effect this had on the rest of my desk.

The kettle started steaming, so I pulled the plug out and poured water into the pot. Everyone was in the room by now. Laura had a sheet of paper with lots of notes on it, the others just sat there and started to slurp their coffees.

I told them about my visit to Neumann, and summarised: "He didn't really tell me anything, but I got the distinct impression that there was something wrong—I don't mean losing an IKM—I mean, like he was out of his depth or something-"

"Oh." A sort of popping noise came from Erika's direction. "I've got a friend who works in *Kripo* Central Co-ordination at Police HQ. When I asked about IKMs she said that officially there aren't any—the experienced handlers have all been discharged from service because they were too close to the Stasi. Basically, there's no-one in the police force with any real experience of running informants."

"What about unofficially? You said officially there were no IKMs. And unofficially?"

"She didn't say, but it sounds like the Ministry is turning a blind eye to the practice."

I'd been idly shovelling up all the files and papers that had cascaded off my desk, trying to persuade them to stay in the general area of my in-tray rather than slide back off onto the floor. Nik helpfully moved his elbows to give me more space, and as he did so a yellow envelope came into view.

"Oh, yes, this came for you by ministry courier. Had to sign for it and everything," he said.

I gave Nik a dirty look, but he didn't notice. The envelope was sealed and had *VS* stamped on it. I slid the short message out.

"They want us to send Evelyn in: undercover operation at the Weitlingstrasse premises." The others looked as astonished as I felt. *"Preparations for operational measures to begin with immediate effect, with a view to said measures being implemented at an early date."*

So the old Ministerial Committee, about to be replaced, were having a last shot at getting into the history books.

There was silence while we digested the news, and I took the opportunity to read the message through again. They wanted evidence for the purposes of criminal prosecutions.

"Well that makes it all a bit final, doesn't it?" I said at last, mostly to break the silence. "Anyone have anything to add?"

Nobody had anything to say, so all in all we weren't that much further.

Except for one thing.

There was no way we were going to allow the *Kripo* to handle Evelyn's operation: they'd either get her killed or lose her.

19:43

Karo

I went to see Antifa Bert. I was pissed off with my housemates and wanted to get another perspective.

"Smuggling," he said after I'd told him about the incident at the East Side yesterday. "So that's why your friend from RS is suddenly interested in the fash?"

He sat there with his chin on his hand, trying to look like

some Greek statue.

"And he's right about the fash getting more active. We've been monitoring this for a while, and we reckon they're gearing up for something big. The referenda, then the *Volkskammer* elections. But they might be planning something else entirely, who knows?"

"So what are we going to do about it?" I was pleased that Bert was taking this as seriously as I was.

"What do you mean? We're already doing loads!" Bert was almost shouting. I'd hurt his pride. Bloody men!

"I know you've been doing stuff. But maybe it's gonna take more than that? We need some new ideas!"

Bert shook his head. "Look you were good the other night, we need more people like you. What we're doing works."

But that was the question: was it really working?

"Look Bert—you and the others, you're doing a good job-"

"Too right we're doing a good job. If it hadn't been for us .... We're the ones who pushed the Nazis out of the centre of Berlin. And we have to do more, we need them out of Berlin and out of the country!"

"But they're coming back! What you've been doing worked for a while, but we're seeing more of them on the streets. More people are getting beaten up—more than have been for years."

"Yeah, so there needs to be more people doing the job. You coming again on Friday?"

"Don't you think there's got to be something else we can do? We've got to be strategic about this—take the fight to them." Bert was shaking his head, but I just carried on. "They're leafleting in our neighbourhoods, we need to do the same. They're recruiting young people, we need to get there first. They meet up at the Weitlingstrasse house before they do their hunting, we need to take the fight there—we need to take the fight to them!"

DAY 10
Wednesday
23rd March 1994

Erfurt: Several Russian citizens were injured at a club in Altenburg last night. Early reports indicate that skinheads were involved, but a police spokesperson declined to confirm whether there was a racist-fascist motivation behind the attack.

10:04
Martin

As soon as the morning meeting was over I headed off to see Dmitri in Karlshorst. As I left, Grit passed me a green A4 envelope.

"This arrived from the Ministry."

I had a quick look. They were release forms for Evelyn Hagenow. I was to sign them if and when we decided that Evelyn had been sufficiently prepared for her mission. Until I signed and returned those forms, Evelyn would be staying where she was.

Getting off the tram in Karlshorst I walked through the Russian colony—a town within a town—schools, shops, offices and military bases for the Russian forces and their families. The red star and the letters CA were still to be seen everywhere, but since the breakup of the Soviet Union this area was under the administration of the Russian Federation. On flagpoles the red banner with hammer and sickle had been replaced by the Russian tricolour.

Showing my RS pass to a guard standing outside the door I went into the nondescript pre-war building that housed Dmitri's office. A Russian non-commissioned officer escorted me up the stairs.

"Martin! Come in, come in and we shall drink a toast!" Dmitri and I had first met during a covert operation, and a bond had grown between us. But now we seemed to be meeting up just to push paper at each other, there was none of the adrenaline and excitement of our first covert meetings. Nevertheless, Dmitri always seemed pleased to see me. He was a large but gentle man with grey hair and a military bearing. About the same age as me, he was usually either cheerfully grinning or else frowning in concentrated thought. To people who didn't know him, his most remarkable feature was a black leather eye patch over his left eye, which, despite his frequent grins, gave him a sinister yet rakish look. I think Dmitri rather liked this image, and that was possibly why he used the patch rather than a less conspicuous glass eye. Perhaps it was for the same reason that he rarely gave a straight answer to a straight question, preferring instead to speak in Sibylline riddles.

"You seem a little pre-occupied today, *tovarishch*," Dmitri said after we'd looked over a few files.

I considered telling him what was on my mind, about the aborted raid, our concerns about the cops, and that my next appointment was with Evelyn, my own personal nemesis. We shouldn't be discussing live cases, and none of this had anything to do with the community of states which had once made up the Soviet Union; it was something I should have left at the door.

"Remember the case last year? The woman who headed up the Stasi task force? She's my next port of call today."

Dmitri grew grave, the joshing grin of a moment ago no longer in evidence.

"I thought that was out of your hands? No longer your responsibility? Evelyn Hagenow, wasn't it? Codename GÄRTNER?" I could see him adding notes to the files he kept in his head. "Where is she now?"

"In Magdalenenstrasse remand prison. I've been ordered to brief her for an undercover operation against a fascist group in Lichtenberg. They're growing in strength, or at the very least they're becoming bolder. There's no longer any doubt that they're a tangible security threat to the future of the Republic." I closed the file I'd been looking at and let if fall onto Dmitri's desk. "But we're in the dark. We need eyes on the ground and we have no-one who can do that kind of thing. The *Kripo* have been worse than useless. That leaves the ex-Stasi. Evelyn has volunteered."

"What is it you are trying to discover?"

"K1 had an IKM in place, but he was beaten and murdered a few days ago-"

"K1? You mean *Kripo*—they had an informant?" Dmitri knew full well that K1 was the shadowy political branch of the police which had once been the link between the Stasi and regular detectives—he was only asking to buy time while he mentally tabulated the information I was giving him.

"Yes, yes. But what we've known for a long time is that they have large amounts of propaganda and agitation materials, presumably brought in from the West. We should assume that they've been receiving financial assistance too. But none of that's new. It's the combination of this material with the recent surge in activity." Dmitri was still frowning, and I wondered what use he would find for this intelligence. "They're far more aggressive on the streets, they're demonstrating regularly, using the current refugee situation to make people scared. Don't tell me you haven't noticed— the target of these activities are often Russians!"

Dmitri's one good eye was intently watching me. Hands folded in his lap, he was a picture of relaxed concentration. But he didn't say anything, just waited for me to continue.

"Is there any intelligence on a link between yours and ours—between the fascists here and Pamyat, Otkasniki, any of the other far-right movements in Russia?"

Dmitri finally responded. He shook his head, then picked up a pencil and started tapping it on a file on his desk. He frowned for a minute or so.

"No, there was nothing flagged as being of interest to the GDR, and there's nothing I've come across. The groups around Shirinovski, the nationalist groups, they're just that: nationalist. They're not looking to support other nationalist movements in what was once the Soviet sphere. If anything they see it as being in their interest to undermine similar groups in other countries, not to support them. I think their main focus at the moment is Russian nationalism and anti-Semitism. They're feeling smug at how successful they've been in forcing so many Jews to leave our country, and they don't care whether they go to Washington, Tel Aviv or Berlin." He thought for a moment longer, tapping the pencil again, then carried on. "No, I don't see a connection there, but I think you're right to be suspicious of the West. You can't expect West Germany to give up so easily—they've wanted to take over East Germany for nearly fifty years—they'll still be doing everything they can to catch the prize."

"So what do you think? Will they be working underground, using the BND intelligence service? Or maybe agitating at a political level?"

"Oh, Martin, you know the answer as well as I do! You're just fishing for information." He dropped the pencil and spread his hands over the desk, palms down, a shrug lifting his shoulders. "You know I'd be the first to give it to you if I had anything at all. But I'm dry. They know where my sympathies lie, and so they keep me dry." Another shrug, the hands gathered back together in prayer. "All I can do is speculate, same as you."

Dmitri picked up the pencil again, playing with it for a moment before getting out a pack of black Russian cigarettes. He offered me one but I shook my head.

"If I were to speculate," he rolled the cigarette between his fingers, the loose paper creasing up as it met his thumbs. "I would say that anyone looking into this matter needs to take great care, yes, to be careful."

He put the cigarette in his mouth and lit it from a desk lighter, drawing in, then breathing out a cloud of dark smoke. "You mention politics," he drew on his cigarette again, speaking as he exhaled. "Have you considered your fifth column: the political parties. So long as you have parties then those involved will be representing a party and not the people. And while you have cross-border party affiliations the Western politicians will be telling their colleagues over here how to think, how to vote-"

"But we can't restrict free political association!"

"No, no, but I like the way your central government and parliament is losing power day by day; I watch with great interest your preparations for a referendum on devolving more power to the Round Tables." Dmitri drew on his acrid cigarette, exhaling again before continuing. "But the Round Tables offer the politically ambitious much less room for manoeuvre, so the parties resist decentralisation. *Power gathers power*, as they say in Moscow." Again Dmitri spread his hands out over the desk, like the wings of a dove, a peace offering. "And remember how well the West-parties played that particular role when they tried to derail the events of 1989 and 1990?"

Re-unification propaganda—mostly sponsored by the West-CDU—had flooded our country even before the Wall opened in November 1989, and that was the start of the rumours of close links between the West-CDU and the far-right.

"Are you suggesting that the parties, the ones *here*, in the GDR, could be supporting or encouraging the fascists?"

"Political groupings may see supporting unrest as a canny move. Oh, it may not be direct support, but they're not exactly going out of their way to deal with the problem either. It's always been that way—remember the SPD in 1919, the workers' own party involved in liquidating the Workers' Councils? How Minister Noske tolerated, even supported the nationalist *Freikorps* in order to preserve his position in government."

I'd long been uneasy about the way the political parties, particularly the CDU and the SPD, with their close links to the West, had continuously spoken out against the Round Tables and the Works Councils. Now Dmitri was drawing parallels between today's situation and the bloody suppression of the Workers' and Soldiers' Councils at the start of the Weimar Republic.

"That's how it will always be," said Dmitri, thoughtfully tapping ash off his cigarette. "If people are scared they will be susceptible to calls for strong leadership. If people are confused they will demand simple solutions. Just listen to the arguments—every day on the radio, in the newspapers: the central government, all the political parties in the *Volkskammer* are saying you need strong leadership and clear policies to deal with the problems. Doesn't matter if they're talking about the referenda, economic restructuring, or the increasing violence by fascists. But your revolution is in the creative phase: the chaos that follows the usurpation of power. You're working out new systems, new ways of doing things. Trial and error: a painful, slow, frustrating process. Without this creative chaos you can't decentralise, you can't have autonomous districts and neighbourhoods. Such things can't be decreed from above, only built from below. I need only refer you to Vladimir Ilyich and his abortive attempts at harnessing the revolutionary power of 1918. And just look where that took us ...."

Sometimes Dmitri had these periods of eloquent contemplation, he would look into the middle distance, seeing beyond the walls of his office, beyond his past as a KGB officer and his present role in the FSK. Ever since we first met there had been an instinctive trust between us, allowing him to voice unorthodox thoughts. Yet each time he did so I was taken by surprise. Still, I enjoyed his ramblings; they helped me remember that the experiment in our little Republic didn't only affect us, it wasn't just for our sake—it represented something much larger for so many people in the world.

"Dmitri, that's all very well, you're as persuasive as ever. But it doesn't actually help me right now, does it?"

Dmitri smiled, shaking his head at my short-sightedness.

"On the contrary, my friend, I rather think it does. I'm telling you that you need to deal with your fascists before they spread too many seeds of doubt. You can't let them give the centralists the excuse they so badly want. You must defend your revolution—and quickly!"

"Again, it doesn't help me, does it? There's not so much we can do to defend the revolution: there aren't any Chekists any more, and we wouldn't want them even if-"

"Martin!" Dmitri shook his head in bafflement. "How is it, you Germans—a culture that gave us Schiller and Goethe, Heine and Hölderlin—not to mention Kant and Arendt—how is it you need everything clearly spelt out? You must deal with your fascist problem promptly, and in my opinion, you must do so without involving any form of central authority. Work at the grassroots, strengthen the basis, not the centre."

"So, we shouldn't let K1 handle Evelyn—we should do it ourselves, but-"

"Yes." Dmitri smiled again, a different smile, pleased that I'd finally cottoned on. "Controlling the operation of a penetration agent could be the first step. But what about the raw intelligence—how will you analyse it, what will you do with it?"

As always, Dmitri was way ahead of me. My colleagues and I were already thinking about bypassing the *Kripo* when it came to running Evelyn but we hadn't thought about what to do with any information she might pass on. I guess we were just going to stay within the remit given to us by the Ministerial Committee: task Evelyn to find evidence that could be used in a criminal case against key individuals—disrupt fascist activities that way. But that's exactly how they did things in the old days—it hadn't worked. Sending fascists to prison only made them and their groups stronger. Dmitri on the other hand was talking about acting on intelligence, he hadn't mentioned prosecuting individuals at all.

"You think that Evelyn would deliver useful intelligence? What could we do with that?"

"I think Evelyn has much experience in this game, and if there is anything to find then she will find it. And she may even give it to you."

"Things like supply lines? Money trails, information about support from the West?"

"Yes, yes." Dmitri nodded earnestly. "And once you have that information you will have the means to disrupt them. You can involve the local Round Tables, the Works Councils in the Border Police regiments and local *Kripo*. Let them take responsibility for stopping these supply routes. You could help with co-ordinating and networking the efforts to discover and disrupt new routes. But you should let those involved take the decisions on how to deal with the problem. You provide the information and let the organisations at the local level decide how best to use it."

"But Evelyn, I don't know if we can trust her."

"Desperate times, my friend, desperate times," Dmitri commiserated, his eye twinkling mischievously.

"I'm not even sure I can brief her. I mean how does one do something like that?" There was silence for a moment while my thoughts wandered on. Then: "Dmitri, would you do it? I could get you access to the files, and-"

"Martin, Martin, no. I'm flattered." He held his hands up. "But no. This is not my struggle. I have my own worries."

"I'm sorry, it was silly of me-"

"Yes, but you know Martin, that's why I like you. You are a breath of fresh air, a refreshing addition to our little clique of spies. When I go to see the French or the Americans, or even my colleagues in the GRU, it is always poker. Here a card, there a bluff. But with you, we can pretend we are still human, and we can talk as friends."

He gave one of his little giggles, followed by a heavy sigh, a sigh that made me feel inexperienced and feckless. Dmitri often helped me put my own thoughts in order, see events and problems from an operational perspective, but always at the price of reminding me of my amateur status.

"Comrade, as I said, I have my own worries. Things can't continue like this much longer. There's too much pressure at home, things are falling apart—we're needed back there, not here. There are already signs of a preparation for withdrawal from Germany: personnel not being replaced, there's been less servicing of materiel, you know the kind of thing. Things are even more chaotic than usual.

"But, wait." Dmitri shuffled through papers on his desk, coming up with a grey-yellow file, a pink stripe splitting its cover from bottom-left to top-right, a long series of Cyrillic characters and numbers handwritten on one corner. "This is for you, my gift, because you are such a naif in our jungle. In the middle of all this chaos there's a young officer in Dresden, one of ours, FSK/KGB. Keen. Eager to make a splash. Ambitious. You know: the dangerous kind, destined to go far. No, wait!" He held out his hand, preventing me from opening the file. "Don't open it yet! And be careful who you show this to. The rumours are that our young officer has been buying up all the left-over IMs in the Dresden area. All the informants that have been left without the father figure of the Stasi, all those who feel they need to confess, report and inform. He's got them. And in there you have a list of previous IMs that we believe he has been in contact with, also the cadre files of the officer in question—redacted, of course. I don't know what he plans to do with all these informants, but then, that's your problem."

Martin
12:12

Normally after meeting Dmitri I would feel reassured—he provided me with a solidity that had become rare in my world—but now I felt less than calm. Certainly not the best mood for a meeting with Evelyn. I sat brooding on the U-Bahn, wondering how best to handle her, but as so often before, I came to the conclusion that I couldn't handle her. I could only wait to see how she would handle me.

I reluctantly climbed the steps out of the U-Bahn station and trailed up Magdalenenstrasse. The few tenement blocks soon petered out, replaced by a five metre high wall topped with barbed wire, lights and contact lines. Arriving at the main entrance, I pressed the buzzer, a wicket gate opened and the guard checked my visitor's papers and RS pass. As a second pair of high steel gates creaked open I walked into the courtyard of the prison, taking in the dozens of blind windows that looked down on me. Behind one of those windows Evelyn had her cell, she'd already been here for several months awaiting trial, or as it might turn out, her chance of restitution.

I followed the guard across the narrow courtyard, heading for the administration wing. They gave me the use of an interrogation room. The usual kind of place: one wall lined with *Sprelakart* cupboards, a desk with telephone, lamp, notepad and a two-reel tape recorder. In front of the desk a plain table, set end on, so that the interviewee couldn't get too close.

The interviewee's chair was in the middle of the floor, and I moved it to the table. For this kind of meeting I should have placed both chairs near to each other, with neither table nor desk between them, but I felt the need to keep my psychological distance to Evelyn so I sat down behind the desk.

I didn't have to wait long before there was a knock on the door.

"Come in!"

In a repeat of the procedure last week, Evelyn said nothing until her wrists had been freed and the prison guard had withdrawn from the room. She stood there, looking at me, a slight smile playing at the corner of her lips.

"Martin, I'm glad you've come to see me again." She sat down, angling her head so that she could look up at me, her eyes wide. "It gets so lonely in here-"

"I've been sent by the Ministry," I interrupted. "If it were down to me there'd be no second chance."

But Evelyn had picked up on my uncertainty. She was good at reading me, she was good at reading everyone. And she knew how to use the skill.

"So the dear old Ministry wants my help now that the house in Weitlingstrasse has been abandoned?" She was doing a damn good job at appearing ingenuous.

I don't think I betrayed my surprise that despite being locked up, Evelyn had somehow found out about yesterday's events.

"Oh, Martin! Don't look so shocked. Of course I'll help! Anything for an old friend."

"Why?"

"Martin, you are a sweetie! This is my country too, no matter what you've done to it. What? You think that just because I'm still faithful to my Chekist colleagues that I don't love our GDR? Listen Martin, those fascists," and for a moment her voice was vicious, "they're scum. What they want goes against everything I've ever worked for and everything I've ever believed in. That's what gives me the right to fight them." She sat back in her chair, hands held open, palms towards me. "And I really can't help if I'm stuck in this shit hole, can I?"

I reached down to my briefcase, taking out a file and slowly opening it on the desk. I was using the time to try to regain some composure—she'd only been here for a few minutes and already she had me on the back foot. I needed to find a way to exert some control over the situation.

"I have been instructed by the Ministry to brief you on current events, and request your assistance in this matter-"

"I'll do it." Evelyn's amiable persona had returned.

"I haven't told you what we want you to do yet!"

"Here, let me have a look, it'll be quicker that way." She stood up and reached across the desk to take the file from me, beginning to scan the pages before she'd even sat down again. "After all," she winked at me, "I am a pro!"

I was about to take the file back from her when I realised that she was right. Just as with Dmitri a couple of hours ago, I was meeting with someone who had undergone both extensive training and years of operational experience. I on the other hand was a mere amateur, one still in denial of his role.

It didn't take Evelyn long to leaf through the whole file. She closed it carefully, pushing it back over the table towards me, then leaned back and let out a sigh.

"You don't have much to go on, do you?" she said, more statement than question. "Don't you have any of the backstory? Haven't you found the files? Lichtenberg K1 should have some of them. A few of the more senior and short-sighted comrades thought it might be a good idea to train up some of these fascists, teach them some discipline then get them to report back on what was happening. They got the whole package: paratrooper training, combat exercises, conspirative-operational instruction, the lot. But we lost control of them. That would have been about 1987, 1988. They just passed their new skills on to their Nazi chums.

"No matter," she tapped her head, "I've got the most important stuff in here. I'll do it."

"But I still haven't told you what we want you to do!" I protested again.

"Well I'm doing it anyway. Time to clean up the mess my comrades left behind. When do you want me to go in?"

It was almost as if Evelyn could no longer surprise me—she knew what we wanted from her, and she knew that I wasn't happy about the plan. But she also knew it wasn't up to me, I'd had my orders from the Ministry.

"I have a release order. Once it's been signed you can leave here. But we'll need to prepare you first: a full briefing, set up your team, contact procedures-"

"Martin," quiet, but determined, almost exasperated, "once again: I'm a pro. Give me the use of that phone now, and I'll be ready by tomorrow midday. Just give me whatever files you have. What, this is all you have, isn't it?"

"The cops have more, but we haven't got copies yet-"

"What about related crime reports, who they've been beating up, intimidating? Good, get copies of those to me, I need to know what they'll be gossiping about, sick bastards. Right." She walked around the desk, dragging her chair behind her. Sitting down next to me she pulled the phone over. "I have work to do. As you said: preparations. If I'm going to do this then I'll be doing it my way: I'll arrange my own conspirative meetings, my own cut-outs, my own fall-backs and safety procedures. What?" She pulled a face at me, trying to make me laugh. "Did you think I'd trust those clowns at K1 to set things up?"

She picked up the phone and dialled. "It's GÄRTNER. Get me DAEDALUS." She gave me a business-like look, gesturing with her thumb towards the door.

I picked up my briefcase, and left the room, leaving Evelyn in charge of phone and file.

"Operation WITHERED VINE—it's on again," I heard as I closed the door behind me.

13:14

Karo

It was a bit of a gamble, calling a Squatters' Council. There hadn't been one since last year when it split in two—the Wessis on the one side and the Ossis on the other. But this was something we could all agree on: we were all against the fash.

It felt like we had to think bigger. Yesterday's argument with Bert had shown me that we can't just rely on the Antifa groups to do everything. But right now the meeting was just about boys telling war stories. The usual crap: late night run-ins with skins, near escapes, standing guard outside refugee hostels ...

"Look, we can spend all day yacking about what's been happening. That's not why we're here," I told them. "So let's just stop with the stories! The fash are preparing to take over our country. It's not just the referenda, it's not just about the Volkskammer elections, it's about more and more people getting beaten up, injured. It's about hate and fear spreading. It's got to stop. And the question is: how are we going to stop it?"

Martin

Part of me was relieved that Evelyn was ready for her task but I couldn't shake the feeling that I'd been out-manoeuvred. Apart from anything else there were serious trust issues. Evelyn had shown herself to be an active opponent of the changes happening in our country; she wasn't in favour of all this freedom and participation—as far as I could tell she wanted the autocratic rule of the Party back. I only had her word for it that she wanted rid of the fascists as much as we did. But once we let her off the leash who knew what she'd get up to?

When I got back to the office I knocked on Erika's open door. She looked up from her typewriter and gestured me in.

"Martin, you're back. How did it go? Want some tea?"

I shook my head and sat down on the visitor's chair in front of her desk.

"How was it? You don't look too happy."

"Oh, the usual. How did we get into this situation?"

"Look, Martin, we're doing the stuff that nobody else wants to do. It's never going to be easy, and it's good that we ask ourselves difficult questions." She patted my hand. "That's what you're doing right now, isn't it? Asking yourself difficult questions?"

Erika and I had worked together for a few years now, we got on well, we understood each other. She was cautious, sometimes even timid, but when she decided that she could trust someone then she trusted them; she didn't try to second guess them, she was there for them, no matter what.

"What did Evelyn say?" she asked eventually.

"She jumped at the chance. In fact, she completely took over and sent me away. Right now she's arranging it all with some of her old friends in the Firm."

It was obvious that many of those who worked for the Stasi still had some kind of network going, but it was unclear just how far it went, or what they were prepared to do. It was yet another threat that we had no kind of handle on.

"I suppose that's good for us this time around," Erika came up with after a while. "They know what they're doing, and they're probably better resourced than us. We'll just have to deal with any consequences when they happen."

"She also confirmed the historic links between the far-right and the Stasi."

"Interesting. I suppose we'd better inform the Ministry." Erika got up and poured herself some tea.

"There's something else?" Erika sat down again.

"I saw Dmitri. I told him about Evelyn, and he gave me a few ideas."

Erika was watching me over the rim of her cup, waiting for me to continue.

"He thinks we should be aiming higher, that we should get Evelyn to do more than gather evidence to prosecute individuals. He thinks she could get useful information, maybe even enough to smash the fascist movement."

Now that I was saying it out loud it sounded obvious, but Erika didn't respond—she had her cup held up to her lips, but wasn't drinking. She was thinking.

"We have clear instructions to brief Evelyn only for gathering evidence for prosecution-"

"And Dmitri also suggested that if we get anything useful from Evelyn we shouldn't just pass it upstairs. He reckons we should be distributing it to local groups: Round Tables, Works Councils, local police and Border Police companies ...."

"Why?"

"Because it's the right thing to do. Because right now we're sleepwalking into a nightmare—the fascists, the nationalists, the skins, it's getting worse. Taken together it's probably a greater threat than the economic crisis. And what Dmitri got me thinking about is that *we* have a choice. For once, we hold the levers: we can give the intelligence to the Ministry and the politicians and the government, or we give it to the grassroots. If Evelyn does her job we could get enough to smash the far-right. If we give it to the central institutions then the politicians will take the credit. They'll turn it into a convincing argument for a strong centralised government here in Berlin."

Erika put her cup down. "And going by their recent behaviour they'll be using that argument to defeat the referendum on devolving power to the Round Tables."

14:19

Karo

We did it—we agreed to hold a mega-demo on Friday afternoon, at rush hour. There was going to be a massive mobilisation over the next two days. I knew we could make it happen: nearly every squat in East Berlin had a representative at this meeting, and we were going to end early so that we could get moving, talk to absolutely everyone we knew. By the end of tonight everyone in the squatting scene would know about the plan. We'd put the word out to Leipzig, Dresden, Rostock, Erfurt and Jena: it was going to be big. No, it was going to be *mega*.

15:01

Martin

After talking to Erika I put a brief summary of my ideas on the agenda sheet for tomorrow morning's meeting and went back to my office. It had been a long day and I was feeling tired, but I wanted to make a start on preparing Evelyn's briefing. I sat at my desk but I wasn't taking any information in. I decided to take the paperwork home.

It was a good move—I felt better as soon as I left the office. The sky was clouding over, and the day was cooling rapidly. Walking in the fresh air was bringing my grey cells up to operating speed, and I wasn't paying attention to where I was going, just letting my feet do the navigation. Before I was properly aware of it, I was climbing the stairs in my tenement, opening the door to my flat.

I decided to go through the case summaries first, get some perspective on what had been going on, see if it gave me any clues as to what we should get Evelyn to watch out for. Dmitri's suggestion had been simple: gain intelligence that could be used by networks and organisations all over the country, help them to shut down fascist activities in their area.

But what kind of intelligence? I'd already been over most of these files once or twice before, and if there were any clues in there then I should have found it by now.

But I hadn't found anything useful, nor had Laura, Erika or Nik. Nor, presumably had K1. Perhaps I should just give all the files to Evelyn, she'd probably be more able than I to ferret out any useful bits.

It was slow, boring work, and I took frequent breaks—standing up, stretching, making coffee, going to the toilet—but I kept at it, hour after hour.

At about eight o'clock I looked through my notes for the thousandth time, wondering how to rationalise them, group things together so that they'd still make sense tomorrow. But it was useless. I gave up and took Evelyn's file over to my armchair, leaving the rest on the kitchen table.

I was much more familiar with Evelyn's file, having worked extensively on it last autumn. We'd pieced together her Stasi career, but it had been well hidden, not recorded in the usual archives at the Normannenstrasse complex. We still didn't know who else had been on the Stasi task force that Evelyn had led until a few months ago. Evelyn had steadfastly refused to answer any questions on operational processes so we were still very much in the dark. We had codenames but had found no records in the old Stasi files—presumably these codenames had been assigned after the end of 1989 when parts of the Stasi went underground.

Nor had we been able to comprehensively track Evelyn's activities over the years. There was still an unexplained period in 1988. After the Luxemburg Affair she had dropped out of sight here in East Berlin and resurfaced a few months later in Moscow. Her time in Moscow was a closed book—even Dmitri was unable or unwilling to shed any light on it.

Too many riddles, too few answers.

Thinking about Evelyn's association with Moscow made me think of Dmitri again—I hadn't yet looked at the file he'd given me. I got out of my chair and made my way over to the kitchen table where I'd stacked all the files, searching through them until I found the yellowish cardboard folder.

Which was when the phone rang.

"Martin, you asked me to chase up those reports Lieutenant Steinlein was supposed to be bringing round." It was Grit—she was still in the office. "I've just had a phone call—comrade Lieutenant Steinlein was taken to hospital last night—he's been badly beaten by skinheads."

Steinlein. The officer in charge of the raid on the fascist house yesterday. A uniformed police officer beaten up by skins.

A revenge attack.

Shaken by the news I returned to my armchair in the living room. I still had Dmitri's file in my hand. I glanced over the Russian text but it made no sense to me, my eyes merely focussing on the few German words and names there: Дрезден, Котвус and the like, but I had no idea what it all meant. I'd have to give it to Klaus to use his Russian skills on.

I thumbed back to the front. A loose sheet had been inserted, noticeably different from the others: this was the first copy from a typewriter, not the indistinct blue of the carbons in the rest of the file. Intrigued, I scanned the Cyrillic script, wondering whether I could decipher any of it. A few words in the first paragraph looked familiar:

Ул. Вытпинг 122, 1134 Берлин-Лихтенберг

The address of the fascist house in Lichtenberg! Cursing myself for not paying more attention at school I started at the top of the sheet, attempting to understand what was typed there. But beyond the Cyrillic rendering of some of the names we already had there was not much I could understand.

Shutting the file again I considered what this meant. Dmitri had let me ramble on in his office about the operation with Evelyn, he'd told me to my face that he knew nothing about our fascist problem. And then he'd given me a document about the Weitlingstrasse house.

It wasn't an oversight, it wasn't a mistake—Dmitri didn't make a move without first considering all the angles. So he was trying to tell me something, something he couldn't say to me in his office or on the phone. But what?

DAY 11
Thursday
24th March 1994

Jena: There were violent scenes last night after football club Dynamo Dresden played away at Carl Zeiss Jena. In a related incident, the Junge Gemeinde Jena, which is active in anti-fascist and refugee support initiatives, was subjected to a sustained attack by hooligans associated with Dynamo. Lieutenant Walther of the VPD Jena stated that negative-hostile groupings had been successfully dispersed following police operations.

05:19
Martin

Little good had come of the telephone since it had been installed a couple of years ago. In the old days I had dreamed of having my own telephone connection, of no longer having to queue at the phone box down the road, no longer relying on friendly neighbours to take a message and leave it on the notepad hanging from my front door. But the reality was that the phone—installed when I began working at RS—was a means of summoning me to work, a way to wake me from slumber, and on not a few occasions, from hangover-induced near-death status.

Today it was an early-morning call.

With the first whirr of the bell I started into wakefulness.

My reading material had long slipped out of my hands, loose sheets had sailed over the floor. By the second ring I'd worked out where I was, and with the third long ring I was out of my chair and on my way into the hall.

"Grobe," I said into the receiver, my voice still encrusted with sleep.

"Martin, it's me. Now I do hope I haven't woken you, but I suspect I may have, I *am* sorry, dear Martin."

Evelyn. Not the first time she had woken me with a telephone call, but how had she managed to get access to a phone in the prison?

"I thought you might like to meet up again before I start my little adventure. I don't have much time, so shall we say one hour from now?" She gave me an address in Hellersdorf and rang off before I could argue.

It was a few moments before my brain engaged. I was splashing water on my face in the kitchen sink before I realised that Evelyn was no longer on remand. Somehow she had been released, even without my signature on the necessary forms. I looked at my reflection in the little shaving mirror that I kept next to the soap dish and the *Fit* washing up liquid. The usual grey, stubbly face looked back. No surprise to be seen on that face. Evelyn, for all her adroitness, had definitely lost her power to shock me.

It wasn't until I reached the S-Bahn station at Nöldnerplatz that I looked at my watch. It was just getting light, and that alone should have told me: not yet six o'clock. Once past the shunting yards at Lichtenberg station the train line runs between allotments, parks and back gardens, the only industrial intrusion a hot-water distributor pipe. The train itself was fairly empty, most people travelling the other way.

I changed onto the U-Bahn at Wuhletal, not having to wait long before the train climbed up out of the tunnel. Sitting down on the blue plastic seat I looked out of the window as we dived underground and screeched around a curve, emerging into a cutting before the next station. Above the banks the sun was spearing light beneath the grey clouds drooping in the sky, glinting windows reflected the steel light down into the cutting.

Getting off at Paul-Verner-Strasse, I walked down the main road before checking my map and turning off onto a service road lined by dusty Trabants and a few Ladas and Wartburgs. Reaching a door—one just like all the other doors in all the other concrete-slab flats—I pushed it open and entered the hallway. Ignoring both the ranks of letterboxes in the hall, and the dented steel door of the lift, I climbed the narrow stairs, feet clattering up the terrazzo steps.

On the first floor I knocked at a flat, a confident double tap, followed by two singles. The door was bright yellow, punctuated by a peep-hole in the dead centre, handle and modern lock on the side. A grey cardboard square was pasted next to the doorbell, the inked name faded to illegibility.

The door opened silently on well-oiled hinges, and a silhouette ushered me in. Evelyn. Through the frosted glass of the lobby door behind her I saw the suggestion of a second figure flitting past. But when I went through, the room beyond was empty. A closed door was next to the kitchen-niche in the corner. I went straight over to the smudged windows, checking the main road I had just left. An Ikarus bus started up, its dark orange paintwork shaded further by dirt, the bendy belly concertinaing as it pulled out of the bus-stop, shuddering across the concrete-roadway. Dark, heavy fumes lay in its wake over the grey surface. No-one was in sight, no-one had got off the bus, and the wide road was now empty of moving vehicles. Rain began to spot the glass.

Turning back to face Evelyn I could see she was in the kitchen, boiling water for tea. She hadn't said anything, and I kept my peace, waiting until she was ready to talk. In the meantime I looked around the room. Sparsely but adequately furnished; the sofa deep, doubling up as a bed. The arm chairs matching the beige and brown of both sofa and thin carpet but clashing nastily with the mint-green diamond patterned wallpaper. Orange curtains, pulled back beside the windows, contributed to the impression that the place was furnished with left-overs, that no-one had ever lived here. Opposite the kitchen stood a wall-unit, no knick-knacks ornamenting the shelves, the cabinet doors ajar, showing equally empty insides.

Evelyn brought a couple of cups over to the low glass coffee-table, placing them next to a box of West German chocolates, then went back to the kitchen to fetch the tea-pot. She still hadn't said a word, and this, rather than any nervous tic or twitch, any fidgety movement in Evelyn's manner, told me just how uneasy she was feeling. Normally so ebullient, Evelyn wooed her conversational partners; a black widow of an operative, she graciously drew you into her scrupulously laid web. She seated herself in one of the armchairs, leaning back comfortably, crossing her legs.

"Are you OK?" I asked her as I sat down opposite her, on the sofa.

"How sweet! Yes, dear Martin, I'm fine." She laughed, a tinkling, false laugh.

I poured out the tea, and leaned over the table to hand her a cup. She took it with a smile, and sat back again, carefully sipping her drink.

I didn't ask whether she was ready, I didn't ask why she'd asked—told—me to come here. The answers were obvious: yes, she was ready, she had the support of her ex-Stasi colleagues, and the less I knew about that, the more comfortable I would feel. And she'd asked me to come here to show me, once again, that she wasn't dependent on me for anything, not even to sign the forms to get her out of jail.

But since I was here I decided to make use of my time.

"We didn't get to talk about your mission yesterday." I ignored the face she was pulling. "The Ministry requests that you gather evidence for the purpose of prosecuting individuals associated with groups using the premises Weitlingstrasse 122, with specific reference to any persons of cadre status."

I paused to sip my tea, Evelyn's face was pointed towards the kitchen, looking deliberately bored. She took out a packet of cigarettes—Russian, the same brand that Dmitri smoked—and carefully lit one. She offered me the pack, but I waved it away.

"Oh Martin, still trying to give up? You know it only makes you crotchety-"

"But my colleagues and I are particularly interested in background intelligence," I spoke over her, determined to say my piece. Evelyn had stiffened, her eyes focussed on mine. I finally had her full attention. "We don't just want to know whether and how materials are being smuggled into the GDR, we want intelligence on the groups' background, their make-up, movements. We want patterning data, connections, interests and influences by and on other groups. And we want to know more about the geographic spread. If you can tell us who we need to be concentrating on, here in Berlin and throughout the Republic-"

"Martin! This is why you're so dear to me—you're always good for a surprise! I should have recruited you years ago, if only so that you could have learned the lingo," she said archly. "But I understand, I know what you're talking about."

She leaned forward, smoke leaking from her mouth as she spoke, a low whisper: "But tell me, darling, why should I give you this information. Do you think you're the only game in town?"

"Your network?" I found that I too was speaking in a low voice, not whispering; whispers carry too easily, a murmur, letting the words get lost in the carpet and the curtains.

Evelyn glanced at the closed door, then brought her cup up to her lips, buying time to think.

"And you have the files for me? The police reports?"

I drew the summary reports, the ones I had taken home with me last night, out of my briefcase, laying them on the coffee table.

"Thank you, Martin." Evelyn put her cup down, and pushed the box of chocolates over to me. "Here, would you call that a fair swap? Some friends gave them to me, a get-out-of-jail present. But you know what? I just don't have any appetite right now. You take them."

She mashed her cigarette into the glass ashtray and picked up the files. She spread them out on the table, checking the reference numbers.

"Nothing from October 1987 then?" She didn't even pause to see what effect her question would have on me. "Might be wise to let that one drop. Some bigwig in the scene doesn't want that particular can of worms being opened up."

With that she picked up the files and stood up. She reached the door next to the kitchen niche and turned, looking me in the eyes, a gaze somewhere between disappointment and apology.

"My network, as you call it, will be watching out for me, they'll be in contact with me, providing me with backup. I shall owe my safety, my life to them. What can you offer? What do you have to bargain with?"

The door had opened, as if by itself, but a figure was standing there, dark blue suit, white shirt, no tie. It wasn't so much the suit that I noticed, nor even the man himself, but the way he stood. Knees slightly bent, feet barely in contact with the floor. Shoulders wide, curved forward, his arms slightly bent at the elbows, hands half closed, held just below his stomach.

Evelyn continued in the same easy tone as before: "Please tell the Minister, or the Ministerial Committee or whatever you call it nowadays, tell them that they'll get their evidence."

"And the other information, the intelligence I mentioned?" I stood up as I asked the question. As I moved, so did the suit. As I sat back again, the suit returned to his position in the doorway, both of us marionettes on the same pulley. Behind him I could see a bathtub, the sides lined with cork tiles.

"I think, dear Martin, that it's time to leave, don't you? Goodbye." Evelyn blew me a kiss and the suit stepped aside as she went into the room beyond.

As I stood up, the suit returned to his position. I looked at him, and he looked back. A steady, hard but not malicious look. A step towards the doorway where he was standing, and the hands came up, clenching into fists.

I considered my options, consulted my experiences with the Stasi, with Evelyn, and decided the other doorway—the one that led to the stairwell and the outside world—might be a safer option.

07:49
Martin

I'd gone straight to the office, it was still early: nobody there. But a telex was waiting in the basket: I'd received the summons. And when you receive the summons you don't delay. Frau Demnitz, the senior civil servant responsible for the sundry agencies attached to the Ministry of the Interior enjoyed summoning her minions. She was old school—like many civil servants she had survived the transition that started at the end of 1989. This was apparent in her arrogance and her bureaucratic manner—she blamed you for everything, even the very fact that she had to deal with you. Reports were always too long or too short, illegible, incomprehensible or inconsistent; you were too late or too early; too well-dressed or too informal. And never, ever had you filled in the correct forms in the correct order using the correct stamp. Her endemic criticism wasn't an expression of political belief or values—although we had never talked about politics, so I couldn't be absolutely certain—but her attitude was typical of civil servants in the GDR. Oh, things had improved: officials were softening, bending in the wind of change, but up in the rare heights of the ministries and the organs of central government the situation had remained much as before.

So when you were summoned by Frau Demnitz it was best to go as soon as you could, and if at all possible, sooner.

As I got off the S-Bahn at Friedrichstrasse my thoughts were on Evelyn and the other person with her this morning. To them I was more a hindrance than any help, and they were probably right about that. Reaching Unter den Linden I headed down the side of the Russian Embassy to reach the neo-classical grandeur of the Ministry of the Interior. I passed the policeman standing under the trinity of flags by the main door, and climbed the marble stairs to Frau Demnitz's office.

I wasn't kept waiting but was immediately ushered in. I greeted Frau Demnitz, but she didn't look up as our hands clasped each other in a handshake. She was looking at a flier on her desk. I noticed it because it wasn't the kind of thing one expected to see there—usually her attention was occupied only by manilla files and heavy, dark archive boxes. But this A5 piece of grey paper, badly mimeographed in purple ink, looked like the samizdat newsletters we produced before the revolution.

"Thank you for coming at such short notice comrade Captain Grobe." She sniffed. She was famous for her sniffing, I often had the impression that my presence was somewhat offensive to her. "I presume you have seen this publication, although why you didn't think to inform the Ministry I cannot conceive."

I reached over and turned the piece of paper round so that I could read it. Although it was badly copied, it looked like the original had been laid out and printed from a modern computer. There was even a picture, taking up nearly half the page: a face. I looked more closely, it was hard to make out the features in the blurry, purple ink, but the person in the photograph looked familiar.

Holding the flier at arm's length, trying to decipher the smeared words: STASI SCUM IN YOUR NEIGHBOURHOOD was the title. Below the picture was my name.

I looked up at Frau Demnitz who was watching me with a calculating gaze.

"I see you aren't familiar with this. Well, you can read it at your leisure, but in short it provides some biographical details, including your current occupation as an officer of the *Republikschutz*, and goes on to encourage the reader to," again the sniff, "take action, shall we say, to deal with what they see as a problem."

"Where did this come from?"

"Well, apparently they're pasted up all over your part of town, although someone was kind enough to deliver a copy to the Ministry at some point in the night."

PARRASITES LIKE SO-CALLED 'CAPTAIN' GROBE ARE LIVING OFF YOUR WORK AND LABOUR! NO BETER THAN THE STASI THIS REPUBLIKSCHUTZ SCUM ARE NOTHING BUT SPYS PREYING ON HONEST WORKING GERMANS! I managed to read before Frau Demnitz continued, her voice betraying her distaste at dealing with such material.

"I expect you, comrade Captain, to deal with this situation. We simply can't allow this ordure to bring the Ministry into disrepute. I would be grateful if you could prioritise dealing with this matter."

I looked at her in disbelief. *Bring the Ministry into disrepute*? She couldn't be serious?

"Is it the spelling mistakes that bother you most, Frau Demnitz, or the threatening nature of the message?"

Demnitz didn't answer, she just fixed me with her glare.

"So, let me get this straight, Frau Demnitz: you demand my presence at the Ministry, make me come all the way into town, present me with a leaflet that is calling for physical violence to be done to me, then demand that *I* do something about it?" I was angry now, standing up and leaning over the desk, hands resting either side of her blotter pad. She didn't even flinch.

"Thank you comrade Captain, as ever you have succeeded in summarising the situation in a commendably succinct fashion. Now perhaps you could find your own way out?"

"Tell me, would you have pulled this trick if the new Ministerial Committee were already in place?"

But she must have pressed a button somewhere because her office door opened, and a young civil servant was standing there, silently but politely inviting me to leave.

I ran down the stairs, my heavy feet sending echoes before me. I pulled open the outside door with a suddenness that caused the policeman standing on the steps to look around, then I stalked off down Mauerstrasse.

As my pace slackened and my pulse slowed I found myself standing at the end of Unter den Linden, looking at the Brandenburg Gate. The Wall glowed white beyond the columns, and over in the West the trees of the Tiergarten were budding, the branches picked out by the early sunlight. Tourists were already passing through the checkpoint, customs and Border Police cursorily checking papers and joking with the Westerners coming over to sightsee in central Berlin. The open space, the calm purpose of the tourists with their cameras and their intent gazes—it was all a million miles away from what was happening in the East Berlin that I knew.

I took the leaflet out of my pocket, but it didn't improve on second reading. Putting it away in my briefcase I found the box of chocolates that Evelyn had given me. Why had she given me chocolates? Had they been tampered with? I checked the cellophane wrapping, but it appeared undamaged. What could Evelyn or her Stasi friends have put in a box of chocolates?

A microphone? Too easy to discover, and why bother?

A transmitter to follow my movements? Again, too bulky to evade detection—I'd discover it as soon as I opened the box.

Poison?

I laughed out loud at the thought, and a policeman who had already been keeping half an eye on me started walking towards me. I continued up Otto-Grotewohl-Strasse, still trying to work it all out.

No, like she said, she just didn't have any appetite right now. Fair enough, given her plans for the day.

The thought of Evelyn going undercover to penetrate a fascist group put my little problems into perspective. Sure, there's a shoddy flier with my picture on it, sure, I've got Frau Demnitz on my case, and yes, I've been considering how to undermine the central government of the GDR. But all of that was a breeze compared to the task Evelyn had volunteered for.

Crossing over Marschall Bridge I paused and looked down at the river Spree. Seeing the barges tied up there, next to the whitewashed concrete slabs of the Wall, I remembered my conversation with Rico the border guard just a few days ago. But it felt like more than a just few days, much more.

By now I was nearly at the Charité, the hospital where Steinlein was being treated for his injuries.

I wondered whether Steinlein might appreciate a box of chocolates.

★

It took a while to persuade the staff on reception that they could admit to having Steinlein as a patient, and a further few minutes for the police officer on the ward entrance to agree that my RS credentials were bona fide. But eventually I was allowed into the private room where Steinlein lay.

He didn't turn his head when I came in, just continued staring at the ceiling. His face was badly bruised, swelling over his left cheekbone, plasters covering most of the right side of his face. His hair had been shaved in patches to allow stitches to be sewn into the scalp. Two fingers were taped together around a splint, and a drip was attached to the back of his right hand. Beyond that I couldn't get an impression of his injuries: a starched white sheet and hospital blankets were drawn tightly around his chest.

I stood by his bedside and touched my right thumb to my forehead in a Pioneer salute. A stupid gesture, one I was hoping would elicit a smile from Steinlein. But he just stared at me, his eyes flickering briefly in greeting. Gone was his sardonic look, his disrespectful attitude. It wasn't just his body that was bruised and battered, I could see that the Nazi boots had kicked his soul around too.

"Comrade Lieutenant Steinlein, I'm sorry to meet you again in these circumstances."

Again the vague flicker of his eyes. There wasn't much to read into that, and I wasn't sure what to say. Steinlein didn't look like he was about to help out with any conversational openings. We looked at each other for a moment before I remembered the chocolates.

"Here, these are for you. Chocolates. *Mon Cheri*—from the West." I waved them around for a bit, then put them on the visitor's chair next to the bed. "I, er, just wanted to say hello. To say sorry. I mean, sorry that this happened to you. But look, you probably need your rest-"

A slight movement on Steinlein's face, his lips parting slightly, then closing again. The tip of his tongue protruded, moistening his lips, his eyes closing at the pain this tiny movement was causing. Then he looked at me again. Intent, trying to communicate.

I bent over, putting my head nearer to Steinlein's, watching his eyes close and open again. A breath taken, then: "*Angst.*"

That was it. Just one word.

Fear.

10:37

Martin

I couldn't get Steinlein's word out of my head. Sitting on the S-Bahn, travelling back to Lichtenberg, the word echoed around my skull. *Fear.*

The train whined and clacked its way around the curves. Opposite me was a young woman, wearing a sweater with the hood pulled over her head. Her toes pointed inward, her eyes unfocussed, deep in thought.

Of course Steinlein was frightened. The hospital staff wouldn't tell me the extent of his injuries, insisted that since I wasn't family I had no right to know. But it had looked pretty bad. Maybe Steinlein was scared that he'd never recover from his injuries. Perhaps there was some sort of spinal injury. Or brain damage?

Or maybe he was scared for his colleagues. Worried that they would be attacked too.

Or his family.

I took the leaflet out of my pocket, smoothing the crumples and folds as I read it through again. Badly written, badly spelt, badly copied. Everything about it was bad, from the politics to the paper it was written on. Despite that, the laughable quality of the whole thing made it hard to take it seriously.

But Steinlein would probably disagree. And so would the informant who had been killed in a West Berlin hospital. Or the man from Mozambique who had been kicked to death a few weeks ago, or the Russian family that had been spat on in the supermarket, or the Vietnamese family who had once had a shop near Lichtenberg station—boarded up since the windows were smashed back in January.

Or the young woman who'd been urinated on in the S-Bahn a couple of weeks ago. I looked at the passenger opposite me, her skin, darker than mine, her hair beneath the hood dark and glossy. It was someone just like her. The skinhead had just got his dick out and pissed on her, shouted "Gypsy scum!" and got off at the next station.

How had we let it get this far?

11:16
Martin

"I guess it's not so surprising, after all," Laura said, not quite looking at me.

"What do you mean? What's that meant to mean?"

There was a pause while Laura contemplated me, measured, disapproving.

"I just meant, well, you've been putting yourself out there. Poster boy of the RS and all that."

How to answer that? If Laura spent less time in the office and being a bit more pro-active then I wouldn't have to put myself out there so much! I looked around at the others, waiting for them to support me. But Klaus was fiddling with a paper clip, and Erika was avoiding my eyes.

"What I meant to say was, you're the best known member of the RS—I mean, if you're not talking to the Border Police about smugglers you're having meetings with the KGB. You were even on *Aktuelle Kamera*. It stands to reason that sooner or later you'd be a target!"

"*Putting myself out there,*" I repeated. "*Poster boy?* I've been doing my job—yes, I've been getting out there, talking to people. Because reading files and fiddling with paper clips isn't ever going to change anything!"

Another pause while I glared at everyone. Only Laura met my eyes—she was glaring right back at me.

"What I think Laura is trying to say," Erika murmured. "She's trying to say that you're good at making contact with people, listening to what they have to say, and using that to get an overview. You're good at seeing the bigger picture. But that perhaps right now, considering what's happened, and what we're planning, perhaps it's a low profile that we need."

I snorted, standing up suddenly, pushing my chair back so that it clanged against the radiator. I needed to move, but Laura was giving me a look, the one that told me she found my behaviour aggressive.

I pulled the chair back in and sat down again, then shoved my feet out, leaned back and stretched my legs. I crossed my arms and looked down at my scuffed, brown shoes.

"So is that it? I've been *a bit too high-profile* for your tastes, have I?"

Nobody answered, and I ventured another look around. They were all watching me—that look that adults use when confronted with a toddler having a tantrum.

Klaus cleared his throat and put the bent paper clip down on my desk.

"Perhaps we should concentrate on the current situation," he said slowly, looking between me and Laura. "Martin is under some kind of threat—we should think about what to do about that."

"Right now I feel like I could use your support, rather than all these accusations!"

Laura rolled her eyes and exhaled, breath hissing between her teeth.

We sat there for a while, avoiding each other's gazes and not saying anything. Uneasy shuffling and scraping of chair legs on the lino.

"Well it must be said that Martin hasn't been respecting the team's decisions." Laura finally broke the silence, voice rising plaintively. "While we've been getting on with the paperwork and the background tasks he's been off gallivanting. Trying to catch smugglers, winding up the *Kripo*, going on raids. It's always like that, it's like he thinks he's Old Shatterhand!"

"You like doing paperwork!"

"Martin, no need to shout." Erika was patting the air in a calming gesture.

"I'm not shouting! But I don't need to take this shit either!" I jumped out of my chair again, and ignoring the surprise on my colleagues' faces I marched out of my office.

Slamming the door behind me helped a bit but it also made Grit jump, so I shut the outer office door more carefully. But I was still pissed off, and I ran down the stairs, fast, aiming for every second step.

Just as I reached the half-landing Nik came up the other way.

"Hi Martin, guess what I've ... Hey! What's up?" he called at my rapidly descending back.

I stopped and took a deep breath. It wasn't Nik's fault, no need to take it out on him.

"I've had a death threat from the fascists and all Laura can do is have a go at me about the way I do my job!"

"Whoah! Hang on, wait. That sounds a bit serious!"

"It is fucking serious. I expected better of them all!" I ignored Nik's puzzled face. "How long have we been working together? And then I get this crap!"

"Martin, I was talking about the death threat. What are you going to do about it?"

"Well seeing as I'm not going to get any help from that lot up there ..." I shook my head, "I don't know."

"Listen, where are you going? Right now?"

I shook my head again. No idea.

"Right, you and me, why don't we go for a walk? Work out what to do?" he asked me, in a calm, patient voice that nearly set me off again.

I was still angry, but Nik meant well, and I appreciated the fact that he was there for me.

"OK." A deep breath. "Thanks Nik."

We left the office and walked in silence, Nik giving me a chance to calm down. It wasn't until we'd reached Pfarrstrasse that he spoke again.

"OK, tell me what's going on."

So I told him. The vague and insubstantial threat from the skinhead who'd been arrested last week, the long list of names that Schimmel had given me, being chased by skins at the East Side, the stupid flier that Demnitz had given me a hard time about, my frustration with my colleagues.

"Look, I'll talk to the others, don't worry about that. Everyone's a bit on edge, we're all a bit concerned that we might have bitten off more than we can chew. Give it a bit of time, let them cool off. You too."

I let Nik woffle on. I wasn't upset or stressed. Maybe the others were, but I certainly wasn't.

"Are you taking all this seriously? Because I think you should." Nik paused for a while, considering something, then he shook his head and continued: "You've heard about last night? In Jena? Really heavy stuff. The Dynamo hools went for an away match with their friends from Zwickau and a few casuals from Lobeda. They were organised, it wasn't just a rampage—they went straight for the JG group. Fireworks, steel bars—the lot. Not really surprising—JG Stadtmitte have been a thorn in the fascists' side since before the revolution started."

I grunted, not really listening, just walking along the road, watching the tips of my shoes as they swung in and out of sight.

"Martin, you have to take this seriously—they've never tried anything this big before. And if Dynamo Dresden have done it then the BFC hools here in Berlin are going to do it too—it's a question of pride for them. And you'll be on the list, won't you? They've already attacked Steinlein, who's to say you won't be next?"

Nik was still talking, we were still walking, but I was still thinking about my colleagues.

"What are you planning on doing? Because you can't just ignore these threats. Martin, are you even listening to me?"

"Well I don't trust the cops to catch whoever's responsible. And I don't trust them to protect me," I snorted.

Nik nodded, agreeing with me.

We carried on walking in silence until we'd nearly reached home.

"Fancy a coffee?"

"Martin ...."

I followed Nik's worried gaze, over to the front door of the house where I have my flat. Red paint, same colour as had been used to daub the walls of the RS2 offices. The swastika was crude, badly drawn, the hooks on the cross bending the wrong way. And it was still wet.

"Fuck ..." I breathed.

"Right, you can't stay here." Nik looked up and down the road before pushing me in through the door to the hallway.

We stood there for a moment, listening. The door creaked shut behind us, slotting back into the frame, the loud click echoing off the high ceiling. Putting a finger to his lips Nik started up the stairs, stopping just before the first bend and signalling that I should follow.

We made it to my flat door. It seemed intact, no signs of damage, no signs of forced entry. The little notebook and pencil still hung from their string—no notes, no threats. Nik put his finger to his lips again, then mimed a key turning in a lock. I gave him my key, and he opened up, peering into the dark hallway of my flat. No noises, nothing to be seen.

We went in.

After scouting through the flat, checking it was empty, Nik came back and closed the front-door, then pulled the bolt across.

"That's it, Martin. You can't stay. Pack some stuff, we have to get you out of here," he whispered.

He followed me into the bedroom, and stood watching me pile some clothes into an old army rucksack.

That's when it hit me. Delayed reaction, I thought glassily as I was pulling clothes out of my cupboard. I could suddenly see the flier that Demnitz had shown me. It was there, clear before my eyes, as if I had it in my hands and was reading it. What Nik had been telling me about, the events in Jena last night. The whole series of demonstrations. The nightly beatings in Lichtenberg, Pankow, Marzahn. The whole ghastly, scary array of actions that the hools, the skins and other bastards had been engaged in.

I was in shock. Not the wide-eyed, panting kind of shock—although I noticed that I was breathing in short gasps, my chest heaving, air bellowing through my throat—but a lost sort of shock, sensory perception reduced, not seeing or hearing very well, not even thinking particularly well. A bled-dry sort of shock.

I slowly finished packing, feeling detached, as if I were watching myself through a thick glass window. "OK, I'll go somewhere, I'll stay out of sight."

"Where can we put you? We need to keep you safe for a few days while we work out what to do."

I nodded again, trying to think clearly. Nik was right, my flat was no longer a place of safety; I couldn't stay here—they obviously knew where I lived. I could go to Katrin's, in West Berlin, but I didn't want to endanger my daughter. Thinking about Katrin made me think of her mother. There was a little hut on a small plot of land, on a lake out to the east, it belonged to the family of Katrin's mother, except they were all gone now. I hadn't been there for years, but I knew where the key was kept, in a little nook under the cover of the well. I could go there.

"Yes, there's a *Datsche* in the woods, the other side of Storkow. It's on a lake. I'll go there."

Nik thought about it for a moment. "OK, that sounds good. Where's your phone?"

I pointed through the door to the hallway, and he went out. I could hear him punching the buttons, then silence as he waited.

"Laura? Listen, I'm at Martin's .... Yes, yes, I know, he told me. Listen, this is important: bring the office Trabant round to Martin's, no, wait, not here. Bring it to the supermarket, leave it on Kernhofer Strasse near the supermarket. Martin's in more danger that we thought, we need the car."

He put the phone down, and gave me a worried smile. "Got everything? Good, let's go." Nik opened the front door and held it open for me before double locking it behind us and giving me the key.

We got to the bottom of the stairs, and we paused in front of the house door.

"Right, we're going to the car, and you're going to go to your *Datsche*. I'll call the cops and get them to put a patrol outside your house. Phone me every evening at 9 o'clock, OK? Find a phone box and ring me to let me know you're OK. I'll tell you when it's safe to come home. Right? Let's go."

We walked out onto the street, past the supermarket and up Kernhofer Strasse until we reached the Trabant. Laura was nowhere to be seen, but the car door wasn't locked, and the keys were on the seat under a blue book of road maps.

"Thanks Nik, but I'm sure we don't need to go to all this effort-"

"Just go, Martin, just go. I'll let you know when it's OK to come back."

I pulled the choke out, opened the fuel cock and turned the key. Pressing the accelerator, I listened to the undulating clatter of the engine racing. Satisfied that it wouldn't die on me, I let up the pressure on the throttle. Giving Nik a brief, nervous smile I pulled out on to the road, heading for the countryside.

DAY 12
Friday
25th March 1994

Berlin: An anti-fascist demonstration will take place in the capital this afternoon. The call for the demonstration has been supported by over four hundred Works Councils and Round Tables across the country.

If the fascists march, so will we!

If the fascists fight, so will we! The anti-fascist bloc calls on all residents of the GDR to defend our Republic against racist hate-speech, against fascist and imperialist threats and to demonstrate for a society of solidarity and respect.

No state, no nation, no borders, no capitalism!

The anti-fascist bloc supports the emancipatory struggle for dignity and freedom, we reject the nationalist and capitalist logic of repression!

This means:

We will stop the race-hate and the marches of the fascists in East Berlin and throughout the GDR!

We support the anti-fascist struggle here and everywhere!

We show solidarity with Roma and Sinti and with refugees from Russia and from the wars in the Balkans! We support their struggles and their right to stay!

We are determined to reject, hinder and obstruct the pro-

grammes of the political parties which support unification with
capitalist West Germany!
Let the city rebel! Collectively organise against political
policing!
Organise in the work place, in the neighbourhoods, for the
independence of the GDR as the basis of social renewal!
Long live the Round Tables and the Works Councils!

15:32

Karo

That was when Schimmel flipped.

He totally lost it. He was shaking, foam flecking his mouth, eyes wide—I could see the whites of his eyes, all the way round—and shouting. I couldn't make out the words, it was just white noise, a background to the chanting and slogans coming from both sides of the demo. It was really fucking freaky, and then it got worse. I was standing next to him, looking at him, thinking *what the fuck is going on?* and he just lunged, he just went straight for a gap in the line of cops. They hadn't clocked him until then, but they must have thought he was going to jump them or something, and the line of cops tightened, the batons and shields held towards us, one of them struck out, catching Schimmel on his forearm. He didn't even notice, just kept trying to push through the cops, trying to get to the Nazis beyond. We held him back, it took three of us, he was flailing around, still shouting as we dragged him back into the crowd behind us.

"Becker! Becker you arse, I'm going to fucking get you!"

I could make out bits of what he was shouting now, he was still pointing at the crowd of fashos hiding behind the cops. It was a load of skins, but one of them, standing at the back, was a bit older, early forties, short-back-and-sides, a snide grin on his face. He was staring at Schimmel, egging him on.

I dragged Schimmel further back into the crowd, and made

sure our affinity group went with us. As soon as we were out of sight of the cops Schimmel just collapsed, he just lay on the wet road, crying, shaking.

"We've got to get him out of here, he's flipped!" I said to the others, and we literally picked him up off the floor, and got him out of the demo, out the other side. He was still crying and shivering. Man, he was totally broken.

"What the fuck's going on, Schimmel?" I kept saying to him, but he didn't answer, just moaned.

We got him to the nearest squat, and we put him on a mattress. It was really scary, and I had no idea what to do, I just pushed the rest of our team out of the room, and went to the kitchen. Somebody had already put some water on to boil, and I filled a tea-egg with peppermint leaves, put it in a cup with loads of sugar.

"Is he going to be alright?" somebody asked me.

"How the fuck should I know? Am I his fucking mother?" I poured hot water into the cup, taking it up to Schimmel. Playing mother.

He had got off the mattress and was crouched in the corner, crying, still shaking. I knelt down next to him, put one arm around his shoulders, holding the cup in front of him with my free hand.

"Here's some tea," I said, as calmly as I could.

There was no reaction, it was like he hadn't even noticed I was back. Then suddenly his arm shot out, spilling the hot tea over the floor.

"Fuck's sake Schimmel! You trying to get me burnt?" I shouted, then tried to calm down again. "Fuck's sake," under my breath this time. "Fuck's sake ...."

"Becker," Schimmel moaned, "it was Becker."

"Who's Becker? What you on about?" I asked him, thinking of the Nazi, grinning. How did they know each other, these two?

I went to the door and shouted down the stairs for another

cup of tea, then went back to Schimmel, put my arm around him, pulled his head onto my shoulder and rocked us both, back and forth, back and forth.

It was ages before I could get any sense out of him. The fresh cup of tea had arrived, and I made him take sips of the hot sweet drink. Then more hugging, rocking, making shushing noises. It started trickling out, strings of words, all knotted up, snarled in memories and emotions, mixed with tears and shivering.

He was 13 when he ran away from home: Lössnitz. Some dump down in Karl-Marx-Stadt district. Edge of the world kind of place, near the uranium mines. No wonder he ran away. He got as far as Berlin before the pigs picked him up. A night in the cells, the next day they took him to a secure home on Stralau. First he was beaten, then he was thrown into solitary for a week. The way he told it, it might have been more than a week—no way of knowing: no light, just a cold brick floor, a musty mattress thrown into his cell in the evening, taken away in the morning, and a bucket to shit in. Dry bread, thin broth, nothing to drink. Shit, he was thirteen! All he did was run away from home, a young punk trying to find somewhere to fit in and they put him in a kids' prison!

But it got worse, it must have done, that's where this Doctor Becker comes in, and Schimmel just started shaking and moaning again, the name Becker coming up again and again. I couldn't get any more out of him, fuck, I didn't want to. What did they do to you, Schimmel?

And then this Becker turns up, at a Nazi demo. Not one of the bovver boys, either, he looked neat, a suit, tidy haircut. He looked like someone with a bit of clout.

I was going to get this Becker bastard, whatever he'd done to my friend, whoever he was, I was going to get the fucker.

★

I left Schimmel at the squat. I didn't feel too good about that, but I reckoned he was going to be OK now, and I really needed a break. The others were looking after him. He's just in shock, I told myself.

Thing is, I'd decided to go to to the meeting at the Lohmühle *Wagenburg*. I'd told Martin I wasn't going to do it, there was no way I was going to talk to them about jumping the Wall. I'd told Martin that I was against all borders, end of. I didn't agree with Martin and his *tactical case* for keeping the Wall, but I wasn't 100% sure he was wrong either, and I wasn't comfortable with the fact that the Nazis wanted to get rid of the Wall too. They wanted to get rid of it for different reasons, I know, but it still didn't feel right. So I'd talk to the Lohmühle people, give them Martin's message. I'd do that for him, but I wouldn't argue the case for him. If he wanted that to happen then he'd have to come down here himself.

I walked down Puschkin Allee as far as the concrete flower pots that were at the end of the road, just before the checkpoint by the bridge to Kreuzberg, then I picked my way through the scrubby wasteland between the road and the camp. I could see a chain of paper-bag lanterns and tea lights in jam jars. Figures showed up black against the flames of a camp fire and on the far side faces wobbled in the smoke. It looked really homely.

They'd already started the meeting, and someone was speaking when I found a space to sit on a half-knackered deck chair. It was still free because it was downwind of the smoky fire.

"Smoke follows beauty," some guy leered at me.

I ignored him, and looked around me, trying to work out who was facilitating, and what people were talking about. It seemed to be the usual stuff—people getting pissed off with each other for things that don't really matter: who's using too much firewood, who's leaving fag butts where the kids play.

Finally, there was a pause in the flow of the discussion and a woman turned to me, asking if I was there for the meeting. She was small, and even though it was getting chilly she was wearing just a vest and some army work trousers. Her bare feet were burrowed in the sand. I was dead embarrassed, and I wondered why the hell I was doing Martin this favour.

"I'm here for a friend, I said I'd ask you about jumping the Wall, you know, because you're not going through the Border Crossing Point." I vaguely waved over my shoulder to the sentry box by the gap in the Wall, maybe a hundred metres away. The people at the meeting behaved themselves: I could see a few of them pull a face, but nobody interrupted me. "Look, I don't agree with him, but this friend of mine asked if I'd have a chat with you about it. See, it seems there's a problem with smuggling going on, and that's going to hurt all of us-"

"Is this about those brew-crew smackheads over on the East Side?" A vague giggle came from somewhere in the dark.

I told them about how Martin reckoned people jumping the Wall was distracting the border guards from concentrating on catching the fash smuggling stuff, and this guy with a Bavarian accent started having a go at me for supporting the system.

"So what if we're going to the Køpi—how's that fucking helping the fash?" he asked, and some idiots nodded along with him.

The thing is, I didn't really know either. I was just here because I was doing Martin a favour, I didn't agree with him, but here I was putting across his opinions. Before I had a chance to answer, the discussion had somehow moved on, and I sat down again, waiting to see which way it would go.

There already seemed to be two sides—a few people were saying that we had to fight the fascists, and that meant we had to sometimes do stuff we didn't want to. The other side were saying that borders and passports were fascist, and you can't fight fascism by giving up your freedom!

I sat there, listening to people getting more and more pissed off with their neighbours. What was the fucking point of coming? I'd just split this group straight down the middle. I sat there feeling sorry for myself. Then I looked over to the person doing the facilitation, she looked younger than me and she was struggling. She was trying to get people to calm down and listen to each other, but they were just ranting away and ignoring her. That made me even more pissed off with everyone. But then I thought about the stuff I'd been practising, this course I'd been doing—the neighbourhood facilitator stuff. Dunno why I didn't think of it before, but I knew how to deal with people having arguments and dissing each other.

I had a quick think, hands over my ears to shut out the ranting, then went over to the facilitator and had a chat with her. She nodded, and we talked for a bit as the meeting fell apart around us. Then she got up, walked over to the middle, right next to the fire, and shouted as loud as she could.

"Shut the fuck up! Shut up for a fucking minute will yous?"

It was ace. Everyone shut the fuck up and looked at this hardcore woman. She was dead small, and really thin, but she shouted so loud that everything just stopped.

"Thank you," she said, in her normal voice. "I'm going to call a break, then we're coming back in ten minutes, and we're going to have a proper discussion. I'm facilitating it, and I'm going to let everyone have their say, and we're all going to *fucking listen to each other!* Anyone got a problem with that?"

Nobody had any problems with that, so she walked out to the edge of the group and I got up out of my broken deckchair again to go and talk to her. Tam, she said her name was. I told her about the ideas I had, and she liked them, so I let her get prepared before the meeting got back together and went over to the watchtower, just a few metres away.

I banged on the door and asked for Rico. He came out, and was a bit gobsmacked to see me standing there. Probably wondered what the fuck a punk was doing banging on the door of his watchtower. It was really funny, this German lad, about the same age as me, with his stupid uniform and his spotty face. But I told him I was a friend of Martin's and about what was going on over in the *Wagenburg* so he agreed to come over. I told him to lose his uniform jacket and cap, so he left them behind, putting a padded blue work jacket on and buttoning it up. He still had his fatigue trousers and boots on, but at least now you couldn't see he was some sort of officer or whatever.

Walking back I could tell he was nervous. He puffed his chest out, and started marching, swinging his arms in time to his strides, but they were short, uneasy strides, and he stayed half a step behind me the whole way. Had to smile to myself.

We got back to the meeting just as it was starting up again, and Tam asked me to speak first.

"Hey, I started off on the wrong foot before. Sorry. I think it's because I've been asked to present something that I don't actually agree with either, so I didn't think it through properly, about how to explain it. But basically, like I said before, you've got people worried about the way you're jumping the Wall here and near the Køpi. But I shouldn't have said it that way, so if we can start again I'd like it if we could let Rico here talk: he's from the Border Police, so perhaps he can explain better than I can what he sees as the problem."

Tam took over then, reminding people that we're not here to just say yes or no to Rico, but to look to see if there are any solutions that work for everyone.

There was a tense silence while people waited to see what Rico had to say. I wasn't the only one feeling unsure about having him here, even though it'd been my idea to bring him over.

Rico began to tell us why he had a problem with people jumping the Wall. He talked a load of tosh about security and order and respect for state borders, and it was dead obvious that people were finding it hard not to get pissed off with him.

But then he started talking about the smugglers. People laughed when he said how the smugglers were taking the piss out of the Border Police. Then he started ranting on about what the smugglers were doing to the economy. There was nothing new there, we knew the score, but it was good to hear it said because it was relevant, it was part of what we were talking about.

When he ran out of steam I spoke again, and talked about how it looked like the smugglers were bringing in stuff for the skins and fash over here. Basically I just said the same as I had before the break but this time people were actually listening to me.

"Do you want to tell us about drugs on the East Side?" I asked the person who'd interrupted me earlier.

"We don't talk to the cops." A head shake.

Yeah, they were right. We don't talk to the cops. People were nodding their heads around the circle, and Rico was getting a few dirty looks. The facilitator stood up and said it was time for another break and would someone put the kettle on.

Rico had got the message, and was about to leave. He looked really sad. A bit pissed off, too, but mainly sad. But before he could go Tam was by his side, asking him to stay until the end of the break. She wanted to ask the group if he could stay for the discussion. He shook his head, but stayed anyway, sitting back down on a log near the fire, nobody looked at him, everyone avoided meeting his eyes.

They got the tea going, and warm cups were passed

around, that was dead good because it was getting a bit nippy, and we sat there slurping, waiting for Tam to start the meeting again.

"I'm going to ask if anyone can tell Rico why we jump the Wall rather than go through the Crossing Point, but first I want to check if it's OK for him to stay. Yeah, alright, he's Border Police, but he's already part of the discussion. We've listened to what he has to say and I think he should be allowed to hear from us too. Maybe he can help us find an answer."

There was a lot of grumbling at that, but no-one blocked it, so Rico was allowed to stay, looking a bit nervous and isolated on his log.

The gobby Bavarian kicked it all off with a rant about why it's ideologically purer to use a ladder to climb over a wall than to show your ID to someone in a uniform. Rico was dead intense, listening to what people said, trying to understand them. After a while he put his hand up, like he was at school. Tam nodded at him, and he stood up again.

"But you end up showing your ID cards to the West German official on the other side of the bridge! Is he better than us? He's the class enemy, but you'll show him your *Ausweis*. And I'm on your side but you're not even comfortable with having me at your meeting! Aren't we meant to be working together now? Aren't we meant to be building our new society together?"

"All cops are bastards!" came a shout from the shadows. "Take off your uniform and join us!" someone else said.

I had to smile, it was quite funny, even though I felt sorry for Rico too.

"Why do you hate us so much?" Rico asked. He was being dead genuine, but everyone laughed anyway.

"You serious? You for real?"

"Rico asked a question," Tam intervened again. "Are we going to give him an answer?"

"Where were you in 1989? And before that? When people like us got beaten up, tortured, sent to jail by people like you? People like you set dogs on us, pointed guns at us; you beat us! Come on, you know the score!"

Rico shook his head slowly: "No, I've only been doing this for three years, I'm just doing it before I go to university. And where I come from, up in Mecklenburg, not much happened in 1989, I kind of missed all of that. And I'm sorry if they treated you that way, but you must have been doing something to make them-"

Groans all round, cries of *What planet you from?*

"Look, Rico, maybe this isn't the time to talk about this stuff, but why don't you hang around afterwards and we'll tell you the stories," Tam said. "Is that OK with everyone?"

A few people reluctantly nodded.

"Rico asked something before," Tam continued. "We still haven't given him an answer. He asked why we won't work together with him and his colleagues?"

There were no offers. I didn't have a good answer either. This naive, liberal uniform had asked us why we weren't prepared to work with him. Wasn't it time to think about that question? We went on marches, we hassled our local Round Table, calling them stick-in-the-muds, saying they had to change with the times, listen to what people wanted. Maybe we had to move with the times too?

Maybe he was right, we ought to talk to him. He was answerable to the Round Tables, and we could get involved as much as we wanted to—the Round Tables were open.

But there was too much hurt, too many good reasons not to trust cops. And I don't want a police force—not any kind of police force, whether on the streets or on the borders. So, no: I couldn't co-operate with them.

And I said that to the group, we can't trust cops, and we don't want cops. People whooped when I'd finished.

"Yeah! No borders, no police!" someone shouted, and

everyone laughed.

Except for Rico. He didn't laugh, he just looked confused. I was starting to feel sorry for him again. How did he do that to me?

I sat there for a bit, thinking, *What would Martin do? What would Martin say?* and for a while I lost track of the discussion. When I tuned in again it had turned back to rants. People were lining up to have a go at Rico and all he stood for. He looked really miserable, but, fair play, he stuck it out, he was still there, listening, trying to understand. More than could be said about any of us.

The whole thing was falling apart. Again. Maybe it just wasn't possible to have a discussion with a cop, to find agreement?

But Tam stood up again and spoke.

"Look, we're going round in circles. We're not going to get any further if we carry on like this. We have a choice now, and we have to be serious about it. We can stop this discussion and carry on jumping the Wall like before, just ignore what we've heard tonight. Or we can think about whether the stuff about fascist smugglers means we have to do something about it!"

"I'm not working with the cops!" shouted the Bavarian.

"So don't! Make a proposal that doesn't involve the cops!" shot Tam straight back. That shut the gobby twat up. She was fucking ace, that woman!

But Rico just sat there through it all, looking lost. It was like he was still there only because he didn't have the energy to get up and walk away.

"I hate myself for saying this," the person next to me said. "But I gotta say, the cop is right—in just over a week there's the referendum on the Wall. Things have changed, we have a say now. We want to get rid of the Wall, but we can't do that just by ignoring it, or *them*." A finger pointed at Rico. "We have to talk to people, get involved in the discussions that are happening at the moment. It's time for us to take part and not just moan and blame others when things don't go the way we want them to!"

That was the point I'd thought about before, but still I shook my head. The Bavarian had something to say about it though. "Fuck's sake—we're *punk*!" he shouted. "We're against all of this shit. Punk means *resistance!*"

"Yeah," I shouted back, irritated by his arrogance, "in Bavaria punk is resistance, but what are we meant to be resisting here? If you want to resist then go back to the fucking West! If you want to help build something new then stay and take responsibility!"

By the light of the fire I could see people nodding their heads, but the smug Bavarian just shook his head in disgust.

"We could just open our own Crossing Point," somebody joked.

But Rico looked up at that, and you could tell he was thinking about it, I could hear the gears working.

Someone else took up the idea: "Yeah, there's a Crossing Point here, but we need one on Köpenicker Strasse so we can get to the Køpi and the Schwarzer Kanal!"

"I guess it would be possible," Rico started, he was still thinking about it, trying to work out how realistic it would be. "We'd need to take a proposal to the neighbourhood Round Table, and the Berlin Regional RT too-"

He was interrupted by groans. Doing it that way would take ages while all the old farts in the Round Tables argued about it—by the time we got a decision the referendum might have already decided to get rid of the Wall anyway.

"But we could get it fast-tracked. If you were serious about it, if you agreed to staff it, and we put in a joint proposal together, I mean, all of you and my lot at the regiment and the customs administration-"

He was interrupted by whoops of laughter and hands waving in the air. People thought the whole idea—working together with the Border Police regiment—was really funny. Despite all that had been said before I could tell they loved it.

"But you'd have to agree to do the border controls-" Rico started again, but nobody heard him in all the laughing and shouting.

"I think we may have a decision." Tam smiled over to me and Rico.

Rico grinned—the first smile I'd seen from him—a big, goofy grin on his pockmarked face, teeth glittering in the firelight.

DAY 13
Saturday
26th March 1994

Berlin: *As the country prepares to vote in three referenda next*
week the Central Round Table has repeated its call for a fair and
fact-based debate on the issues. In a statement issued this morning
the body said: 'Only by informing ourselves and only after careful
consideration and discussion will we be able to help our Republic
reach appropriate decisions.'
The Round Table was responding to statements recently made by
the main parliamentary political parties.

06:50
Martin

When I woke up this morning the mist still covered the far
bank, a smoky veil hanging in the moisture-laden air. It was
a queer feeling, opening my eyes and expecting to see dawn,
but being greeted instead by blankness. Everything else:
white. Sheer nothingness.

I took the rowing boat out onto the lake, the water
rippling away before dissolving into that impossible
emptiness. So beautiful, yet—in an atavistic way—terrifying.
A canvas of a world, ready to fill with hope and fears. If I
were to take my brush, what would I paint on this
emptiness? Would I make the same awkward political

181

landscape of Round Tables nudging up against layers of parliaments? Would there be a more elegant way to give people the chance of self-determination? Would there still be the egoists, the oddballs, the power-hungry and those who just wanted to be led? Would there be any people at all? Or just me, the last loner?

After all, we have the system that history has bequeathed us. We can fiddle with the knobs and dials and valves of society, but we are moulded by our pasts. There's no scientifically determinable march through social progression. Each advance has to be fought for, then fought over, again and again, lest it become jaded, corroded, worthless.

Alone in that white mist I'd felt the weight of the world on my shoulders, and my heart lifted when the fog thinned. The fir trees to the left and right materialised, grey, then black, finally their true green darkness showing up against the light tips of fresh growth.

The wind soughed across the water to keep me company on my watch.

07:40

Karo

I ended up spending the night at the Lohmühle, staying in an empty wagon. Only problem was that the person whose wagon it was turned up really early the next morning, still pissed out of his skull. He woke me up by crashing through the door and then falling on top of me. Then he wanted to talk to me, he sat there on the bed, slurring total shite.

So I left.

I wasn't happy about getting up so early, but the low sun was glinting off the shiny buds of the plane-trees on Puschkin Allee and that was nice—it felt good to be out and about. I walked all the way over the bridge to Friedrichshain, and by the time I'd got to Ostkreuz station I'd decided to go and see Martin. He lived quite near by, and I was sure he'd want to hear about the meeting last night—I felt quite proud of what we'd achieved.

So I walked a bit further and went under the railway bridge onto Martin's street.

But when I banged on his door there was no answer. I wrote a message on the notebook that was hanging there: *I came to see you but you were still asleep you lazy git. PS You need to clean up the graffiti on the front of your building—you'll give your neighbourhood a bad rep.*

I stood outside Martin's tenement wondering what to do now. The original plan had been to go home and go back to bed, but I was awake now and buzzing with the memory of last night. I could go and see if Martin was at his office, it was on my way anyway. And it would be just like Martin to go to work on a Saturday. Sad case.

It's not far to walk to the RS office, and I was there in no time. The aluminium and glass door stuck a bit and I had to give it a good push to get past. Why do all offices smell the same? That official floor-wax-and-detergent smell. And soap too—the same grey, hard soap that you get in schools. Not a good smell.

I was still wrinkling my nose when I knocked at the door of the RS office up on the first floor. Laura answered and she must have seen me pulling a face because she didn't look very pleased to see me. Or maybe that was just her usual sour-puss.

"What do you want?"

"Good morning to you, Frau Laura," I answered, all nice and sweet. "Is Martin here?"

"No. He's out of town on important business." I could tell Laura wanted to get rid of me so I tried to think of something else to say, just to piss her off.

But I wasn't quick enough and Laura gave me a curt *Tschüss* and shut the door on me.

I last saw Martin on Wednesday, just a few days ago. It's

not like he reports all his movements to me or anything, but he hadn't mentioned any important meetings outside Berlin.

I shrugged and started skipping back down the stairs. Sour Laura wasn't going to spoil *my* day with her bad manners.

When I got to the bottom somebody was trying to push the front door open, but it was jammed again, so I helped out. It opened with a jerk and Erika fell through the gap, almost landing on top of me.

"Hey Erika!" I laughed. "Bit early for drinking isn't it?"

Erika looked sombre. Grey. She always looked a bit worried, but this was different. She didn't even say hello back to me, just sort of nodded and tried to push past me.

This wasn't like her at all. I liked Erika, she was the best of Martin's colleagues. She always said hello and how-are-you, and she listened to the answers too. Something was up.

"Erika? You OK?"

She just nodded again, not stopping.

"Erika, I'm looking for Martin, do you know where he is?"

That stopped her. She'd reached the bottom of the stairs, but now turned round to face me.

"What's up? What's going on, Erika?"

Erika looked up the stairs, then went to the door that was still jammed open and looked outside before answering.

"Karo, it's all gone horribly wrong. I'm really worried about Martin, about all of us-"

"Erika, what is it? Erika?"

"It's the Nazis. They're after Martin. He's had to leave town, he's gone to some *Datsche* out of town. I don't know where it is, somewhere near Storkow? But I'm worried about him. About all of us. We were meant to have a police officer on the door but they haven't sent one yet."

"Shit, you serious? Like, they're *really* after Martin?" I thought of the graffiti on Martin's door—I'd assumed it was just a random tagging, but from what Erika was saying … "Fucking hell!" I hissed. "I've got to find him."

Erika looked surprised, but didn't ask me why I needed to find Martin.

"A *Datsche* you said? Like in an allotment garden? Out of town? Where? Katrin will know where it is, won't she? Do you have her phone number?"

Erika shook her head.

"Fuck! How do I get hold of Katrin?" My mind was whizzing. My address book was at home, that was nearly as far as Katrin's, and to get to either place would take ages, I'd have to walk loads and get a tram and a bus. "Erika, have you got your bike with you? Can I borrow it?"

12:20

Karo

Martin was well fucked when we arrived. Not the welcome I'd been expecting after tracking him half way across Brandenburg. The journey had taken us ages. From Katrin's we had to get back to East Berlin, take the S-Bahn all the way to Königs Wusterhausen then change onto a stopping train. After all that there was a hike through the woods from the station. Under different circumstances it could have been quite nice, like in the summer when we have a bit of a party down in the woods by the Müggelsee. You know, get a bit of a camp fire going, couple of crates of beer, bit of a swim. But this was different. Katrin was dead worried and didn't say a word for the whole journey. On the train she sat in the seat opposite me, and there was an empty cigarette packet scrunched up on the floor, I could only see *Cab* written on it, the *inet* bit was lost in a crumple. An empty beer bottle rolled around whenever the train slowed down or sped up or went round a curve. A dark, sticky stain of dry beer was spread between our feet. That's not the kind of thing I'd normally pay attention to, but there wasn't anything else to do was there? Not with Katrin pretending to be mute.

We got off the train and went down the sandy road. At

some point the forest just started, a wall of pine trees—it was really dark in there, the road got narrower and sandier and we went down the middle of the track, tripping over tree roots and avoiding deep holes filled with loose sand.

We passed an empty holiday camp, witches' cabins with steep roofs, all standing empty in the woods, waiting for summer—they were well spooky. I pointed them out to Katrin and she just looked around and said *they're not witches' cabins, they're just holiday chalets.*

After that I kept my gob shut.

We walked for miles through those woods. It was dead creepy, no birds, nobody else, just us. And when we got there and I gave Martin a hug I could smell schnapps on his breath. Katrin noticed it too, she was freaked out by that but tried hard not to show it. She held her father by his shoulders for a while, looking into his eyes as if she could read his soul or something. And then she started talking again.

"Papa, what's going on?" she asked him.

Martin just shrugged, looked away from her. As if he was embarrassed or something.

I hate scenes, and I thought this was going to turn into one of those family rows, so I decided to try to lighten the atmosphere.

"Took us ages to get here, Martin, you're totally in the middle of nowhere!"

Martin just turned round, turned his back on us. He was looking out over the water. I'd never seen him like this, well, apart from last week when we crashed at Katrin's. He looked dishevelled, crumpled. He'd definitely slept in his clothes if you ask me. I decided I was being a bit mean, so I didn't say anything—I just thought it in my head. But it still wasn't fair.

So I decided to be a bit more charitable: maybe the smell of schnapps wasn't on his breath, but coming off his clothes? Maybe he drank himself into a stupor last night, and hadn't had time to have a wash and change. Or clean his teeth. Even though it was already past midday.

"Papa?" Katrin touched her dad's elbow, trying to draw him back, find out what was going on.

"It feels like I've failed." Martin still had his back to us, being all dark and mysterious and fucking rude too, if you ask me. He was still looking out over the water.

I gave Katrin a look that said *what the hell?*, and she moved around to stand in front of Martin.

"Failed? How?"

Martin shook his head, looked at Katrin, then turned around a bit so he could see me too, like he'd just realised that we were both there. And then he must have decided to get his shit together because otherwise Katrin was going to lose her rag. He looked around the garden, then extended his arm, pointing to the Hollywood swing.

"Why don't you girls sit down? I'll go and make coffee."

I studiously avoided reacting—Martin wouldn't normally be that crass—he must be in a pretty bad state to call me girl. So Katrin and I shared another look, and Martin bimbled off into the *Datsche*. It was one of those wooden frame and hardboard jobs, with a slanting roof covered in tar paper. Looked like it hadn't been used for a few years: moss was growing up the outside and the windows were so dusty I couldn't see through them, but I could hear the clattering of pans and cups. We sat down on the swing, looking down the garden to the lake. A beech tree was just coming out in leaf, and it cast a soft green light. Further down the garden, bushes were growing wild, blocking the pathway, but between them I could see a small boat tied up next to the bank.

When Martin came out again he was carrying a tray with three cups of coffee. He looked more human, more like the Martin I knew. He'd made an effort, changed into fresh clothes, washed his face. He didn't smell so much any more either. Just a bit musty, but that was fine. Meant I could look him in the eye again.

"Sorry, haven't got anything to eat," he said as he sat down. "I was just thinking about going to the village *Konsum* when you arrived."

"Papa, are you going to tell us what's going on? Why did you say you've failed?"

He kept shtum for a bit, and then that weird, faraway look —the same one he'd been wearing when we arrived—it came back. He didn't look at us, just stared down the garden. Then he began to speak slowly and irregularly, as if he was in a ket-loop.

"I haven't got the energy for this kind of thing any more. All these years I've been fighting, the whole time, and it never seemed like we'd ever get anywhere—up against the Party, the Stasi. And then the revolution began, and when it was clear that we had won, that the people had won, no more Party, no more Stasi, just the will of the people ... once we got that far I thought I could relax. And I did, just helped out a bit, stayed in the background, doing boring stuff that nobody else wanted to do."

Martin was still staring at the water, as if we weren't there, or maybe he was just pretending we weren't there.

"But that business last year, with the Minister. And then this, the fascists," he continued, still speaking slowly, quietly, as if to himself. "I feel like I have a duty to get involved, to continue defending the revolution, the will of the people ...." He trailed off, and his eyes shifted to mine, daring me to disagree, to argue with him.

He was really starting to freak me out now. He was just staring, not blinking. I swallowed, and thought, *he needs you, just listen to what he has to say.* I just nodded—a smile would have felt a bit stupid right then.

"Look, I can see you're upset-" I started, but he cut me off.

"No, not upset. Not upset. Wrong word. It's a kind of, no .... I feel a kind of *Weltschmerz*."

I wasn't even sure what that meant, but Martin didn't give me any time to ask.

"I have this sense of duty in me, this feeling it's my responsibility. But it costs so much, it's already cost too much. I think it was last year—it was when they started targeting me—it wasn't just that they were following me round, but they'd been in my flat, they'd messed with my things, messed with my head. It was like nothing had changed, like I was back in the bad old days. Too much. All too much. And I don't know how much longer I can keep going, not with all this shit that's happening."

There was this moment of total silence in the garden. None of us said anything. None of us even moved at all. I sat there thinking *shit, shit, shit, what the fuck do I do?*

But it was obvious what I had to do, and you're probably reading this and thinking, course it's fucking obvious. But it wasn't until that moment, just then, that I knew what to do. So I kind of got up a bit so that I could reach over to him and put my arms around my friend. He didn't move, he was really stiff, and his eyes were welling up, and I was nearly welling up too, had to really bite my lip to stop from laughing or crying or both at once.

Katrin knew what to do—no-one had to tell her. She just put her arms around both of us, and we just stood there, hunched over the table and the coffees, all hugging each other for what seemed like hours.

"Come on, let's go and get some stuff from the *Konsum* for dinner," Katrin said at last, and we stopped all the touchy-feely stuff and Katrin and I headed around the side of the *Datsche* towards the lane. I didn't look back at Martin. He needed space. Probably needed to repair his bruised ego or rebuild his emotional wall or whatever.

★

It took us about half an hour to walk to the village and buy some stuff for a salad, some bread and a jar of plum purée from the shop. The woman behind the counter was dead nosy, wanting to know who we were and whether we were on holiday. As if that wasn't enough there was a skinhead in there, buying milk and Katrin had to put her hand on my arm to stop me saying anything. But he clocked me alright, and swore at me as we left the shop. Fucker.

When we got back Martin was looking loads better. He'd put an oil cloth with a flowery pattern over the garden table and laid out plates and cutlery. A fresh pot of coffee was keeping warm on the little candle stove and he sat there, looking nervous, waiting for us.

He'd put some music on the tape player in the hut and noise leaked out of the window. He's always got some music on the go—typical of Martin to take some tapes with him when he left. Normally he listened to some old-school rock or blues from some has-been GDR band but this time it was some stuff I've never heard him play before, something in English. Katrin gives him these tapes, and he's always really chuffed to get them, it's really sweet. Then he plays whatever he's been given, listening to it like she's sending him some message, dead serious like. But his English is a bit shit, so I don't think he knows what he's even listening to half the time. I looked at the cassette insert and worked out what song was playing: *I've been left on the shelf*, about some old dude who pretends not to be sad that he's all by himself, feeding the ducks for company and he's only got his hot water bottle to take to bed. But there's Martin, like, *yeah, Katrin gave me this tape: Jake Thackrey, some Englishman. It's really nice, isn't it?* He didn't even get that Katrin was taking the piss! I was really good and didn't say anything to him about it, just told him it was cute and gave Katrin a sharp look. She did the innocent act and pretended she didn't know what was going on.

Katrin and I sat down at the table in the garden, waiting for Martin to finish getting everything together for our midday meal. A book was splayed out on the table, I picked it up. Erich Fromm, The Fear of Freedom. I glanced over at Katrin, pulling a face: heavy reading. Looking at the page Martin had dog-eared I read a sentence that had been underlined in pencil. Scanning up and down a few paragraphs I could see it was a commentary on policing; or rather crime, how crime is caused by restricted lifestyles, by fear and deprivation and poverty. And how prison is just one more restriction, so can never be an answer to criminality.

"Good book that—borrow it if you want." Martin had come out of the hut, carrying the bread and a bowl of salad.

I shook my head. It looked a bit too heavy for me. I mean, life was a bit too heavy for me right then, I didn't need to add to the burden.

"It's another of those things we have to find an answer for. Prison isn't a solution, it's just another problem."

I didn't respond so we all sat there for a while, chewing away at our rubbery village bread, wondering what to say about Martin's little speech. It was like we were all pretending that the little scene from an hour ago had never even happened.

So I just dived straight in.

"What the fuck's going on, Martin?"

Katrin looked really pissed off, as if she was the only one allowed to be direct with her dad. But Martin started telling us about this demo he'd been 'observing'. It was gross, all these fucking Nazis marching, chanting, and he'd just stood there watching them. I had a bit of a go at him. I shouldn't have, but I couldn't help myself, sometimes he's such a *mensch*, being all reasonable, trying to see all sides of any argument, and it pisses me off because we're in the middle of a fucking revolution! I told him we had to take sides.

"So what should we do about them?" he asked, all

reasonable-like.

"Shoot 'em!" I didn't really mean it, just wanted to provoke him a bit, but he was shocked.

"Really?" he asked, taking me seriously, again.

I sighed, then looked him in the eye and shook my head.

"No, but it's my first reaction. It's what they want to do to us." I watched him think about that for a bit. "And you've got to admit, the Antifa have done a lot of good: hitting Nazis keeps them from spreading so fast."

I was right and he had to admit it. If the Antifa weren't prepared to beat the shit out of fascists then the whole situation would be loads worse. The fash just want to attack, kill off anything different: punks, anarchists, foreigners, queers, the disabled. They even had a go at the Central Round Table building once.

I could see Martin thinking about it, his face moving as the thoughts passed behind his eyes. In my head I could almost hear him think: *but we overthrew the Party*, he'd say in that old-fart way of his. *We ended a dictatorship and started a revolution without violence. The only violence came from the security forces.*

He didn't say it, and it's not like he needed to. We all knew that. But even he had to admit that it was kind of ironic that our oh-so-peaceful revolution had led to a gang-war. Fash against Antifa. Yeah, the fascists started it, but you have to admit that it's not like the Antifa aren't up for a scrap, is it? Far too much fucking testosterone in that scene if you ask me.

"But beating Nazis up isn't going to solve the problem," he finally came up with. "It might keep them in check, but we're not going to get rid of them that way. The more violent we are to them, the more violent they are back, so then we have to up the stakes to keep them down. Using that logic we'll end up shooting them, unless they shoot us first."

He looked so self-satisfied, as if he'd been really

perceptive. I groaned again. Times like this I wonder why I hang out with Martin. I looked at the beech tree, the one growing in the middle of the path, trying to work up a bit of patience.

"So what do you suggest we do, then, Mr. Clever Clogs?" I asked him.

"In the medium term, well, we know the answer already—some people are doing it. We need to talk to the young skins, people who are getting dragged in. They need to be listened to, made to feel part of our society, our revolution."

"What, you mean we should just tell them they can take part in our revolution, integrate their fascist filth into our society?" I threw back at him, he was really starting to piss me off now.

"No, no, I didn't mean that. I mean, get them before they've really bought into the whole ideology of hate. Or if they're already part of that, get them to start thinking, asking questions. I don't mean we should give them a chance to sow their hatred. I meant we should welcome them as individuals and encourage them to feel respected, just as they should respect others. We need to give them back their sense of self-worth, their place in society, so that they don't feel that hate, so they don't have the need to destroy everything that is different."

The most annoying thing about Martin is that he's usually right. I guess he's been around for so long that he's thought about practically everything there is to think about. Doesn't make it any easier to listen to him being all opinionated though.

"But what about the short term?" I asked him.

"I don't know." He shrugged at me. "You got any ideas?"

Great.

If not even Martin knew what we had to do then we really were fucked!

★

193

Katrin had gone inside while Martin and I were arguing, I could hear her clattering around, washing up our plates, tidying up the little hut. I wondered what it was like in there, probably a total tip.

But our little talk had ground to a halt, and Martin just sat there, gawping at the little candle under the coffee pot. And I was just sat there too. Probably gawping into space as well. Thinking about the fash had made me think of Schimmel again. I couldn't get what he'd told me out of my head. The stuff about being abused in the secure homes they'd put him in when he was a kid.

And that was when I realised that I really wanted to tell Martin about it all.

Which made me realise just how much I trusted Martin.

But Martin had his own problems right now. *Fucking ace friend I am*, I thought to myself, *I've got two friends having a really hard time of it and I've got no clue how to help either of them!*

Under normal circumstances I would tell Martin about Schimmel, and he'd know what to do. Then again he'd probably tell me to go to the Reconciliation Commission. Yeah, right, as if I'd do that! I didn't want reconciliation for my friend. I wanted fucking revenge.

I smiled, thinking about what Martin would say to that.

"Something amusing you?" he asked me, the ghost of a smile crossing his lips too.

"Nah." I shook my head. "Just wondering how to deal with this current situation."

"What?"

"You know the fasho-squat on Weitlingstrasse? They've only gone and moved back in again."

Martin was gobsmacked.

"Yeah, seems the cops didn't bother to guard the place after the raid, lazy eejits. And before the District Housing Association could change the locks the place was overrun with Nazis again!"

His face was a picture. It was almost worth it just to see his coupon. But, let's be honest, it was a shit situation.

"So what are we going to do about it?" I asked him.

He just shook his head, as if he didn't want to answer. That just wound me up again.

"I'll tell you what we're going to do," I told him. "We're going to get a bunch of good people together, and we're going to take that house right back off those bastards. We're going to re-socialise it, give it to someone who needs it, like those people who've come from Russia, or the families from Serbia and Croatia."

"We can't do that! It's just too much. Too undemocratic." He was still shaking his head, as if I was suggesting we build a missile or a tank or something.

"Yes we can! Come on, we did it before! That's what direct action is all about!"

"What? Setting ourselves up to be the vanguard of the revolution? No."

"It's not a fucking vanguard! We're stopping the bloody counter-revolution. We're stopping the fascists from being the vanguard of the counter-revolution! The time for talking is gone. We need new impetus in this revolution of ours!"

"Maybe you're right." But he was still shaking his head, like it was on a spring or something. "But I've been wondering whether we even have a consensus in our society-"

"What are you on about now?"

"Well, look, we're trying to set up this independent, grassroots GDR. But does *everyone* actually want it-"

"Course they fucking do!" I interrupted, but he carried on as if I hadn't said anything.

"But back in 1989, all those people marching, they said they wanted the end of Communist rule. But did they say what they wanted to replace it with? Or did we just make assumptions? Did we just think this was our revolution because we'd been resisting for so long, opposing the state, encouraging debate?" He paused for a bit, he had wrinkles on his forehead, as if he'd been thinking too hard. "What I'm trying to say is, back in 1989 and 1990, did we just assume the privilege of influence, use the Round Tables to push our agenda, just because we were there already, because we were already organised?"

I shook my head. He was talking bollocks. It wasn't just him and his cronies, for fuck's sake, there were literally millions of us marching back then—of course we wanted this!

"So these skins and fascists," he was still wittering on, thinking aloud. "Maybe they're not just a small minority, maybe lots of other people feel the same way—*Foreigners Out, Germany for the Germans, Time for Strong Leadership*? Or even *One Germany*? Maybe no-one's interested in all this stuff about solidarity, a progressive society, freedom, fairness, grassroots democracy, respect for one another ...." He tailed off, lost in a pit of thinking inside his head.

"Bollocks! Fucking shitey bollocks, Martin!"

He grinned at my fierceness, but let me continue.

"You know what, you're not the only one who thinks about this shit! Because I think about it too, and so do my friends. And we're out there, on the streets. We hear what people are saying and they say some pretty shit things! Know how many times I've been told that I should be gassed? Just because I'm a punk, just because people don't like the way I look? People spit at me, and I spit right back and give them the finger too. Cos some people have an ugly side. Jealous, scared, bitter, whatever. Fuck, we've all got an ugly side, just some people are more ugly than others. Yeah, and that's gonna come out when they're frightened, and you know what, these are fucking frightening times—hell, even I'm a bit frightened sometimes, and I love all this chaos!

Thing is, Martin, just because some people are bitter, twisted shits doesn't mean that we have to give up, does it?" I stared at him, daring him to disagree, daring him to interrupt.

"Know what I think?" I carried on ranting—nothing could stop me now. "You know what? All that shit that the Communists used to spout? Well here's the news: all their talk about scientific socialism was just cronyism, privileges, authoritarianism. And the funny thing is, people knew they were talking shite, and still the propaganda stuck. I reckon people in this country believe in fairness, believe in helping each other out, sharing. Soli-*fucking*-darity. The labels were all bollocks, all a sham, but what those labels should mean, that's what stuck with us."

I sat back, arms crossed, feeling a bit better for having got that off my chest. Except now I felt a bit bad, because Martin was already giving himself a hard time, and now he'd got me ranting at him as well.

I felt something move behind me, a stir of the air, or maybe a faint breath. Looking over my shoulder I could see Katrin had come back out of the hut.

"Come on you two let's go inside, it's getting chilly" Katrin was looking at her dad, dead tender. She looked sad.

We sat together on the train, heading back to Berlin. There wasn't much to say, we were both a bit shocked by Martin's behaviour. At some point, Katrin started talking.

"I think it started last autumn, he's been different since then. I've always thought of him like a bear. A big bear of a man. Large, generous. And quick to anger. But since last year he's been, I don't know, pensive? Thoughtful?"

I only got to know Martin last autumn, so I had nothing to say. I let Katrin do the talking.

"But maybe it goes further back. My mum. Maybe it was when she went ...." She shook her head, looking out of the window. There was nothing to see out there, it was already dark. But looking out of the window meant she didn't have to look at me.

She told me about her mum, about how she left the country when Katrin was still young, leaving Martin to look after her. "The personal cost you had to pay for wanting to leave the country .... I often wonder what it cost her. But the thing is, it cost *us* a lot, too. Me and Papa, particularly Papa. It cost him too much."

I put my arm around her, and she snuggled up against me, burying her head in my shoulder, still avoiding eye contact.

"Too much," she repeated. She told me that her mum had written to her, wanted to have contact. I knew there was something going on, something about Katrin writing to her mum—I'd overheard that much on the morning when Martin and I had stayed at hers.

"What are you going to do?"

Katrin glanced up, then hid her face again.

"I don't know," came the muffled reply. "Don't know. I'm curious. But then I think of what happened .... actually I don't really know what happened, I don't know her."

"What about your dad? What are you going to do about him?"

Katrin froze for a moment, as if this were a new thought for her. She shook her head again, still buried in my side.

"Oh, who knows? He's always asking me what I want. But yeah, what about him? I don't know. Perhaps it's time for me to be there for him. For my whole life he's been there for me, looking out for me, always there if I want help or advice. And I just get annoyed by him, lose patience with him. I've been unfair, maybe. But now it looks like he's the one that needs some help."

I stroked Katrin's hair. She was right, it was time for us to be there for him.

DAY 14
Sunday
27th March 1994

Magdeburg: The Sascha Berkmann Brigade at the SKET factory in Magdeburg have written an appeal to mobilise support for widespread anti-fascist action in the GDR. In their statement the brigade call on humanist, anti-fascist and peace-loving citizens and residents to unite in their opposition to the negative-reactionary forces that are attempting to disrupt and destroy the Social Experiment in the GDR.

15:27

Karo

I spent most of Sunday with Schimmel. He was fine, or at least he was pretending to be fine. He didn't mention what had happened on Friday, so I didn't ask him about it either. We just hung out, played music and went up to Forcki park with a few beers. I told him about Martin, not the bit about Martin breaking down, just that the fash were after him and that he'd had to leave town.

By mid-afternoon it had clouded over and was getting chilly so we went back to our squat on Thaerstrasse. When we got there Katrin was waiting for me in my room, huddled against the wall, chewing her bottom lip.

"Papa's gone missing! Karo, he's gone, they've taken him

—I don't know where he is!"

I put my hands on her shoulders just as she'd done to her dad yesterday.

"OK, calm down. Tell me what's happened."

"I got the train out to the *Datsche* this morning, but when I got there the place was empty, the door was smashed in, the place was a mess. I went straight back to the village and dialled 110. I said it was the Nazis, that they'd taken Papa. But the dispatcher wouldn't take me seriously, she just told me to go back to the *Datsche* and wait for him there. They weren't going to help so I came here-"

I put my arms around her, held her close until she stopped talking. She was right to be scared about her dad's safety. But what to do? Schimmel was standing in the doorway, he'd heard what Katrin had said, it was like it had woken him up.

"I'll go round to Rigaer, get Antifa Rex, he might have some ideas-"

"Wait! Phone Erika too, Martin's colleague. The number's in my address book—over there."

Schimmel got the address book then stopped, patting his pockets.

"You got twenty Pfennigs for the phone box?"

Erika came straight round, she was here even before Schimmel got back. If she'd looked worried yesterday morning she was positively scared now. Katrin and I were on the bed, next to each other. She'd stopped crying, but I still had my arm around her. I filled Erika in on what I knew and she sat for a while frowning.

"We need to talk to Captain Neumann from K1. He'll know what to do. And if you ask me this is probably his fault too. I'll go and give him a ring, get him to come-"

"No! No cops are coming in here! Ring him if you want, but he's not coming here."

Erika stopped in the doorway, working out how to react,

then nodded. "Before I go to the phone box though, maybe I should tell you something. There's someone else who might be able to help." She gave me a look, glanced towards Katrin, then moved her eyes towards the door. She wanted to speak to me without Katrin overhearing.

"No, Erika, tell me now. Come on, we haven't got any time to lose!"

Another of her long pauses. Erika always has to think before she says anything, normally it's annoying but right now I was getting really impatient and was ready to shout at her.

"Evelyn." Erika took a step backwards. "Evelyn could be able to help-"

"For fuck's sake!" I shouted. "What the fuck has that bitch got to do with this? Isn't she locked up in fucking prison?" I think I'd prefer to get help from the cops than from that Stasi sow!

"Karo, it doesn't matter how you feel about Evelyn, I shouldn't have told you anyway. I'm going to the phone box now-"

"Oh no you don't!" I jumped off the bed and grabbed Erika by the elbow. "You've started so you'll finish. How is Evelyn involved?"

"She's gone undercover in the fascist scene. She's got her own support team, from her old Firm. They may be able to locate Martin, and if he's in danger-"

"You're saying the Stasi can help us? Didn't we deal with them last year? Tell me they're not still around!"

Erika stood there, saying nothing.

Great. Not only had Martin probably been kidnapped by the fucking fash, but the only people who could help us were the bloody Stasi, because the cops sure as hell weren't going to be any fucking use.

"So are you going to ask them for help?" I asked Erika.

"Martin was handling Evelyn." She shrugged. "Nobody

else knows how to get hold of her."

"And Klaus? Nik? What about Laura, she's always on top of everything, doesn't she know?"

Another shrug.

"Can't find Rex!" Schimmel pushed past Erika, breathing heavily. "But I've sent everyone out to find him or anyone else from the Antifa core-group."

"I'll go and phone Neumann from K1," said Erika, ignoring Schimmel. "He may still have some contacts in the Firm. Don't worry, I won't bring him back here. I'll come back after and tell you how I got on."

"K1? The Firm? What's going on?" demanded Schimmel as Erika went down the hall.

"It's Evelyn. She's back. She may be able to help Martin," I told him.

Schimmel slowly shook his head and came to sit down on the bed with Katrin and me.

"So what are we going to do now?" he asked.

The three of us sat there in silence. Katrin hadn't said anything the whole time Erika was here, and when I looked at her now I could see she was staring into space, a hard, stony look on her face. I put my hand on her knee to reassure her.

"Don't worry. We'll work it out."

Except I didn't sound very convincing, not even to myself.

19:50

Karo

We waited by the telephone box on Forckenbeckplatz. It was dark already, and the occasional car threw its headlights at us, making the railings dial shadows across the park. I leaned against Schimmel, and shivered. I was glad I'd brought him along.

Schimmel was bricking it, but he'd been a total star. After a bit of a think he'd told us about the Stasi man who'd tried to recruit him, back when he'd first been released from the secure home.

"I followed him home once. I don't know why, maybe because it felt like turning the tables. Spying on the spies, you know?"

Schimmel told us all this and then went round to this bloke's house and demanded that he put the word out: we wanted to speak to Evelyn's support team.

"He denied he'd even been in the Stasi," Schimmel reported when he got back. "He pretended he didn't know what I was talking about, so I told him that lives were in danger, that it was about Evelyn Hagenow. He shut up when I mentioned Evelyn's name. He shut up and shut the door on me."

But Schimmel didn't go away. He stayed on the staircase outside the man's flat, hammering on the door. None of the neighbours complained, nobody came to see what the fuss was about. Eventually the man opened up again, he said: *2100 hours. Telephone box. Forckenbeckplatz. One person.* Then he'd banged the door shut again.

And that was it. Easy as that.

Except for Schimmel it hadn't been easy. For him it had meant facing up to the ghosts of his past.

But here he was, waiting in the cold with me. We didn't know what to expect, whether the phone would ring, or a car would arrive. Maybe someone in a leather jacket or a trenchcoat would come along and slip a note into our hands. Thinking about it now it's easy to make it sound like some stupid American spy movie, but I was well scared at the time.

I don't know how long we'd been stood there waiting, watching the cars go past, waiting, waiting. But at some point a Barka van pulled out of a side road and slowly climbed the hill towards us. Schimmel and I both held our silence as the van struggled up the cobbles.

"You were told to come alone." A Saxon voice from behind

the steering wheel. "He stays. You get in."

I looked at Schimmel and shrugged. He looked like he was going to try to stop me.

"You're not going by yourself, Karo, who knows what these bastards will do to you!"

The driver revved the engine, and the Barka inched forward before stopping again.

"Your choice, young lady. It's you and your friends who wanted to speak to us, remember?"

I opened the side door and got into the back of the van, it was too dim to see anything, the windows covered by purple polyester curtains. Schimmel made to follow me in, but I held my hand out, stopping him and pulling the door shut on his taut face.

The small engine howled again, and the van drew away, turning right, juddering over the uneven road.

"Sit down." It was a different voice this time, Berlin accent, gravelly from cigarettes. A man was with me in the back of the van.

Enough light from the orange street lamps penetrated the thin curtains to let me see the bench down the side, and I sank onto it, facing the dark figure that was my companion for the ride. I had to grip the edge of the slatted seat to stop myself from sliding off as we went around each corner. Don't ask me how long the journey took—I don't know the answer. At least ten minutes. Maybe half an hour? We sat there in silence, the whining of the engine and the strobe of the passing street lamps the only way to mark time and distance.

There must have been some kind of signal, a knock I didn't hear, a sequence of corners, a change in the quality of the lights outside, who knows? But the shadow stood up, and efficiently pulled a cloth bag over my head. Before I could react the job was done. I clawed the bottom of the cloth, trying to pull it off my face.

"Leave it on." That voice again, calm. "If you take it off

then that's the end of the meeting, we'll take you back and you'll never see us again."

A deep breath, trying not to gag on the mustiness of the bag.

The van stopped, and the door was opened. A hand gripped my elbow and I was roughly guided through the low doorway, down the step onto the ground. It was flat and even: concrete or tarmac. The hand on my elbow was removed, then it came back again, perhaps it was a different one.

Across a short stretch, ten paces, no more, then up some steps. Four, five? We were in a corridor, I could tell by the lights and the echoes of our footsteps. Not far before we rounded a corner, and I was pushed onto a chair. I was afraid I would fall, gasping by now, trying to keep a grip on myself. It wasn't easy, not easy at all.

The bag was pulled off my head, and I found myself in a room I'd been in before. Maybe not this exact one, but definitely one like it: a small room, lino, desk, a few chairs. You can find this room in any police station, or in the old days, any Stasi building.

Opposite me was an old man. Grey suit, grey hair combed over the top of his bald head, the smell of *Atoll* deodorant emanating from his armpits. I'd met him before too. Him or one of his many clones.

"Why are you here?" he asked. Pleasant enough, but with just the right dose of menace to make the situation clear to even the most stubborn punk. It probably took years of practice to get it just right.

"Cos I was dragged here!"

"Miss Rengold, I think we should start again, don't you? Why are you here?"

God, some things never change! What do we have to do to get rid of pricks like this? We already started a revolution and they're still here!

"I'm here because I need to get in touch with Evelyn Hagenow."

"Now that wasn't difficult, was it, Miss Rengold?" The prick smiled, wiping his hand over his head, making sure his comb-over was holding.

God, I wanted to punch him! Shout in his smug face, tell him his time was up, his time was over—the future belonged to us, not fucking Stalinists! A swallow, *keep calm Karo*, I told myself, *this is for Martin, and he's going to owe you for this. Big time.*

But Martin already owed me big time, I'd already saved his arse more than once! Another deep breath.

"You know my name already, so who are you?" I asked, civilly enough.

"Why do you wish to speak to comrade Hagenow?" the prick demanded, as if I hadn't spoken.

This was hard work. I didn't know what was worse, being kidnapped off the streets, or having to deal with Mr. Prick.

"Martin Grobe's gone missing. We think the fascists have got him. We know they were after him, and he left town to get away from them, but now he's gone missing and the place where he was staying has been trashed."

"Miss Rengold, or may I call you Karoline? Well, Karoline, I think you need to tell us how you know about comrade Hagenow, and exactly what it is you want of her."

"I was told about the operation, about Evelyn going undercover. They told me after Martin went missing."

"They? Please do try to be precise. Who are *they*?"

"His colleagues. At RS." I didn't want to tell the Prick anything, but if he could help Martin ....

"I see. Not too difficult is it now? And perhaps you can tell me why you wish to speak to comrade Hagenow?"

"We're hoping she can find Martin. If the fash have him then who knows what they'll do to him-"

"We? Who is this *we*? Who thinks comrade Hagenow

might be able to help?"

"His colleagues. And friends."

The prick made a note, then nodded to himself.

"His colleagues. I see, how moving. Well, we'll be in touch, Karoline."

This time I screamed when the bag went over my head, trying to lash out at whoever was behind me. A sharp jab to the kidneys and I went over, retching and moaning on the floor. I couldn't see it, but I definitely felt the prick's smile as I was bundled along the corridor, dragged down the steps, back to the van.

DAY 15
Monday
28th March 1994

Berlin: Far-right groups have registered demonstrations in each of the Regional capitals for this evening. Counter-demonstrations have also been announced under the motto "We are the people!"

02:17

Martin

What can I tell you?

I blacked out, I must have done. I remember being hit. The ears, they aimed for the ears: once, twice, once again. After that, nothing. It must have been a blackout. There's no other way of describing it. If I try to concentrate on that moment, remember when I was next conscious, the memories just skitter away, and all I can see are crowds of people. We're standing shoulder to shoulder in the streets, candles lighting hands and faces. Standing, waiting. The fear, *that* fear again. Men in green uniforms and white helmets running towards us, shields raised, truncheons raised, running, running, running towards us; running away from them. The silence, no noise. Was it because they hit me on the ears? Or did we not scream and shout in our terror? Being hit, back of the head, a truncheon, a fist. On the floor, boot to the stomach, dragged along the road, by the hair, screaming. Yes, there was noise, they were screaming at us, swearing at us, threatening us. Lifted, thrown onto a lorry, kicked again, move, move, move avoid the boots, avoid the fists, move back, further into the truck. Movement, truck rumbling, shouting get off, get down, get out. Down the steps, stumbling, falling onto the backs of others, Katrin, where's Katrin? Is she safe, is she in a hole like this? Down the steps, face the wall, legs spread, arms up, hands on head, shouting, shouting, fall over, boot to the back of the head, stand up, stand up, screaming, shouting can't stand must lie still can't move stop just stop please stop.

Please.

A fever? Concussion? My mind delivering false memories to cover the confusion, the blankness, the blackout? 1989. So long ago, so recent. Whatever you want to call it I saw a different future that day, in the cellar. We were there, with our candles, every night, we went out, we faced down the dogs and the pigs of the Party. They beat us and we didn't back down. But bit by bit the Party did: they crumbled. They were leaderless, they had no plan, no scientific socialism to guide them any more. Grasping at straws, they take their cues from the West. Propaganda flooding the country, *Deutschland einig Vaterland*, the promises, the Deutsche Mark: whatever you want to buy, you buy it with your Westmarks. Work: we'll have all the work we want—well paid, good clean jobs, short hours, long holidays. Join the West, West is best, *test the West*. Let them tell us what to do and they'll see us right. They promise the Earth. Currency union, the Westmark comes, destroying industry, jobs, communities in its wake. And soon after that, the coup de grace for our all our hopes: unification with West Germany.

Feverish hallucination? A dream?

Nightmare, more like. Another universe. One I wouldn't want to be in.

Karo

Katrin was still in my room. She'd been really quiet since yesterday, but I guess I hadn't said much either. There wasn't much to say. I didn't want to tell her about my trip to see the Stasi and what else was there to talk about?

We spent the night lying next to each other, just holding each other. Exactly like last Sunday. It was becoming a habit.

But now it was morning and I was in the kitchen, Schimmel was making a pot of coffee, and Antifa Bert and Antifa Rex were at the table.

"Look guys, it's really straightforward. The fash are organising demos all over the country. We've been mobilising for counter-demos, and after last Friday I reckon we can get enough people-"

Bert had been nodding to everything I'd said so far, but now he broke in. "Precisely. We need to outnumber them, make it clear to everyone that there's a vast majority of people who don't agree with the Nazis and who aren't going to let them spread their poison."

"No!" I banged my cup down on the table. "We need to take it to them. Mass demonstrations aren't going to do the job, we need lots of small groups. While they're busy marching down Frankfurter Allee and Unter den Linden or wherever, we need to be hitting all the different places they hang out—including Weitlingstrasse! When they come back they'll have been evicted. Game over. Martin is probably in one of those places—he's in danger!"

"And that's why we can't do that—it's too dodgy. They'll fight back, it'll get nasty. You're talking about putting normal people without any experience into a dangerous situation!"

Martin

They were holding me by the shoulders. I was sitting on the cement floor, a skinhead either side of me, and another one standing behind me, holding my head, making me look at a figure in the shadows. It was the size of a person, the approximate shape of a person. But it was lying on the floor in a way that looked like no human body. Arms and legs were bent in an attitude that no person could achieve. Not without broken bones.

"Don't worry, *Zecke*. He's probably dead already." The skinhead behind me had a slow, deliberate way of speaking. There was no sense of emotion in how he talked. "But we need you to give us a hand."

My head was released from the tight grip, and the skin holding my right shoulder let go, but grabbed my hand instead, holding it up. The speaker came into sight, dressed much the same as the others: stonewashed jeans, a t-shirt and denim jacket, shorn head. He was wiping something on his t-shirt, a gun. He held the barrel through the material and placed the grip in my hand. I tried to make a fist to stop him, but the skin holding my wrist squeezed a pressure point. My hand went limp and the pistol was placed inside it.

My index finger was forced into the trigger guard, my arm extended, gun pointing at the body, and with a sharp strike on my knuckle they made me squeeze the trigger.

09:40

Karo

"Karo's right." Rex poured another cup of coffee for himself. "It's time to take the fight to them. *This* feels like the right time. People will join in. People are pissed off, and they're scared. The attacks all over the place, the way the fash are mobilising for the referenda next week—people can't ignore them any more. And that's our chance."

"It's this afternoon we're talking about! We've left it too late." Bert wasn't about to give in.

"It's not. We can still do it." Schimmel spoke up for the first time. "This is what we've got phone trees for. We can reach nearly every Antifa group in the country in a matter of hours. And we'll get Martin's colleagues to start sending telexes to the Round Tables and Works Councils that are likely to be up for it—like the Berkmann Brigade at SKET. We've already started the mobilisation, the people are coming already—we just need to redirect them."

Bert shook his head. "It's not going to work."

17:02

Martin

The strip-light quivered into life.

I started to move my hand up to my eyes, shielding them from the glare. The dull ache in my chest changed to a sharp pain. Without instructions from my brain my movements were slowing down. A gasp, heard as from someone else's throat, a scrape as a door opened. Instinct demanded that I turn my head, look towards the door, see who was coming into the room. Slowly I turned onto my side, ribs stabbing into my lungs, panting in pain. I lay there waiting until I could breathe again, waiting for the burning in my side to recede. More aches began to make themselves known. Left knee: throbbing. Right eye: swollen, restricting vision. Right ear: nagging pain, dampness.

Enough.

I moved my concentration away from my body, towards my situation. A cellar. In a Nazi house. Weitlingstrasse maybe. Perhaps they've moved me somewhere else. Perhaps I was no longer even in Berlin.

Another scraping noise: a boot against grit. I lifted my head, turning it slightly, ignoring new messages of pain coming from my neck. A pair of para-boots, soles worn on the inside edges. Toe caps scuffed, marked with dark stains. White laces, above them white socks. Then the turn ups of stone-washed jeans, cut tight. My eyes carried on up the body. Green bomber jacket hanging open over white Lonsdale t-shirt. Above all of that, the head. Hair shorn, a fringe around the neck and face. A face I recognised. Blue eyes, pointed chin. But I didn't recognise the hardness to the eyes, the determined set to the chin, making it appear more prominent. But it was still her: Evelyn.

I gasped her name as she advanced, she checked over her shoulder, nobody behind her, then hissed at me: "Shut it!"

She put her hand over my mouth, with the other she pushed my head back on to the floor. Thoughts whirred through my mind: *Why? What does she want? Revenge?*

I struggled, feeble, muscles aching. I could feel my energy slipping away. My lungs fought for breath. A fight I lost as I slipped back out of consciousness.

17:08

Karo

There were already loads of people at Lichtenberg station, and more kept arriving every time a U-Bahn train rolled in. The fash were starting their march a couple of stops away, down the road at Frankfurter Tor, and they must have wondered where our counter-demo was. Well, we were here, and we were going to take back their precious fucking Weitlingstrasse 122.

Schimmel was pushing his way through the crowds, ducking under banners, looking around, trying to find me.

"Hard to say how many," he panted, out of breath. "But there's definitely someone in the house—it's not empty. We need to be careful."

We'd wait a bit longer, see how many more people came. The more the better, because Bert was right—it could get dangerous.

Martin

A pulling on my wrists, constant, nagging. I still couldn't breathe, my throat scratching, making me want to cough, but coughing would hurt too much. My shoulders ached. I opened my eyes, Evelyn was above me, she was holding my arms, pulling me up, making me sit up.

"Where were you? Evelyn, where were you?"

Evelyn looked down, breathing heavily.

"Saxony. I got word and came back to get you, you fool. Now shut it." She looked up, talking to someone else. "Let's get him up the stairs before they find us."

Hands grasped my wrists, my ankles, my back was scraped against steps as I was carried up the stairs. My eyes closed, it was too much.

The bang of a door, shouting. I'm lowered onto the floor, none too gently. Forcing open my eyes: two skins, shouting, pushing Evelyn around, punching her in the belly. There was another man there, another skin, the one who'd had hold of my feet, he was trying to pull the others away from Evelyn. She was screaming at them, spittle flecking her lips, her eyes wide in fear and hate. I turned over, and got to my knees, crawling away, into the corner. The screaming had stopped, I could hear grunts and whimpering.

"That's enough! We don't want to kill them. Not yet." A strong Berlin accent, sounding disinterested.

I propped myself up against a wall. The two skins were standing over Evelyn, she was lying on the floor, not moving. The other guy, the one who had been helping her, was slumped against the wall. Close enough that I could see the blood flowing from his nose, his eyes tight shut. But he was breathing. One of the fascists aimed another kick at Evelyn. Right in the stomach. She whimpered again, but didn't move.

"Lock 'em in the storage room, the boss will know what to

do with them when he gets back."

The other skin grunted, grabbing Evelyn under the arms and dragging her towards a doorway. He returned for Evelyn's friend. His colleague stood there, watching while the work was done. Finally, they came for me.

"Awake are you? Too soft on you, were we?" This time both skins took hold, pulling me up by the arms, then pushing me into the same room as Evelyn and the other guy.

I stumbled as they let go, nearly falling onto a pile of placards. Leaning against the wall, I watched as the door was slammed shut.

17:10
Karo

We were about forty or fifty people now, plus Rex and the Friedrichshain Antifa group. There was no way of knowing how many people had turned up at the other meeting places, but there were enough of us here to take over a nearly empty house. I was about to say that when Schimmel and this kid who should have been at school dashed up to me and Rex.

"It's all kicking off at Frankfurter Tor—a bunch of people turned up for the counter-demo, they didn't hear about the change of plan. They're getting their heads kicked in! We've got to go there, help them out!"

A few people had heard what Schimmel had said and were already moving towards the U-Bahn entrance.

"Wait!" I yelled, but nobody took any notice. "Schimmel, get them to wait just two secs will you? Rex, do you reckon your lot can deal with what's happening at Frankfurter Tor?"

"Yeah, get everyone to stay here, we'll sort it." Rex was already on his way. "We'll be back in thirty."

"Wait here! Wait! Everything is under control!" I bawled.

The crowd was already breaking up.

Martin

I staggered over to Evelyn, then sank down next to her. I shook her arm, but there was no reaction. I put my fingers on her wrist, her pulse was slow, much too slow. Running my hands over her body, checking for blood, they came away dry. Didn't mean there wasn't any internal bleeding or broken bones though.

Turning to the man lying next to Evelyn I did the same thing. Similar results, except for his nose and the fact that his pulse was stronger. There was movement beneath his eyelids. I slapped his cheeks gently, he groaned, his eyes twitched.

Good, that counted as progress. They were both alive.

I sat between Evelyn and the stranger and looked around the room: the pile of placards that I'd nearly fallen onto, several boxes of leaflets, another box with what looked like black, white and red striped armbands. On the other side of the room was a neat stack of torches, the kind that the FDJ used to have for their torch-lit parades past the tribune on which the *Bonzen* stood smiling down at us.

Uncalled for, a child's song came into my head: *Am Kindertag, beim Fackelzug, da darf ich auch mitgehn*—'on Children's Day, on the torch-lit parade, I'll go with the others'.

Shaking my head, trying to clear it, I stood up again to look at the window. A normal window, but the kind that doesn't open. I was sure we were on the ground floor, but the frosted glass meant there was no way to tell how far the drop from the window sill to ground would be.

Turning my attention back to my fellow prisoners, I slapped each gently on the cheeks again, hoping for a reaction. The man stirred, groaned, his eyes trying to focus.

"Are you OK?" I asked him. The man just stared at me, his eyes unfocussed. "Listen, can you get up?"

Obediently, he stood up. He winced in pain, but he

managed it.

Standing up, he didn't look in bad shape. He looked much fitter than I felt. That was good enough for me.

"Do you smoke? Have you got any matches?"

The man just stared at me, not understanding what I wanted. I patted down his pockets, finding a soft-pack of *Juwel* cigarettes. Tucked inside was a brass cigarette lighter. Perfect.

"Listen, get Evelyn on her feet, we need her awake," I told the man, speaking slowly, trying to get through to him.

I hobbled across to the boxes of leaflets and pulled out handfuls of the paper, scrunching them into a big pile on the floor. I tugged at the stack of torches, trying to drag them into the centre of the room. They toppled over with an echoing clatter. The man's scared eyes fixed on the door, listening for any sounds from the other side.

A pause, nothing happened, nobody came. I carried on dragging the torches over to the pile of leaflets, laying them around and over the paper, keeping a couple back.

Exhausted for the moment, I sagged down to the floor again, holding my side and trying to ignore the pain of breathing. The man was holding Evelyn up, he still didn't look particularly aware of his surroundings, but he was doing a good job. Evelyn's head was lolling, but her eyes were open. More progress.

Back onto my feet, trying not to breathe too deeply, I made my way around the pile of paper and torches on the floor. I picked up a couple of the placards and tore the hardboard messages off the poles, letting the black-red-gold propaganda fall onto the pile already spilling across the floor.

A moment to gather myself, then back to the man. I gave him one of the poles and looked him in the eye.

"We have two chances," I told him, still speaking slowly, checking to see whether he understood me. He nodded in a vague but committed way, the way a drunk would. "If we can't get out that way," I pointed at the window, "then we have to shout and make noise. When they come to see what's going on ..." I shook the pole I was holding in my right fist, and for good measure picked up a torch with my left hand.

He nodded. He didn't ask any questions, like how do we get Evelyn out of the window? Or how do we manage to get past whoever comes to find out what's going on.

It was a crap plan, but in his concussed state he didn't realise it.

Another pause for thought, the song still going around in my head. *Ich zünde mein Laternchen an, das leuchtet hell im Dunkeln dann. Am Kindertag, beim Fackelzug könnt ihr es alle sehn.* 'I light my little lantern, so it glows in the dark. On Children's Day, at the torchlit parade, you'll see it then.'

I used the brass lighter to light one of the torches, thrusting it into the pile of placards and leaflets. Another torch caught fire, and a few leaflets started curling brown at the edges before bursting into a blue and green flame. I watched for a few seconds. The fire was going well, dark smoke was gathering into a fine column, mushrooming out below the ceiling. Already the wooden poles of the placards were starting to catch fire here and there, adding to the smoke.

It was time. With one of the poles I smashed the window, quickly knocking the remaining shards of glass out of the frame.

"Get her through the window! Now! Come on!"

The man heaved Evelyn up onto his shoulder in a fireman's lift. He was strong, and that's what we needed.

The smoke was filling the room, flowing and ebbing. I was choking, each cough a stab in my side.

Evelyn was through the window, the man had lifted her onto the sill and she managed to get through by herself. He was climbing after her. I was right behind him, I could see his head and shoulders as he stood outside, holding his hands out to me, waiting to help me through.

"Fuck's sake!" Swearing, coming from behind me.

I looked over my shoulder, the door was open, and in the cross draught the fire climbed higher, the leaflets and placards flaming upwards.

"Get the sand buckets!" Behind the flames and smoke a figure impotently waved at the heat. Other skins came, forearms over faces, trying to push through the blaze. "They're fucking escaping!"

17:20

Karo

We'd just managed to get everyone to calm down, but some tosser was arguing with me, the kind that talks shit and never actually does anything.

"Look, it's under control—we've got our own mission here!" I told him. "And if you don't like it then why don't you go to Frankfurter Tor and help out there?"

Schimmel was doing a better job, he and a few other people from the squat were going around, telling people what was happening, why we were delaying the march down Weitlingstrasse.

Ignoring the argumentative tosser I looked around, it was going to be OK, people had calmed down, and somebody had brought a guitar out and a group was sitting in the middle of the road, singing *Give Peace A Chance.*

Bloody hippies, can't take them anywhere.

I was keeping an eye on the station, waiting for Bert and Rex and the others to come back, and that's why I was first to notice the skins come up the steps from the U-Bahn. There were about ten of them, and they looked like they fancied their chances against forty assorted hippies, grandmas and punks.

Martin

Using a placard I shovelled against the heat, pushing the burning torches and leaflets towards the door, towards the skins.

"Martin! Come on!" Evelyn was shouting from the window. The smell of scorching hair, the hot tingling of eyebrows sizzling, pushing a bit further, pushing the fascists back out of the room. The placard ignited, flames running up the pole towards my hands.

Chucking the burning pole towards the doorway I twisted round and stepped over to the window. Evelyn's colleague was reaching in, he grabbed my forearms, dragged me over the sill. The window frame pressed into my ribs but I didn't feel the pain. I was panicking, trying to get out. I fell down the outside wall of the building, but strong hands held me up. With an arm around my shoulder I was half pushed, half carried down the road. I didn't look round, but behind us I could hear the drumming of boots on the pavement, almost feel the ground shivering beneath my legs.

"Get the fuckers!"

They sounded close, too close.

I was only holding the others back. I willed power into my legs and tried to shrug Evelyn and her colleague off, but they held fast, dragging me on.

Karo

Everyone had seen the skins by now, but they were just standing around like a load of muppets. If I didn't act soon then we'd lose this battle before we even started it. I had to buy time for the Antifa to get back here.

But how?

"Right everyone, just like the plan." Schimmel was by my side again—he'd climbed up on a railing so that everyone could see him. "Move down Weitlingstrasse, nice and slow. Don't worry about the skins, we're gonna deal with them."

Like how the fuck are we gonna deal with them? The fash were standing just outside the station entrance, taking their time, enjoying the smell of fear.

"OK, you get the people away," he said to me. "I'll stay here and ..." But Schimmel didn't finish his sentence. The fash were watching him, he was marked.

"Like fuck you will! Anyway I'm staying," I told him.

We shared a scared grin as the people around us melted away, moving down Weitlingstrasse in one big block.

"C'mon Bert, c'mon Rex—we need you!"

17:22
Martin

"Shit! It's like 1989 again! Martin, we're going to need your help." Evelyn's voice was calm, almost slow. But it carried a brittleness that made me try to look over my shoulder, catch sight of our pursuers.

"No, the other way." Evelyn turned my head with her free hand, lifting my chin so I could see the mob blocking the road ahead.

I sank down to the pavement. I'd failed. We were sandwiched between two gangs of skins.

"Martin!" Evelyn's voice was more urgent now, "Martin, come on, help us out. Just one last time." Evelyn was crouched down next to me, why wasn't she running? She could make it without me, she'd get through somehow. I turned my head, looking back down the road, wondering how long we had, how many seconds before boots and fists smashed into us.

Karo

It wasn't Bert, or Rex, or any of the Antifa crowd that came—
it was Erika.

She appeared behind the fascists, and she'd brought a
whole bunch of very angry looking refugees with her. They
just surrounded the skins, disarmed them, just like that.
Erika had gone to the refugee hostel near the station, told
them what was happening, and brought them all here:
Russian Jews, Roma, Sinti, Croatians, Serbians,
Montenegrins. They'd all been on the receiving end of fascist
violence. For them it was payback time.

Behind us the original crowd were still marching down
the street. There were more of them now, local residents had
come out and were marching too. I wanted to go and join
them. But first I gave Erika a hug.

"You rock!"

Erika blushed and looked away, but before she could say
anything Rex ran out of the station.

"Karo! Message from your neighbour, Frau Kembowski! I
saw her go into the U-Bahn, she says she's going on the
march over in Berlin-Biesdorf!"

Frau Kembowski? Going up against the Nazis in Biesdorf?
"Is anyone with her? She's not going by herself?"

He nodded, and I knew what I had to do, I had to go and
be with Frau Kembowski. But I wanted to take the
Weitlingstrasse house. I was standing there dithering, not
knowing which way to go.

"You go to your neighbour. I'll help out here." Erika gently
pushed me towards the station.

Martin

Four skins, ten, twenty yards away. Behind them, smoke was billowing out of the house on the corner, flames licked the window frames, glass littered the pavement. But the skins stood there, not making a move. They weren't staring at us, but past us, towards the big group on our other side. I looked the other way, focussing for the first time on the larger group.

They were people.

Ordinary people.

And they looked very pissed off.

They were nearly upon us, most were concentrating on the skins, but a few were glaring at Evelyn and her friend.

"Martin, tell them!" Evelyn was no longer calm, she was frightened. She shook my shoulder as about twenty people surrounded us. They were young, old, men, women, punks and workers—there was no common feature, other than determination.

"Call an ambulance." Evelyn had stood up again, she spoke with authority. "This man needs an ambulance. We rescued him."

A figure from the back of the group split off and ran across the road to a shop, I could see him through the window, talking to the shopkeeper. The rest of them stood around, staring at us. They didn't do anything, just held us with their eyes.

"Martin, if you don't say something soon then it's going to get nasty," Evelyn hissed into my ear. "They think we're skins."

"These people." My voice croaked, I struggled up, and Evelyn held my arm, supporting me as I stood there. My throat was raw and what sounds came were rasping out of my mouth. "These two rescued me. They're not skins. They're in disguise ...." I looked to see what was happening behind us. About twenty people were surrounding the skins, a further group was standing at the end of the street, waiting for anyone fleeing the burning house. Evelyn's words from a minute ago penetrated the smoke that still fogged my mind: *It's like 1989 again.*

My head dropped until my chin was on my chest, I was exhausted, I had no more to give.

17:39

Karo

We got off the U-Bahn and ran down the road, Rex seemed to know where he was going. Turning off into an alley, it was obvious that we'd arrived. A crowd of people swelled out of a gap between some garages. We pushed our way through until we were standing in the forgotten garden of a ramshackle old villa. There must have been about a hundred people, and they'd made space for about half a dozen skins whose eyes darted around, trying to find a way through the mob.

"What's happening?" Rex asked.

"We cornered them, in their nest, and now they're trying to fly!" A middle aged woman in a pinny laughed. "Fly, little birds, run little rabbits!"

I was trying to spot Frau Kembowski—what was she thinking of, coming here, she'd be crushed by the crowd! Standing on tiptoes, craning my neck, scanning the crowds, but no sign of her, she was too little, she'd be hidden by all the people around her.

There was a sudden hush, and my eyes switched to the front. One of the skins had a knife, he was holding it out, threatening the people closest to him. The blade was already red, he'd already slashed someone. *Shit*, what to do? This was going to turn nasty. I grabbed Rex by the arm and pushed my way through the crowd.

There she was! Frau Kembowski was standing in front of

the Nazi with the knife.

"I'm Frau Kembowski," she said. "I lived here in Biesdorf for sixty years. I know you, and you know me." She stared at the skinhead until his arm dropped.

I managed to get through, and I stood by Frau Kembowski's side. Her hand clasped mine, it was shaking, but she stood there, as tall as she could.

"I know you, and I knew your father and your mother. Ashamed they'd be, ashamed of you. And so are we. We've all had enough." Frau Kembowski was pointing at each of the skins in turn, using her stick. "Young men, listen to me: you've got a choice, either you bugger off and leave Biesdorf —no, make that: you leave Berlin. Or you stay, you make amends. Your choice. You want to stay, you come to the Round Table. Tonight at eight."

Frau Kembowski shook her head in disgust, then reached forward and took the knife off the skin.

"Come on, young Karo," she whispered to me. "Time for us to go."

I tried to fix the skins with a stare, but they were all looking at their feet, and Frau Kembowski was pulling me back into the crowd.

"Run hares, run like rabbits! We'll catch you!" The crowd was chanting, but they made way for the skins who legged it, shitting themselves all the way.

17:42

Martin

"Goodbye, dear Martin, I doubt we'll meet again."

I opened my eyes. A blue light lunged at me, swept on then came round again.

"It's a shame, really. We never did get together, did we?" Evelyn whispered. She was holding my hand, her face was close to mine. I felt something soft touch my lips, pressing on them, the smell of *Florena* hand cream. It wasn't unpleasant, but it didn't feel right either.

A kiss.

"Come on, get him to hospital—we haven't got all night!"

The last thing I saw before my stretcher was loaded into the ambulance was Evelyn's silent friend.

"*Dmitriy Alexandrovich peredayet privet*," he said as he lifted his hand in a clenched fist salute: greetings from Dmitri Alexandrovich.

DAYS 16–20
Tuesday 29th March
to Saturday 2nd April 1994

Berlin: Across the Republic celebrations are being held after yesterday's extraordinary events. Last night, in spontaneous demonstrations across the Republic, communities took over buildings used by right-wing groups and parties. The events have been compared to the Monday demonstrations of 1989.

Martin

For the first day in hospital I had refused all visits, knowing that K1 would be the first in the queue. I wanted to wait until I had a clear head before they tackled me.

"Could you describe the one they called the boss?"

"Comrade Captain Neumann, I've told you twice already. I know how this works, but I've given you descriptions, and now I'm feeling tired. It's time you went." I reached for the button that would summon the nurse.

It was true, I was tired, but Neumann was also taking an unhealthy interest in getting an exact timeline of my imprisonment.

I'd decided not to tell him about the gun. The whole thing had been a set up—they'd been trying to frame me for murder, or maybe they had intended to blackmail me at some point in the future. I knew how to deal with such Stasi tricks: just tell everyone. And I would, but I'd start with my colleagues, and not with K1.

And with any luck it might not come to that. The gun was probably still in the building when it went up in flames, burning off my prints. The powder residue on my hands had long since been removed by careful nurses treating my burns. My burnt and sooty clothes had already been disposed of.

"Just one more thing, then I'll go. A body was found on the premises. It was another of our IKMs," Neumann continued. At this stage I wasn't particularly surprised that he'd had another informant in there, but I wasn't particularly interested any more either. "He died before the fire, shot several times. Can you tell me anything about that? Did you hear any shots?"

I was saved from answering by an efficient nurse who ushered the policeman out.

Karo

I went to see Martin again today. They wouldn't let me in yesterday, even when I told them we were best mates. I guess he must have been in a serious state.

"Yay—my favourite old fart! Look, I've brought you some oranges."

"Yay—my favourite punk." Martin was trying to be witty but he didn't have the energy.

He looked pretty done in. Eyebrows burnt off, hair singed, burns on his hands and arms, bandages around his chest and a nasty cough.

"You look like shit," I told him.

"So what have you been up to?"

"What? You don't know? I saved your ass, man!" I said in a cowboy drawl. "While you were lounging around in your luxury cellar we were kicking off—big-style."

Martin propped himself up on a million pillows while I told him what we'd been doing, hassling the Stasi, the demos, getting people sorted, kicking the fash out. He looked impressed.

"So now Antifa groups are working with Neighbourhood and District Round Tables." I took one of Martin's oranges and started peeling it. Little green things they were, Cuban. "They're doing the debriefing—loads of the skins are talking, saying they didn't actually want to be Nazis, they just got dragged into it. I don't believe the fuckers for a minute, but Rex said that they're getting loads of info, they're tracking down the people who were pulling all the strings—the suits. Fuckers."

I started on another orange, offering one to Martin, but he shook his head.

"And you know that house you set fire to? Totally burnt down. The fire brigade turned up, but they just stood there and watched it burn." I grinned.

I could see Martin was getting tired so I told him I'd see him the next day.

Outside in the corridor I bumped into Erika.

"Erika!" I gave her a hug and she gave me a squeeze back. That was nice, it felt like we were a team now.

"Karo, I'm glad I bumped into you. I wanted to ask you about giving us a hand with investigating the Nazi structures."

"You'd be better off talking to the Antifa—that's Rex's department."

"Yeah, I know, but I thought it would be good to work with you. You'd be our link to the Antifa and the other grassroots groups around the country—we need some help with keeping in touch with them all."

I thought about it. It sounded a bit boring, but kind of cool as well. "Martin's good at that kind of thing—why can't he do it?"

Erika looked down the corridor, towards the ward where Martin was. "I think he needs a break, don't you?"

"He needs more than a break—you should have seen him at the *Datsche*!"

Erika nodded. She knew what I meant.

"Laura's sorted it out with the Ministry. He's going to get paid leave."

"Laura? Would I have to work with her? And that Nik too?"

"Give them a chance. We've all been a bit stressed lately."

"OK, I'll think about it. But on one condition." There was a promise I'd made to myself, and working with RS could help me with that. "There's one particular Nazi I need to track down—it's a personal score I need to settle."

"OK, but nothing illegal."

I just laughed.

The next time I went to see Martin I bumped into Rico, the cute Border Guard. We had a quick chat near the entrance. He was dead embarrassed, blushing and stammering, poor sap.

"Martin says you're going to tidy up the East Side."

It's not the way I'd have put it myself, but yep, I'd had a chat with some of the *Wagenburgs* in Berlin and they were going to go and sort out the East Side—both the site and the people. All part of the new job at RS I told him, breathing on my nails and polishing them on my chest.

"I know that Customs *Obersekretär* Reinhardt wants to investigate the smuggling that's been going on there"

I was confused for a moment, and then I worked out who he was talking about. "Kalle? Yeah, all sorted. I'm seeing him about it this afternoon, we're going to go and have a look."

Rico blushed again.

REFERENDUM DAY
Sunday
3rd April 1994

Berlin: *Polling stations have been busy throughout the Republic as citizens and residents vote in the triple referendum. Voting closes at 10 o'clock this evening.*

Dresden: *The State Prosecutor for Saxony, Dr. Harry Kern, will announce immunity from prosecution for those involved in the events of last Monday. Criminal proceedings will only be opened at the specific request of a Neighbourhood or District Round Table, he said. The Central Round Table in Berlin has welcomed the statement, commenting that it will give communities the room to implement local accountability processes against offenders. Similar statements are expected to be made by State Prosecution Offices in the other Regions.*

13:29
Martin

I didn't have far to go—the local polling station was just next door in the *Kulturbund* rooms. But in my mind I had a much longer journey to make. I hobbled down the stairs, putting my bad leg down first, then gingerly hopping after it. My stick tapped each time I winced down another step.

It was my first full day at home. I'd insisted on leaving the hospital, I couldn't stand lying around on the overheated ward. I wanted to be at home, responsible for looking after myself, not having my food wheeled in and a nurse tutting at me whenever I asked to be let out. They'd been worried about my burns and my head, wanted to keep me in longer.

Bottom step, pause, breathe deeply to settle the pain, then down the hall, past the letter boxes.

I turned sideways to haul open the heavy front door, standing on my good leg and using the stick for balance. Then a few steps down the street, into the next building.

I stood in the entrance of the *Kulturbund* centre. To my right was the polling station, and on the other side was the hall where we held our communal Sunday lunch. I could hear voices, laughter coming from the hall, human warmth emanating through the half-open door. I decided I could use some of that warmth. I would eat before I voted.

I went over to the food table, looking at the dishes that my neighbours had brought. Picking up a plate I hesitated for a moment, unsure where to put my stick while I served myself.

"Here, you can give me that." It was Margrit, smiling at me, laughing at my clumsiness.

But before I could give her my stick she'd stepped forward and enveloped me in a hug. I gasped and Margrit stepped back sharply.

"Sorry! Oh, Martin, you look terrible—are you in a lot of pain?" She stroked a burnt eyebrow with her forefinger.

I shook my head and eased myself out of her clasp.

"If I go and sit down would you bring me a plate of food?"

I tapped over to the nearest table, and lowered myself into a seat, stretching out my dodgy leg, trying not to look too much like the invalid I obviously was. As soon as I'd got myself settled more neighbours came over, clapping me on the shoulder, shaking my hand. It was kindly meant, and in a way I appreciated it, but I was embarrassed all the same.

Margrit came over with my plate.

"What a week! I'm so proud of all of us." She gave me a

serious look, "I'm so proud of you."

I muttered something and started eating my food.

"I was at EKL, sitting at my workbench, minding my own business. And then the word went around—we're dealing with the fascists. The whole factory marched out, and I had the same feeling as I did that night, in Leipzig. Back then we were worried about the Chinese Solution. Remember, they brought in the army, we thought they were going to shoot us." Margrit's eyes were seeing the past, she was part of her story. "But still we marched."

Her eyes sought out mine, needing to share the fear and the strength and the determination of that time. "And last Monday was just like that."

She paused, putting her hand on my sleeve. I wasn't eating now, just listening to her. I'd heard the story already. Everyone who'd come to visit me at hospital, colleagues and friends alike, they'd all told me. Karo had come every day, and she'd told me every day. It was the same story, everyone had the same story, but different. Different for each person, each *Kiez*, each neighbourhood, each town and each village.

She shook her head again, astounded at how easy it had been. When the word went out about the demonstrations, when the Weitlingstrasse squat went up in flames something snapped. People said *enough*. They went out there and raided the places the fascists meet: the flats and factories, meeting places, everywhere. There were a few injuries, rumour of a death down in Saxony. But people gave the fascists a choice: go, or stay and make amends to the community.

Margrit was jubilant, still on a high after experiencing once again the power of the people, the ability to make change happen. But her face grew suddenly serious. "But that was the easy part. Now the hard work begins." She looked towards the window, at the town outside. "There's a lot of tidying up to do, isn't there?"

★

Standing in the booth I studied the slip of paper on the table.

"1. Should the existing installations along the State Border with the Federal Republic of Germany and between West Berlin and Berlin, Capital of the GDR, as well as between West Berlin and the Region Brandenburg be retained, including the maintenance of forward barrier-elements, metal lattice-fencing, observation and command-towers?"

I picked up the pencil and put my cross in the *yes* box.

"2. Should the *Volkskammer* be mandated to approve the Round Table (Constitutional Amendment) 1994 Bill?"

Another vote for *yes*, anchoring the role of the Round Tables and the Works Councils into our democratic institutions, with a clear timetable for further devolution of power away from the *Volkskammer* and the six regional parliaments, giving more say to Round Tables at every level.

So far, so good. Next came the question on the Police (Constitutional Amendment) 1994 Bill. We were asked whether we thought Paragraph 96, article 15 of our constitution should be changed to explicitly forbid the establishment of counter-espionage bodies. If I put my cross in the *yes* box I would be voting myself out of a job.

I thought of all the arguments I'd heard. I remembered all the pain caused by secret police and intelligence agencies in the past, the anti-democratic nature of their work. I thought of all the good we'd done at the *Republikschutz*. Was it possible to have an agency that defended its people from outside threats without itself becoming a threat to the people's power? If that were possible, if there were any example of how to do it differently then my colleagues and I were that example. But we'd had little power, even fewer resources. What we'd achieved had been more through luck than intelligence.

I wielded the pencil, the tip almost grazing the paper as it wandered between the three boxes: *Yes. No. Re-open Discussion.*

In order to be democratic the organs of a state need to be accountable. But by the very nature of the work it was practically impossible to make counter-espionage agencies open and accountable, at least not in real time. I'd been thinking for weeks about this problem, about accountability. The secrecy surrounding the work. The complicated and political nature of it all. The real risks and danger involved. All these factors militated against accountability to anything but a closed committee with long-term membership. But by its nature such a committee would become corrupted, seduced by the cloak and dagger games of the spies.

There were no answers. We could only experiment, that was what the GDR was all about: experimentation.

I pressed the pencil to the paper, and with a hard, quick movement I voted myself out of a job.

PREVIEW
OF
SPECTRE AT THE FEAST
Book 3 of the East Berlin Series

SUNDAY
12th June 1994

Kaminsky stood on scaffolding at the end of Alexanderplatz.

One arm raised, fist clenched, saluting the crowds below. He stared out at thousands of faces, at hundreds of placards and banners, flags and flaming torches.

The crowd chanted. *Kaminsky Kaminsky Kaminsky.*

But Kaminsky stood above them all, stock still, fist raised, saying not a word.

The crowd hushed itself, the shouts and chants dying back, murmuring to a standstill.

Only when he had absolute silence did Kaminsky lower his arm and step up to the microphones and cameras.

The government is weak.

The government has lost its way.

They even held a referendum to ask us what to do, but they're still unsure: parliament and Round Tables are bickering.

Our government is paralysed.

But we, the people, we are making history. Right now, all of us here are making history.

And more than ever, in this historical time we need a capable leader. A leader to steer a steady course for our Republic. We need a leader with strength, a leader of ability and moral fibre.

It is time to end the political corruption—but the establishment doesn't recognise this.

It is time to renew our democratic system—but the establish-

ment won't do this.

It is time for real leadership—but the establishment can't provide this!

Again the chant *Kaminsky Kaminsky Kaminsky* swept through the crowd. Kaminsky himself stood back, let the wave of words break on the stage and surge around again.

Look at the Resurgence: just a few weeks ago the government of this country was unable to deal with violence and criminality from skinheads and far-right extremists. The establishment showed itself unable to act.

We, the people, took matters into our own hands.

We, the people, cleared up the mess they couldn't handle.

We, the people, exposed the weakness of the elite!

It is time for us, the people, to take back control.

It is time for us, the people, to take back power.

Because we are the people!

Kaminsky stood back, his fist raised again, smiling and acknowledging the chants of the crowd.

We are the people! We are the people! We are the people!

20:13

Karo

I don't think anyone saw us.

My mate Schimmel was on the street corner, keeping a lookout while I decorated the window with red paint. I'd only got as far as RACIST SCUM before I was overcome by the sour taste of anger that rippled up my throat. *Fuck it.* With the heel of my boot I kicked a cobble loose and levered it out.

I took a few steps back, turned, and lobbed the stone.

The window of Kaminsky's office cracked, the glass hanging for a moment before sliding down, shattering as it went. Schimmel twisted around, shock splashed over his face. I grabbed his hand as I legged past him.

At the U-Bahn station we jumped down the steps as a

train pulled in and I sat down, laughing at the dismay on my friend's coupon.

"That wasn't the deal!" he said.

"You feeling sorry for Kaminsky?"

Schimmel didn't answer, and I stopped grinning. It was no fun any more, not with my friend looking so pissed off all the time.

"Oh, come on." I tried again. "He deserves more than a smashed window!"

"He does. But what about sticking to agreements?"

"Fuck off!"

The train was pulling into the next station. As I stepped onto the platform my anger and frustration felt like a kick in the back.

20:46
Martin

The police lieutenant limped into my flat on a Sunday evening. He wasn't in uniform and I was just about naïve enough to assume this might be a social visit: *just passing, thought I'd pop in.*

"They let you out?" I asked as I held the door open.

"Had to argue with the surgeon." Steinlein's stick tapped over my painted floorboards.

I offered my visitor the comfy seat, but he preferred the hard kitchen chair at the table. I was about to offer him coffee too, but he lit a cigarette and started to speak.

"I know you're still on leave but I was hoping you could help me with a case. It's sensitive."

The shift in his voice warned me even before his words reached me. This was work. This was police work. I got up, carefully pushed my chair back under the table and stood by the door, pointing out into the hallway.

"You want a cup of coffee, you're welcome. But if you want to get me involved in something ... You know why I'm still on leave? It's not because of this," I touched my bruised panda eyes, the eyebrows that were still growing back, "nor because of this," I pointed at my left knee. "They say it's because I need a rest." I tapped the side of my head. "I think I've had enough of *sensitive*, don't you, comrade Lieutenant?"

"When the fascists attacked me, when I was in hospital, you were the only one to come to visit." Steinlein was still sitting there, hands clasped over the top of his walking stick.

"Doesn't make me responsible for you."

"Think about it. Call me when you're ready to talk." Steinlein got to his feet, holding on to the table for support, then tapped his way back into the hall, as slowly as he'd come in. By the time he was at the door, curiosity had got the better of me.

A curiosity I thought long gone. A curiosity I should have known better than to allow myself.

"What is it? What's so bloody *sensitive*?"

With one hand on the latch Steinlein half turned to meet my gaze. "They want to kill Kaminsky."